Love is Patient

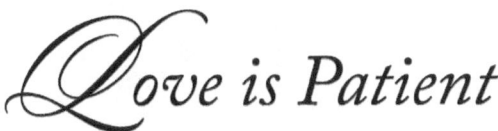

Love is Patient

KIMBERLY LOGSDON

JOYIN PUBLISHING INC
Where joy finds a voice

Ajoyin Publishing is honored to present this title in partnership with the author. The views expressed or implied in this work are those of the author. Ajoyin provides our imprint seal representing design excellence, creative content and high quality production. To learn more visit www. ajoyin.com.

ISBN 13: 978-1-60920-095-4

Prologue

ELANIE SNATCHED JONATHAN'S satchel from his hands and stepped back out of reach. She tried to be strong, but her voice wavered when she spoke. "Please don't leave me."

Jonathan sighed deeply and rolled his eyes. They'd had this conversation numerous times before, but always in the past Melanie had been able to convince him to stay. Never had Jonathan gone as far as packing.

"Mel, I don't love you. I'm young and I have my whole life ahead of me." His words ripped her heart wide open and she suddenly felt as if she were drowning in a sea of hopelessness. Jonathan reached out his hand. "Give me my bag."

Melanie clutched the satchel to her chest and shook her head. Tears burned her eyes but she blinked them back, refusing to admit that he was really leaving her this time. Her lips trembled as she spoke. "Bu-but, you said we'd get married. You're all I have." An uncontrollable sob broke through her lips. "I gave myself to you because you said we'd get married!"

Her fiancé and lover of three years ran a hand down his face. "I know, and I'm sorry; but this isn't what I want anymore."

Melanie gasped. Could this truly be the end then? Jonathan stepped closer and wrapped his arms around her thick waist. Or was it? He was barely as tall as her so he had to tilt his head back to kiss her forehead. Desperation flared in Melanie's heart and she decided to resort to old tactics to convince Jonathan to stay. That he needed her. Wanted her. Melanie's stomach tightened, because the truth was, *she* needed *him*. She dropped her eyelids slowly and looked up at him with the seductive look that had always convinced him to stay in the past. She slowly licked her lips to draw attention to her mouth and he easily took the bait. Jonathan leaned forward and kissed her softly. She dropped his satchel safely behind her and slid her hands up his chest and around his neck. She kissed along his jaw and down his neck. A low grumble emitted from his throat, and she smiled, knowing she had just convinced him to stay.

Jonathan pulled his arms tighter around her waist so their bodies were touching from chest to thighs. His kiss turned to a hungry passion and he began walking her backwards toward the bed they shared. He lowered her to the thin mattress and ran his hand up her leg, pulling her dress hem up in the process.

Melanie woke with a smile on her face and turned to kiss Jonathan good morning. At the sight of the empty space next to her, her eyes widened and she became fully alert. She bolted up and looked around the small apartment. His satchel was gone.

Melanie thumped the thin mattress with her fist as the first tear rolled down her cheek. She looked around the apartment searching for some sign that Jonathan would be back. When her eyes came to the window, she bolted off the mattress and raced for the loose floorboard beneath the windowsill.

She chanted, "No, no, no, no, no," as she dashed across the small room.

Dropping to her knees, she dug her nails between the floorboards to wrench the loose board out. The small leather pouch containing their savings was gone. Melanie felt the wind suddenly rush out of her lungs at the sight of the empty hole. She fell onto her backside and dropped her head in her hands as deep sobs racked her body. The man she loved, the man she gave every ounce of her heart and soul to, had left her. Not just left her, but left her penniless.

Shame shrouded her as she thought back to the first night she had allowed him to convince her with his sweet words and even sweeter kisses that they had been meant for each other and that he wanted to show his love as a husband does. She had protested at first, knowing it was wrong, but his promises of marriage and a future together had lulled her into a false sense of rationality. After their first night together he had argued that the damage was already done, so why not continue enjoying each other? So for the last three years they had shared a bed, all the while Melanie thinking, hoping, that one day they'd right it all by getting married.

Melanie lay on her side and allowed the full weight of her shame and guilt to wash over her like a wave. Pain radiated from her heart as she thought of Jonathan, her love and her lover, leaving her with no second thoughts or regrets after having her one last time. She felt used and empty.

Melanie jumped when a gentle hand rested on her shoulder. "Melanie? Are you OK?"

Melanie gasped for a steadying breath and leaned on her elbow to see who had come into her apartment. Relief and embarrassment fought for reign in her heart at the sight of her friendly neighbor, Charlotte.

"J-J-Jonathan," was all she could choke out.

Charlotte looked around the apartment. "Did he leave, honey?"

Melanie couldn't speak, too embarrassed and torn with grief to respond, so she simply nodded her head.

Charlotte must have seen the loosened floorboard exposing the hole where they had kept their savings. She sighed. "He take all your money?"

For the first time the fear of not knowing how she would eat or pay rent entered her thoughts, and now that fear tore up through her throat and burst from her mouth in a loud exclamation. "Yes!"

Charlotte clucked her tongue sympathetically. She stuck her hands under Melanie's arms and helped her to her feet. "Come on, honey, you'll just have to come stay with me."

Several weeks later Charlotte and Melanie were having tea.

"You know what you need, honey?" Charlotte pointed a long, slender finger at Melanie. "You need yourself a good man."

Melanie rolled her eyes. "I *had* a good man and he left me!"

Charlotte snorted. "That worm was *not* a good man." Charlotte shrugged and sat across from Melanie with a cup of weak tea. "But if you're interested, I might just know the perfect man for you."

Melanie strolled down the street with her hand securely tucked into the elbow of Tom Graves, the gentleman to whom Charlotte had introduced her. He was tall and lean with dark hair and even darker eyes. He opened every door, pulled out every chair, and said all the right things at just the right moments. At first she felt even more paunchy next to his lean stature, but his constant compliments soon drove all thoughts of insecurity out of her mind. His gentlemanly attention was a cool balm to Melanie's battered heart.

Tom stopped in front of her building and reached to hold her hand. "I was wondering," she saw his Adam's apple bob up and down as he gulped. "Would you mind if I kissed you?"

Melanie looked down at their hands, stalling for time. Jonathan was the only man who had ever kissed her. His kisses were soft and warm and usually led to something more. Melanie glanced around nervously. They were standing in front of her building on a busy street. Obviously, nothing more would happen. Melanie looked up and simply nodded her head. Tom leaned down and kissed her lips. Sloppily. When he finally pulled away she had to resist the urge to wipe her mouth. Instead, she put on her best smile and thanked him for seeing her home. As she climbed the stairs to the apartment she shared with Charlotte, a sick, foreboding feeling of dread churned in her stomach. She paused briefly on the staircase to consider it but quickly brushed it off as a reaction to the inexperienced kiss.

Two weeks later Tom took her to a community musical program. He picked her up in a small rented buggy and presented her with a red rose. At the end of the night he drove her home and she invited him in for coffee, as was their custom now. Melanie's stomach flip-flopped with nerves when she realized Charlotte wasn't home from work yet. She ran her hands down her skirt to wipe away the moisture. She hadn't been alone with a man since Jonathan dominated her life, and being alone with Tom now suddenly made the apartment she shared with Charlotte seem incredibly small. Melanie set the coffee pot to boil on their small woodstove, then took a seat across from Tom.

He scooted his chair closer and reached for her hand, stroking her palm with his thumb. "You're so beautiful."

Melanie's cheeks flushed. In the three years she had spent with Jonathan she could probably count on one hand the times he had said she was beautiful.

She smiled up into Tom's eyes. "Thank you."

He reached forward and brusquely ran a shaking finger down her cheek, along her jaw and finally across her lips. Jonathan used to caress her face the same way except his touch had been gentle and had made her shiver. Tom's touch made her want to pull away—but she didn't. She spread her lips in a smile and tried to remain still as she figured out if there was a motive behind his awkward affections.

Tom moved his chair even closer to her. Tension knotted in Melanie's stomach and she fought to remain calm. Behind her she heard the coffee begin to boil and she jumped up to get it. She poured two cups and placed one in front of Tom.

He made a sour face after taking a timid sip. "Can I have some sugar, please?"

Melanie eyed him curiously. Tom had never asked for sugar before, but Melanie rose to get the small tin of sugar. When she turned back around she paused. Tom's hand was hovering over the top of her coffee cup.

She furrowed her brow. "Is something wrong?"

Tom smiled. "No, not at all. I was just feeling the steam."

Melanie quirked an eyebrow but nodded nonetheless. She placed the tin of sugar on the table with a clean spoon. Tom stirred a small amount of sugar into his coffee then lifted his cup to his lips.

"Bottoms up."

Melanie smiled and drank of the warm liquid. They discussed the musical production put on by the community for a few minutes, and then Melanie began to feel odd. It was still early, yet her eyelids suddenly wanted to do nothing more than droop closed. She told Tom that maybe it was time for him to go. He stood and took her hand to help her out of her seat and they walked to the door together. He wrapped his arms around her and whispered sweet nothings in her ear. Melanie was feeling so drowsy his whispered words droned in and out. Melanie felt the first twinge of irritation spark when he began kissing her with his usual wet and sloppy kisses.

She pushed against his chest and opened the door. "Goodnight, Tom." She had to lean heavily against the door to prevent buckling to her knees.

Tom shut the door and turned the lock. "No." He drew her back into his embrace and kissed her roughly. "You're so beautiful."

Melanie rolled her eyes, the compliment suddenly no longer as dear as it had originally been. She tried pushing against his chest again but couldn't find enough strength in her arms to do her any good.

He scooped her up into his wiry strong arms and took her to the corner of the apartment where her mattress was shielded by a pinned up sheet and he gently placed her on her feet. She stood there, her mind incapable of comprehending what was happening, as he began undressing her.

Her eyes slid shut and he jarred her, "Stay awake. I want you awake."

He gently laid her down on her mattress. Her body demanded sleep with each heartbeat. Through slitted eyelids she saw him undress. He knelt beside her and stroked her hair back out of her face. Her groggy mind raced to figure out why they were both undressed, but the fog only continued to thicken. He positioned himself on top of her and suddenly she realized what was about to happen. Her eyes widened and she pushed against his bare chest with all the strength she could muster.

"NO!"

Her heart beat wildly as he spread her legs. She begged, "No." She tried to squirm away from him. "Please don't."

He quieted her with another sloppy, disgusting kiss. She turned her head to avoid his mouth and gasped a lung full of air to scream. She paused, her eyes wide. Tears began to streak down her face as she realized that he had entered her during his disgusting kiss.

He stroked her cheek. "You're so beautiful."

What once had been a compliment and set butterflies to fluttering in her stomach and her heart to racing now felt like a hard slap in the face. She felt insulted and disgusted, and used by yet another man. Her eyelids began shutting on their own accord again, even as she willed them to stay open.

She begged him through her pitiful sobs, "Please stop."

Her body ached to cry out, to beat against his chest, but she didn't feel right. She felt sick and weak and it took all of her strength just to beg him to stop. She thought of the odd way he had held his hand over her coffee cup, and it suddenly dawned on her that he must have put something in it. Tears streamed across her temples and into her hair as she begged him over and over to stop, but he continued to insult her with fake compliments as he invaded her body. When she didn't think she could bear the abuse anymore, she allowed whatever drug he had put in her coffee to take over and slipped into a soundless, dreamless sleep.

Melanie awoke just before dawn and felt a heavy hand resting on her hip. She glanced over her shoulder and saw Tom. She jerked in surprise, accidentally waking him. As pieces of the night before flooded back into her memory, she frantically tried to get up, but he slid his hand around her waist and pulled her up against his body.

He whispered into her ear, "Don't get up yet, I like the feel of you against me."

Melanie tried to remove his arm from around her waist but he only held her tighter. Painfully tight. She gave up, frightened he would hurt her to get what he wanted. Minutes later she heard his breathing return to the shallow, steady breathing of sleep. She laid there, ramrod straight, waiting for him to get up and leave.

Two hours later the rat finally woke up. He rubbed his hand against her hip and whispered into her ear, "Morning, beautiful."

Melanie scowled, now hating the compliment and taking it for the worst insult ever flung in her face. She elbowed him hard, her strength finally returning.

She nearly growled between clenched teeth, "Get out."

He chuckled and patted her bare rear before getting up and dressing himself. Melanie wrapped her quilt around her, ashamed and embarrassed to have him see her naked. He followed her to the door and bent low to kiss her cheek.

"I loved making love to you."

Melanie reared back, the full hate she felt for the man burning through her eyes. "That was *not* making love."

LOVE IS PATIENT

He had the audacity to laugh in her face before turning on his heel and walking down the hallway. As Melanie watched the devil retreat down the hall, her heart froze solid and she vowed never to trust another man.

WESTERN UNION

Received at

Great-Uncle Brooks passed on STOP

Left you ranch in Sterling Canyon TX STOP

Days ride southeast of town STOP

So big you can't miss it STOP

P.H.

Chapter 1

ELANIE STARED LONG and hard at her reflection. Rouge tainted her full cheeks an unflattering shade of red to match the lipstick she wore. She bared her teeth like an unruly mule and cringed at how the vibrant red lipstick made her teeth look yellow in comparison. Is this how men really liked their women to look? Melanie snorted in disgust and grabbed a nearby handkerchief and began rubbing all the red off her face. Once her face was freshly scrubbed, she began taking the long pins out of her curls and nearly sighed with relief as the pins released their biting hold. She smiled at her reflection and turned her head to one side, batting her eyelashes all the while. And men were truly that easy to lure. Melanie snorted and rolled her eyes.

"Men are idiots."

She picked up her brush and began brushing out her long, brown curls. She smiled at herself as they sprung back and nestled against her cheeks. Her hair was definitely her finest quality. In the dim light of a lamp, her eyes flashed a golden brown and she considered that they may be her second and other finest quality. Once her hair was brushed and then neatly braided down her back, Melanie stood up from her vanity chair to dress for bed. She unbuttoned the tiny jet black buttons trooping down her bodice and inhaled deeply once the tightly-corseted dress was loose. She allowed the short dress to fall to the ground and turned to see her reflection in the tall, full-length mirror in the corner.

She cringed at the sight of her thick arms and wide hips that rounded into an expansive backside. Men paid for *this?* She shook her head as she retrieved a cotton chemise from her trunk and pulled it over her head, then bent and picked up her dress to hang in her wardrobe. Before shutting the wardrobe doors she stared at all of her fine dresses and wondered if she'd miss them. She made a disgusted face as she thought of the kind of work that came with the silks and satins, and immediately decided no clothing was fine enough to warrant what she had been doing. It had been mere survival from starvation that had brought her so low.

Melanie walked to the gleaming, ornate table beside her large poster bed and opened the drawer. She pulled out her Bible and affectionately stroked the cover before clutching it to her ample bosom. She sat on the edge of her plush, featherbed and placed the Bible in her lap. She opened the cover and stroked the wad of cash inside her hollowed out Bible.

"This is my new beginning. No more fancy luxuries." Melanie sighed as she looked around the beautifully decorated room that had been hers for nearly five years now. "But no more carnivorous men either."

CHAPTER 1

Melanie placed her Bible back in its place and shut the drawer. She lay down on her side facing the ornate table that held her precious Bible and pulled her thick down comforter over her, relishing its plush softness and warmth for the last time. She slid her hand under her pillow until it touched her derringer. She gently rocked from side to side, lulling herself to sleep while pushing the small twinge of fear and anxiety at leaving a roof, three square meals a day, and a steady income behind for an even wilder country than the place where this brothel was located.

The morning light dawned brightly and shone through her sheer curtains. She grumbled at waking so early when she had gone to bed so late, but the importance of today immediately rushed back to her. She sprang out of bed, and racing to the end of her bed she flung her trunk wide open. On top was her favorite ready-made calico dress purchased for her journey. It was a light blue fabric covered in small yellow flowers. The other dresses she had purchased were much more practical for work, being various shades of brown and gray. She also had bought plain, cotton petticoats and the chemise she had worn to bed. All of the intricately embroidered petticoats, chemises, and corsets of silk, satin, lace, and ribbon would stay behind at the brothel. She pulled the blue calico covered in tiny yellow flowers over her head and quickly buttoned the white buttons trooping up the front. Melanie took a deep, bracing breath and turned to see her reflection. This was the first time she had worn a calico dress in five years.

Her lips immediately formed a frown at the slight bulge of her stomach and the taut fabric across her bosom. She glanced at the wardrobe filled with corseted dresses that at least gave the illusion she had an appealing figure. Melanie rolled her eyes at her reflection. *What were you expecting? To be transformed into a slim beauty by a simple calico?*

Melanie hated admitting it, but yes, she had thought she would be transformed. The blue calico with tiny yellow flowers was so beautiful that she secretly thought by simply wearing something beautiful, she herself would, for once, seem beautiful too. She shook her head at her foolishness and sat down at her vanity. She brushed her hair and then attempted to pin it back into a bun. She was happy to see she had accomplished a smooth bun with only a few rebellious curls springing out to line her neck and temples.

Melanie retrieved her Bible from the ornate table and placed it on top of the bed. She lifted her pillow and picked up the derringer. Opening the cover of her Bible, she tucked the small gun beside her savings in the hollow. She quickly put on fresh stockings followed by the new, sturdy boots she had purchased to wear with her ready-made dresses. She fetched a new gray shawl and took her Stetson from a hook by the door. Wrapping the shawl around her shoulders, she crammed the hat down on her head, her bun low enough to be out of the hat's way. She picked up her Bible and clutched it to her side, then turned to her full length mirror for one final look.

The fabric across her bosom pulled so tightly the white buttons threatened to pop out of their buttonholes. She slouched her shoulders forward to see if it would help ease the tension on the fabric, but it only made her look hunched. She straightened her shoulders and figured she should be grateful the high necked dress she wore allowed no cleavage to show. It was almost as if she were a respectable young lady and not a brothel girl. The dress fabric circling her arms was a bit tight as well, but no one would be able to tell unless she took the shawl off. Her eyes went to the bulge in her stomach and she glared at it as if the heat from her stare could melt the fat away. She took a deep breath and held her stomach in, then turned sideways. She arched an eyebrow, "That's a little better."

She looked her reflection in the eye and said, "Well, I guess that's as good as it's gonna get." She nodded and her reflection nodded, agreeing with her.

As she headed for the door, a loud knock sounded. Outside she heard the trusty bodyguard to all the girls at the brothel announce himself. "It's me, Amos. Are ya decent?"

Instead of responding, Melanie opened the door and nearly burst into laughter as Amos's jaw dropped open. "Miz Melanie, you almost look like a preacher's wife with that Bible there." At that, Melanie did burst into laughter.

"I know, it doesn't suit me at all." Melanie turned and pointed toward her trunk. "Can you haul that to the stagecoach, Amos?"

The middle-aged grizzly of a man nodded and stepped over her threshold. Well, not her threshold anymore. Now it belonged to whichever girl Minnie put in her place. Amos heaved the trunk up and Melanie turned to hurry down the hall in front of him. As she descended the stairs to the large parlor Melanie looked up and was shocked still to see all of the brothel girls (her friends and adopted sisters) clustered together holding a banner that said, "Farewell, Friend." Melanie knew the banner was used for any girl who left Minnie's tightly-knit flock. Melanie had held it for a dozen or so girls herself, but she hadn't expected the old dusty cloth to be brought out on her account. Tears shone in all of the girls' eyes and Melanie raced forward to embrace each one. In the midst of her life falling apart, these women had brought her out of the cold, tucked her into their unique version of a tightly knit sisterhood, and cared for her for the last five years.

The last woman who came to hug was Minnie, the woman who owned and ran the cleanest, friendliest brothel in all of Wisconsin. As a young woman, Minnie had been trapped working in a brothel bossed by a brutal man with a heavy hand. Fortunately, she had escaped during the chaos of a fire that burned the brothel down. She decided to start her own business doing the only thing she knew how to do. She had vowed to only serve clean, peaceable men and in return they got freshly scrubbed girls in clean, provocative gowns, and were entertained in luxuriously decorated rooms. Over the years, Amos had hauled many a man out for being unruly or raising a hand to one of the girls. Minnie also gave each girl a fair percentage of a customer's payment and encouraged them to save that money for a new start. Melanie had taken her advice and today she was making her new start.

Minnie hugged Melanie tighter and whispered in her ear, "Come with me to my office."

Melanie obediently followed Minnie into her office. Once inside, Minnie shut the door and opened the small safe underneath her desk. Before Melanie even had an inkling of an idea of what Minnie might be up to, the petite, middle-aged woman handed Melanie a large bundle of cash that had a small note attached with her name neatly written on it. Melanie looked at Minnie, confused. "What's this for? You've already paid me." Minnie shook her head and leaned in to whisper, as if someone could actually overhear through the thick, polished oak door. "I take an extra five percent of what a customer pays and I stash it away for the customer's girl. When the girl leaves, I give it to her. Kind of like a little going away present."

Melanie looked at her boss, speechless. Minnie shrugged. "I only keep this place because it's the only thing I know to do and if being here helps a few girls get off their backs, then I'm happy to do it. I take peace in knowing at least my girls are safe, unlike at some other places."

Melanie thought the brothel-owning woman was a saint. She threw her arms around Minnie's neck and kissed her cheek. "I can't think of a way to thank you."

Minnie hugged her back and laughed. "Not like you didn't bring in a tidy profit over the years, girl. You've earned that money."

Melanie tried not to cringe at the thought of *how* she had earned the thick bundle of money in her hands. At first she had felt so used and worthless she hadn't minded selling her body for money. She was too numb with heartache to truly notice. In fact, for a while, the more generous lovers had helped ease that numbing pain for at least a few moments of un-matrimonial bliss. But always, afterward, the black disgusting taint of a whore would move in on her soul and she would often cry herself to sleep after the last customer had gone. A chill ran down her spine and she fought an urge to shiver.

Minnie pulled back and held her at arm's length. "Just look at you. All ready for the world."

This time Melanie couldn't help but shiver. Minnie gave her a knowing smile and winked, "You'll be just fine, honey." Melanie tried to smile and nod. Minnie squeezed her arms, "But if you ever need a place to stay, my doors are open."

Melanie's smile was genuine this time. She hugged Minnie one last time and thanked her again. Minnie handed Melanie a garter and this time Melanie was the one with a knowing smile. She placed her new, shiny boot atop a wooden chair and pulled up her dress hem. She slid the garter up her thick thigh and tucked the wad of cash into the garter so it was snuggly held against her leg. Melanie dropped her foot back to the floor and smoothed out the front of her dress.

"Perfect!" Minnie turned and pulled the door open, "Let's go, kiddo, the stage waits for no one."

Chapter 2

ELANIE'S BELOVED FRIENDS followed her outside with their handkerchiefs transitioning from wiping tears to waving farewell. As the stage coach lurched forward, Melanie leaned out the window to wave goodbye and soak in the last look she might ever see of her adopted sisters.

A short redhead, Sarah, who went by the name of "Candy" at night, jumped up and down as she called, "Goodbye, Melanie, I'll miss you!" A tall black-haired girl, Jewel, vigorously waved her handkerchief in the air. "We love you, Melanie!"

The slender blonde who had taken her in all those years ago, Charlotte, her dearest friend in the entire bunch, covered her mouth with her handkerchief as if holding back sobs. She raced a few steps forward and cupped her hands around her mouth as she shouted, "Don't forget to write!"

A large lump situated itself in Melanie's throat rendering her unable to speak. Instead, she met Charlotte's gaze and nodded vigorously. She had spent weeks trying to convince her friend to come with her, but Charlotte was still convinced the only place she'd be safe from her abusive pa was under Amos's watchful eye at Minnie's Dollhouse. Melanie hoped that in time she still might be able to convince Charlotte to leave.

The coach picked up speed and Melanie worried she'd lose her new Stetson, so she popped back inside and began righting herself in her seat. When she looked up, she saw her fellow passengers, a preacher and his wife. Amos' words about how she looked like a preacher's wife came flooding back to her. She appraised the woman and figured that except for her Stetson as compared to the woman's simple bonnet, she supposed they were dressed similarly. Melanie gulped as she turned her eyes to the preacher in his tidy black suit and caught sight of a Bible resting on his lap. Melanie clutched hers tighter to her chest.

The preacher's wife cleared her throat and Melanie was surprised to see her smiling with her hand sticking out in midair. "My name is Louisa. Louisa Merryweather. And my husband," the young woman motioned toward her husband who was looking at Melanie with a smile that matched his wife's, "Reverend Tom Merryweather."

Melanie kept her hands tightly clutched around her Bible, too afraid she'd taint the young preacher's wife by touching her. Surely the woman knew that the building they just pulled away from with the gaggle of women waving farewell was a brothel. Why would this perfectly righteous woman want to shake hands with a whore? To see if it made her skin burn?

Just in case the young woman was too naïve to know she was offering her hand to a brothel girl, Melanie simply nodded and smiled in return. "Melanie Brooks. Pleased to meet you both."

CHAPTER 2

Louisa Merryweather allowed her hand to fall back to her lap but her smile remained strong as if Melanie had just shaken her hand with all dignity and politeness. "So, Miss Brooks, where are you headed?"

Melanie twitched at being called "Miss Brooks," but she didn't insist on being called by her first name. If she did it would only prompt the preacher's wife to do the same and there was no way she was calling a preacher's wife by her first name. She didn't know much about God but she knew her soul was as dark as a moonless, starless night and that she must have committed enough sins to see her burn in Hades for the rest of eternity. No way was she dirtying her new start so soon by calling a respectful preacher's wife by her first name.

Melanie smiled through her discomfort. "Texas."

The preacher's wife squealed with delight and turned to her husband, her hand resting on his arm. "Did you hear that, Tom? Texas! Maybe I *will* have a woman friend!"

Reverend Merryweather smiled at his wife. "Wouldn't that be an answer to prayer, dear?"

Louisa pivoted her attention back to Melanie. "Where exactly in Texas?"

Melanie felt the sweat drip down her back. The preacher's wife wanted to be her friend? Melanie must have pegged her right, she was too naïve to know they had just left a brothel. What was the preacher's excuse? Wasn't he supposed to be aware of all evil? Maybe he was a little naïve too.

Melanie swallowed past the lump in her throat. "Sterling Canyon."

The woman's eyes rounded wide and she clapped her hands. Melanie swallowed hard but this time the lump wouldn't budge. It couldn't be. It felt like too great of a coincidence.

11

The preacher's wife pivoted in her seat toward her husband and clutched at his arm. "Tom, I *will* have a friend!"

Reverend Merryweather patted his wife's hands and smiled at her with what Melanie thought was more than all the love and tenderness a man was capable of feeling for a woman. He leaned forward and surprised Melanie by kissing his wife's cheek. "I'm so glad, darling." He turned to Melanie, "We heard Sterling Canyon was widely populated by men and my dear little wife was worried she'd grow lonesome for female companionship."

Melanie's face blanched. Sterling Canyon was mostly men? When she had received the telegram notifying her that a great-uncle she never knew existed left her his ranch, Melanie imagined finally living a wholesome, solitary life outside a cozy, quiet town. Now, however, with Reverend Merryweather's description of Sterling Canyon, she could only imagine a town teeming with men. Melanie straightened in her seat and strengthened her spine with as much steel as she could muster. She knew how to handle men, and if she couldn't fend them off with threats she'd just have to resort to her derringer. She silently thanked Minnie for insisting each girl learn to shoot and carry a gun of their choice. She glanced down and hoped that with her new conservative dress she'd hardly be noticed, much less bothered by the opposite sex.

Louisa Merryweather, giddy with the possibility that she had just found her new bosom buddy, leaned forward and squeezed Melanie's hand. Melanie gasped and pulled her hand back before she could stop herself. Reverend and Louisa Merryweather stared at her with mouths gaping, shocked by her reaction.

Melanie quickly rubbed her wrist and smiled apologetically. "I recently wrenched it, I'm afraid it's still a bit sore."

CHAPTER 2

While Reverend Tom and Louisa Merryweather made soft sympathetic noises of understanding, Melanie inwardly cursed herself. Fifteen minutes. That's how long it took her to foul up her fresh start with a lie.

Disgusted with herself she leaned back against the seat of the coach and closed her eyes, hoping the reverend and his wife got the hint that she wanted to be alone. Or at least as alone as one can be on a stagecoach.

The coach lurched to a stop and nearly threw Melanie out of her seat as she startled awake. She peered out the window to see the sun was far to the east and the sky was turning swirled shades of maroon and blue. From outside the stage master called, "Stretch your legs!"

Melanie quickly moved to open the door and stepped down. The stage master was already changing out the horses for a fresh team. Reverend Merryweather followed Melanie out and turned back to assist his wife. Melanie arched her back, then stomped her feet up and down a few times to get the circulation moving in her legs. She realized she hadn't eaten all day, and as if on cue, her stomach rumbled. The reverend's perfect wife came over with a basket in hand and offered her a biscuit sandwiching a thick slice of ham. Melanie's mouth watered and she wondered how sinful it would be to accept food from a preacher's wife.

As if sensing her hesitation Louisa Merryweather smiled sweetly and shoved the biscuit into Melanie's hands. Softly, she whispered so no one could overhear, "You're going to be OK, Melanie."

Melanie looked up, startled, but before she could reply or even thank her for sharing their supper, the young woman had turned and was heading back toward her husband. Melanie stood watching the sun's descent as she ate her biscuit sandwich and pondered what the preacher's wife could have meant. The only thing Melanie could decide on was that maybe Louisa Merryweather wasn't as naïve as Melanie had first assumed.

Chapter 3

T TOOK FIVE long, hard-riding, non-stop-chatter-from-the-preacher's-wife days to get to Sterling Canyon, Texas. Melanie felt ready to stumble out and kiss the ground. The door swung open and the stage master announced, "Sterling Canyon, everyone out."

The scruffy looking stage master held his hand up and Melanie allowed him to assist her down. Surely she couldn't taint a man as salty looking as him. A second man was climbing on top of the coach, and once the stage master was finished assisting his passengers down, he began relieving the coach of their luggage with the second man's assistance. Melanie directed the stage master to place her trunk inside. Then she asked for directions to the livery. As she walked in the direction the stage master had indicated, Melanie was quite relieved to see the preacher and his wife occupied with greeting a man in a worn, yet tidy, gray suit.

Melanie hurried toward the livery which was conveniently located right across the street. Two large doors hung open at the front so Melanie walked in and announced herself. "Hello? Is anyone here?"

A young man with a head full of fiery red hair poked his head out of one of the stalls. "'Ello there, be with you in a moment." True to his word the young man quickly stepped out of the stall moments later. He dusted his hands on his pants and smiled broadly. "Now, what can I do for such a lovely lady, miss?"

Melanie's cheeks flamed red but not from embarrassment or shyness. She absolutely hated a man calling her lovely or beautiful or pretty or any other such nonsense. She knew she was a fat, homely whore and didn't appreciate being teased about being pretty. She gritted her teeth and resisted the urge to pound the young man with her Bible.

"I'm looking to rent a wagon and a team."

The young man's eyebrows shot straight up to his hairline. "Most women are more suited to a buggy."

Melanie glared at the young man. "I'm not most women. Do you have a wagon and team I can rent or not?"

The young man quickly nodded. "Yes, ma'am!" He immediately went to work harnessing a pair of strong-looking geldings to a rough, but sturdy, wagon. As he worked he called out, "About how long will you need the team and wagon?"

Melanie slipped into one of the stalls and looked to make sure the young man was too busy working to notice her, then she slid her dress up to remove a few bills from the garter. She quickly tucked them inside her long shirt sleeve and let her dress fall back into place. As she worked she called back to the young man, "Until I can have my own wagon made."

The jangling of leather, metal and wood suddenly ceased. "So you're plannin' on stayin'?"

Melanie rolled her eyes as she thought of what the preacher and his wife said about Sterling Canyon being mostly men. "Yes. And if you could please hurry I'll gladly be on my way."

The young man brought the wagon around and Melanie pulled out a couple of the bills she had tucked in her sleeve. "About how long until my wagon is ready?"

The young man seemed to think intently. "No longer than a week."

Melanie nodded. She inquired about where she could purchase a team of her own and the young man directed her to a farm northwest of town. Once they finished talking business, Melanie shook the young man's hand. "I'll be back in exactly a week for my wagon." She strode to the rented wagon, hopped up, perched herself on the front bench, and placing her Bible securely under her thigh, she clicked the horses into action before the young man could even think to assist her into the wagon.

Melanie darted across the street in the wagon and requested the stage master to put her trunk in the back. After a generous tip, he kindly obliged, and in mere minutes Melanie was on her way down the long main street of Sterling Canyon.

According to the telegram she had received, her departed great-uncle's ranch was roughly a day's ride southeast of town, so big you couldn't miss it. As she drove down the street, she spotted a general store. She pulled the wagon over in front of the general store and set the brake. With her Bible firmly in her grasp, she marched up the steps and into the shop.

Two women talking over a bolt of fabric immediately looked up and appraised Melanie with their eyes. Melanie tried to smile and the two women shyly smiled in return. An older man with gray shot all through his hair nearly bellowed, "Good afternoon, and welcome to the Sterling Canyon General Store! How can I help you?"

Melanie smiled, mostly out of amusement at his enthusiastic greeting. "I'm looking to purchase a few supplies."

The man spread his arms wide to gesture at the entire store. "Then you've come to the right place." The man placed his hands on top of the smooth wooden counter. "So, are you just off the coach?"

Melanie nodded. No sense in hiding why she was here, in a small town like this people would know before the day's end. "Apparently my great-uncle left me a ranch."

The man's eyebrows shot up and Melanie noticed the two women put the bolt of cloth down and inch closer. "You're Old Brooks' niece?"

Melanie shrugged. "I suppose I am." She glanced outside and saw the sun was heading higher into the sky. If she didn't hurry it would be well past noon before she lit out for the ranch. Walking over to large sacks of dry staples she ticked off on her fingers what she would need. The general store owner bellowed to a curtain behind him and a scrawny boy no older than thirteen came hustling out. The boy began scooping the staples into smaller burlap sacks as the older man weighed each one.

While the two of them hurried to fill her order, she scanned the shelves of canned goods and selected several cans of fruit. She placed the cans on top of the counter near the register. The general store owner looked up from weighing a sack of sugar and smiled. Melanie turned and noticed a crate of vegetables by the front door. She tapped her nail against her teeth as she tried to decide if she should buy some. Since she had no way of knowing if this old uncle of hers had kept a kitchen garden she decided it'd be wise to purchase a few of the vegetables. She strode over and picked up an empty burlap sack next to the crate. She selected a couple of potatoes, a few carrots, two turnips, and a very large onion.

As she stood up from bending over the crate of vegetables, the window display caught her eye, and she wondered how she had missed it on her way in. There in the window sat a small collection of six-shooters and rifles surrounded by boxes of ammunition. Melanie recognized the gun Amos had taught her to shoot. She grabbed a long barreled Winchester and hefted it out of the display. She grabbed a couple of boxes of ammunition with her free hand and walked back to the counter, quite aware of the women's staring eyes. She placed the bag of vegetables, the ammunition, and the rifle on the counter.

The older man behind the counter had finished weighing all of her food items. He smiled. "Will that be all for today, Miss Brooks?"

Melanie cringed at being addressed so formally. She smiled demurely and cocked her head to the side slightly, slowly dropping her eyelids then looking up at the general store owner as her eyes opened again. "Please, call me Melanie."

The older man's cheeks flamed red and he began to stutter. "Y-y-yes ma'am!" His cheeks flushed an even brighter red and he gulped. "I mean, Melanie." He named the price she owed and she withdrew more bills from her sleeve to pay him. When he handed her the change, she looked at the coins in his outstretched hand.

"I don't have anything to carry those in."

One of the women who had been gawking at her spoke up. "You can sell her one of my reticules, Mr. Jenkins."

The general store owner's eyes widened. "Why, what a lovely idea, Mrs. Burmood!"

The older man, apparently Mr. Jenkins, quickly stepped from behind the counter and ushered Melanie toward a table scattered with different sized, shaped, and colored reticules. A yellow floral one immediately caught her eye, and she picked it up. Surely it wouldn't hurt to have a little something pretty.

"I think I'll take this one. How much would you like for it?"

Mr. Jenkins smiled. "Please, take it as a welcoming gift."

Melanie smiled kindly and thanked Mr. Jenkins, half regretting having used her brothel charms to fluster the man into calling her by her first name. She slipped her change into her new reticule and the same young boy assisted Mr. Jenkins in carrying her supplies to the wagon.

Once securely seated on the wagon bench, Melanie lifted one leg and firmly wedged her Bible underneath it. She looked over her shoulder and spotted her new rifle. "I'll take that up here with me, Mr. Jenkins." The general store owner nodded and handed her the rifle. "And a box of that ammunition; if you'd be so kind." Mr. Jenkins motioned for the younger boy to hand up a box of ammunition from the satchel he had just deposited into the back of her wagon. Melanie immediately loaded the rifle and placed it on the seat next to her.

When all of her supplies were loaded into the wagon, Melanie picked up the reins and released the brake. "Thank you for all your help today, Mr. Jenkins."

The older man wiped his brow and smiled. "Pleasure meeting you, Melanie." His face flushed red again when he said her name.

Melanie nodded and slapped the reins across the horse's backs to get them moving. Once out of town she urged the able geldings faster, wanting to get as far today as possible. After a few miles of the faster pace, the trail began to thin out and become

CHAPTER 3

rockier. Melanie pulled up on the reins to slow the team and began to maneuver around holes and large rocks.

As the sun began its descent, Melanie stopped the wagon in the middle of the trail, doubting anyone would come by to make her move. She jumped over the seat to the back of the wagon. She pushed her supplies to one side and knelt down in front of her trunk. Unlatching the leather straps, she opened the top and reached in to grab a quilt she knew was on top. As she did, her fingers came into contact with a burlap sack. Melanie pulled it out and noticed a small note pinned to the front that read, "Good luck, kiddo. Minnie."

Melanie untied the strings at the top and peered in. It was a dinner sack. Gratitude flooded Melanie's heart for she hadn't thought of buying anything at the general store for her supper. Inside were several biscuits, jerky, and a chunk of cheese. Melanie ate two stale biscuits, some jerky, and half the chunk of cheese right away, deciding to leave the rest for morning. Once supper was finished and the remainder tucked safely back into her trunk, she pulled out her favorite quilt, one she had somehow managed to hold onto since both of her parents had been taken by yellow fever and she had been left to raise herself. She laid down in the back of her wagon, tucking the blanket securely around herself, her Bible safely hidden in her trunk and the Winchester snug at her side.

Chapter 4

ELANIE WAS AWAKE before the sun split the sky. She sat up and stretched her arms wide as she yawned. She had slept so well she nearly forgot she was in the back of a wagon with just a quilt to protect her from the night air. She wondered if that was what it was like to sleep without degrading yourself first. It ate at her that she couldn't remember that feeling. It had been too long. Shrugging off the guilt, she wrapped her quilt around her shoulders and pulled from the dinner sack in her trunk—the one Minnie had packed for her. By the time she had eaten and repacked her quilt, the sun was cresting the horizon.

As the sun peaked high in the sky, Melanie drove the geldings up a hill and stopped at the top, too frozen in awe to drive down into the valley below. Just east of her position she could see a large, two-story house. Painted yellow. Melanie smiled to herself. "Guess me and Uncle Brooks had something in common."

CHAPTER 4

She let the geldings pick their way along down the hill. Glancing up every few seconds she watched as more outbuildings came into view, and smiled her delight to see each outbuilding was painted the same sunshine yellow as the main house. The only exception was the great big red barn located just to the right of the house. As she descended the hill, she turned the horses and headed straight for the large ranch house. When she was closer, she noticed a worn trail leading from town to the ranch and made a mental note next time to use the worn trail rather than trying to traipse over the rocky hills. She directed the geldings along the long drive and pulled to a stop directly in front of the house.

Up close Melanie could see the sunshine yellow house had white shutters, neat white trim, and the large porch that wrapped around the entire house looked to be sturdy and freshly painted white as well. Melanie grabbed her valuable Bible from under her thigh, and picked up the Winchester before jumping out of the wagon. She clutched the Bible to her side and loosely balanced the long rifle in her other arm. She called out her presence, not sure if any employees still worked the ranch or if someone had taken up squatting on the property. When she didn't get a reply she climbed the porch steps to get a better view over the wagon. No one in sight.

Melanie felt a surge of relief. No one around to bother her. She smiled to herself as she thought of the quiet life she could build for herself here. She turned back to the house and tried the door. Unlocked. Not so unusual. Great-Uncle Brooks was dead; what would he need to lock the door for? She walked in and was surprised to see the house decorated with plush furniture, lace curtains, and vases of wildflowers. She walked

23

into a small parlor to the left and ran her finger across a small table situated in front of an elegantly upholstered lounge and two chairs. No dust. Her brow furrowed. She had received the telegram saying her Great-Uncle Brooks had died nearly two months ago. Melanie had fully expected the house to be full of dust, cobwebs, and rodents, not vases of wildflowers.

She shrugged. "This must be the wrong place."

"Nope, you're at the right place, girly."

Melanie whirled around at the sound of a rusty, old voice. She clutched her Bible tighter and leveled the Winchester with one hand hoping she wouldn't have to drop the Bible to fire the gun.

A tall, old man stood before her, his face covered in white whiskers. He held up his hands, his cheeks bulging as he smiled. "Sorry, Little Missy, didn't mean to scare ya."

Melanie eyed him carefully. "Who are you and what are you doing on my property?"

The old man's smile seemed to grow and he chuckled. "I'm Pappy. I sent for ya."

"Pappy?"

The old man slid his thumbs under his suspenders. "Yup. P.H. Pappy Henderson."

Melanie quirked an eyebrow. "Pappy?" Who named their child Pappy?

The old man leaned back and laughed. "Real name's Paul, but I reared my nephew and once when he was younger he accidentally called me Pappy in front of all the Brooks riders. They teased him something fierce, but eventually they all got used to calling me Pappy as a joke. It just stuck."

CHAPTER 4

Melanie nodded slowly. "I see. And you're the one who sent me a telegram about my Great-Uncle Brooks?"

Pappy looked pleased with himself. "Yup, and took plenty of years to find ya too. Your uncle searched for nearly fifteen years trying to track you down."

Melanie's mouth gaped open. Fifteen years ago she was still an innocent young girl living in Wisconsin trying to ignore the deep ache of losing her parents in order to survive in the world on her own.

Melanie shook her head in disbelief. "Fifteen years?"

Pappy nodded. "Yup, ever since he heard your parents passed. Toward the end he begged me to keep lookin' 'til I found ya." Pappy lifted his face to the ceiling and held up his hands. "Well, you old coot, I found her. I hope you're happy!"

Melanie darted her gaze to the ceiling, not quite sure what the old man was seeing. Surely he didn't have the power to look directly into Heaven. Or did he? She took a step back from the old man. She heard that sometimes old people lost their minds.

Pappy stopped talking to the ceiling and looked back at her. "So, young lady, you hungry? I've got rabbit stew on the stove."

Before she could reply the old man walked away, gesturing for her to follow. They walked out of the parlor, down the hall and toward the back of the house where a large kitchen took up nearly the entire back of the house. In one corner stood a large counter that branched out to a stove on the right and a sink on the left. A small work table with a couple of chairs sat a few feet from the counter. Behind that was what Melanie assumed to be a pantry, built into the back of the stairs. On the other side of the kitchen was a long table with what Melanie guessed to be twenty chairs around it. To her upmost delight, windows lined the entire kitchen and dining area so it was almost more window than wall. All those windows looked like picture frames for the Texas landscape.

Between the windows, a large door divided the kitchen and dining areas that seemed cut in half. She approached the door and pulled the handle. To her surprise only the top half swung out, while the bottom half stayed bolted into the threshold.

"My goodness."

Pappy nodded. "Yup. Your great-uncle sure didn't spare any expense. He wanted to make sure you'd like it."

Melanie turned to the old man. Surely she hadn't heard him right. "He wanted to make sure *I'd* like it?"

Pappy threw his hands in the air and shook his head. "Well sure! Haven't you heard a word I said? He had been lookin' for you for quite some time."

Before she could ask any more questions, the old codger pulled out a glass bowl from a cabinet hanging in the corner and ladled steaming stew into it. He retrieved a silver spoon from a drawer and placed it on the work table. He filled one more bowl, retrieved one more spoon, and grabbed a loaf of bread which he put in the middle of the table.

He pulled out a chair and gestured for her to sit. "Have a seat, Little Missy."

Melanie stared at the offered chair. She wasn't quite comfortable with a man pulling out chairs for her, even if it was just this old, grizzled-looking man. She stepped around the other side, pulled out the other chair and seated herself with her Bible securely under her thigh and her Winchester propped against the table leg.

CHAPTER 4

Pappy's brow rose, but much to Melanie's relief he didn't comment. Instead, to her horror, he removed his hat, reached across the table, grabbed her hand, bowed his head, and began to pray. "Dear Heavenly Father, we thank You this day for our daily bread. We also thank You for Miss Brooks' safe travels."

While he prayed Melanie stared at his bowed head, which she was surprised to see was covered in thick, white hair. She felt the dirtiness creep up inside of her and she knew she must be committing another sin by touching this old man while he spoke to God. Her fingers itched to pull out of his grip, but she restrained herself. Surely, the only thing worse than touching a man while he spoke to God was interrupting him.

"Amen." Finally the old man lifted his head and beamed a smile at her. "Well, Little Missy, let's dig in."

Melanie dipped her silver spoon into the thick stew and spooned in her first mouthful of *real* food since leaving the brothel almost a week ago. Despite the presence of large chunks of meat and vegetables the stew was quite bland except for a slight lingering burnt taste. She looked over at the large pot simmering over the stove and wondered how many days it would take her to finish it. She reached for the bread and ripped a chunk off, thinking the stew might not be so bad soaked up in the bread. She dipped her bread in the thick stew. Her teeth ground against the hard bread until her jaw ached.

She looked up and saw Pappy watching her intently. She forced a smile. "It's delicious, thank you."

Pappy tossed his head back and howled in laughter. "You sure are a sweet one, Little Missy. But you don't have to lie, the boys tell me enough for me to know I'm not a good cook."

The only thing Melanie had heard was the old man's mention of "the boys." Melanie turned her head to scan each window, but didn't see anyone moving about the yard. Maybe this old man was a bit off his rocker. He must have noticed her looking out the windows in search of people, for he began to explain.

"Oh, you won't find anyone out there now. All the boys have gone to take the cattle to market. They should be back in six weeks or so."

Melanie's heart pounded in her chest. Men worked here? Men lived on her property? She came out all this way to get away from men, not be surrounded by them!

"H-h-how many men work here?"

Pappy smiled as if he were proud. "Fifteen. We did have twenty but some took off once the old boss passed on. They weren't too keen on having a woman be their new boss."

Fifteen men. Fifteen stinky, filthy, lust-driven men. Melanie's mind whirled. How ever would she survive among fifteen men? She reached down and stroked the barrel of the gun. Well, that would be one way.

Pappy obviously didn't notice her discomfort for he continued shoveling the tasteless stew into his mouth. He paused briefly to ask, "Have you ever bossed a ranch before?"

Melanie laughed bitterly. Surely the old coot was just messing with her now. He found her didn't he? So he must know where she had been working. She glared at the old man across from her. "Why no, *Pappy*, whores don't get much opportunity to boss ranches."

She stood so fast her chair clattered over. She grabbed her Bible and Winchester and headed for the front door. She pushed the front door open and allowed it to slam shut behind her. She grabbed the reins of her rented geldings and turned them around to head for the barn. Friend or no friend of her great-uncle's, Melanie decided she'd send that old man on his way down the road if he made one more joke about her past. Suddenly the reins were torn from her hands and she turned to see Pappy towering over her. She hadn't even heard the door open.

"Now you listen here, Little Missy!"

Melanie gulped. Before the old man seemed fragile and half out of his mind, but now standing directly in front of him Melanie could see the alert and dangerous anger burning in his eyes. As he held the reins away from her, she noticed his shirt was still pulled tight with muscle and she wondered how she had missed that before. Melanie looked directly up into his fiery eyes.

"I don't ever, and I mean *ever,* want to hear you say that blasted word again. You are *not* and will never be –"

Melanie waved her hand and cut him off. "Pappy, I'm sorry that word upsets you but surely you know the truth. You found me after all." He looked at her with one eyebrow raised. Was it possible he didn't know what 'Minnie's Dollhouse' meant? She sighed, she might as well explain. "Minnie's Dollhouse is a b-"

Now Pappy cut her off. "I know; a brothel."

Melanie stared at him astonished. "Then surely you realize it's true, I'm a whore." Pappy's face flushed bright red. Melanie placed her hands firmly on her hips. "Well come on, Pappy. It's not like I was polishing shoes in there."

Melanie saw a vein pop out on Pappy's neck, and she unconsciously took a step backward. He immediately schooled his emotions and dropped his head. "I know what kind of work you did, but I still don't believe that you're – *that.*"

"A whore?"

Pappy glared down at her. "Don't use that word, Little Missy."

Melanie tilted her head back and nearly screeched. "But it's true! I slept with men for money. I am a whore!"

Before she could move out of his way, Pappy grabbed her by her shoulders and shook her. "Listen here, Little Missy, you did what you had to do to survive. Your great-uncle understood that and I think that's why he worked so hard to make this place so enjoyable for a lady. He wanted you to have the best." He shook her hard. "Do you hear me? He cared enough to spend the last fifteen years of his life searching for you and all the while he was spending a fortune building this great big house and filling it with lacy curtains and glass doo-dads."

Pappy released her shoulders and Melanie glanced at the great big, yellow house that stood behind him. Tears began to rim her eyes as the full impact of what Pappy said penetrated her frozen heart. Someone cared enough to search her out and build this near-mansion-sized house with careful thought as to what a woman would like. What *she* would like.

Melanie turned on her heel and ran.

Chapter 5

APPY LIT ANOTHER lantern and placed it on a windowsill. Satisfied that enough lanterns were lit and shining through the open windows to be seen from far away, he stepped out onto the porch. He peered into the darkness and wondered if he should saddle up and go looking for the girl. He had promised Old Brooks he'd care for the girl—but thus far he didn't feel he had done a great job. He had tried hunching himself over, thinking the girl would be more comfortable with a feeble old man. But then he lost his temper when she went and called herself a—well he couldn't even bring himself to think the word. He shook his head. The kid had had a hard life, and from everything Old Brooks had learned of her over the years, time hadn't lessened her hardship. Pappy shook his head.

"God show me how to help her," he prayed.

Pappy scanned the yard once more but saw no sign of the fiery young woman. With shoulders slumped, he walked back inside. He went into the large sitting area and checked the clock on the mantle of the huge rock fireplace. It was barely seven o'clock. One more hour. That's how long he'd wait before saddling up to go look for her.

Melanie pushed up from the ground from where she had fallen asleep. She wasn't quite sure how far she had run from the ranch house, but from the ache in her legs it was definitely far. She stretched her arms wide and yawned. Her face still felt warm and her eyes were swollen from all of the tears she had shed. Suddenly she realized it was sunset and she wondered just how long she had been sleeping on the soft ground. Not wanting to waste a moment more, she began trudging back toward the house.

She broke through a grove of trees and looked up to scan her surroundings. Directly in front of her, no more than five hundred yards away, was the ranch house, *her* ranch house, each window glowing with golden light. Tears stung her eyes as she thought of the kind gesture. Pappy was trying to help her home. The thought nearly startled her. *Home.* She hadn't had a real home since her parents had passed. A new home for a new beginning. A smile broke across her face and she ran for the house.

She raced up the porch steps and flew through the front door. "Pappy? Pappy I'm *home!*"

The old man lumbered out of a room to the right that she hadn't yet gone into. He quickly approached her, and before she could protest he had her in a fierce bear hug.

"Don't run out on me like that again. Ya hear me, Little Missy?"

CHAPTER 5

Melanie was surprised when that old repulsive feeling didn't start knotting up in her stomach as Pappy held her. She allowed the tension to ease out of her shoulders and she slowly wrapped her own arms around his middle.

"Yes, Pappy, I hear you."

He held her out at arm's length. "Good. Now do you want to talk about what happened?"

Melanie hung her head, suddenly ashamed at how she had acted after this family friend had shown her nothing but kindness. Slowly, she shook her head. All she wanted now was to go to bed.

Pappy grunted. "Too bad." He grabbed her elbow and wheeled her around toward the room to the right. Inside was a large fireplace made of stone with two plush arm chairs on either side. Between the two armchairs, directly in front of the fireplace, was a wooden rocking chair. Pappy seated her in the rocking chair and sat himself in one of the armchairs.

Pappy folded his hands neatly across his stomach. "Now, Little Missy, just what was all that running off nonsense about?"

Melanie gulped. She knew she was technically the boss but this new confident, strong side of Pappy was almost frightening, and she didn't want to see him truly upset by not answering. "Everything you said—about Great-Uncle Brooks, how he did all this," she gestured all around herself. "It just hit me full force." Melanie sniffed back the beginning of tears. "No one has ever done something like that for me. I could almost believe he truly cared."

Pappy nearly guffawed. "That old geezer did care!" He leaned forward and pointed a rough finger at her. "Do you truly think he'd have done all of this if he hadn't?"

33

Melanie's voice came out in a weak, whimper. "I guess not." Melanie looked directly into Pappy's eyes. "But doesn't mean I deserve it." She stood and quickly strode to the doorway, safe from Pappy holding her back. "I want you to show me around tomorrow. I need to see my land and know what's been done and what needs doing." She took a step into the hallway and paused, remembering one more thing, "And tomorrow, I'll make breakfast."

Melanie thought she heard Pappy snicker as she began to climb the stairs but she wasn't sure. As she reached the second floor she looked down the long hallway at its many closed doors. With her Bible and Winchester tucked against her body with one arm, she used her free hand to open and close doors. The second door on the right had a lantern inside, illuminating the yellow quilt that had been placed across the bed and the lace curtains that fluttered in the night breeze coming through the open window. This must be her room.

Melanie shut the door and placed her Bible inside the small table beside the bed and leaned her gun against the wall. She turned to further inspect the room and noticed her trunk had been brought up and was sitting along the wall behind the door. She smiled at what, yet again, must have been Pappy's thoughtfulness. On the wall adjacent to her bed was a small vanity with its own mirror. She took a deep, shuddering breath. She'd definitely have to work hard to earn each luxury her great-uncle had thought to shower upon her.

Pappy leaned forward resting his elbows on his knees. So that was the problem. The girl didn't feel worthy of this place.

He shook his head. "I guess any girl coming out of a situation like hers wouldn't." He scrubbed his face with his palms. "Help me, Father. Show me how to help her."

Pappy sat in his chair praying for a long time. By the time he was done, it was nearly eleven o'clock. He grunted as he stood to his feet, stiff from sitting so long in one position. He arched his back and yawned.

"Well, at least breakfast won't be burned tomorrow."

Chapter 6

ELANIE WOKE BEFORE the sun rose and dressed quickly in one of her brown calicos. She braided her hair down her back and quickly laced her boots. She grabbed her Stetson and rifle and quietly tip-toed down the stairs. She knew Pappy slept down the hall from her because she had heard him retire late last night. Now she didn't want to wake him. She went out the front and carefully closed the door instead of allowing it to bang shut. She turned left and headed toward the barn.

She heaved the heavy door open and began walking down the aisle, looking for the milk cow she had heard lowing from her bedroom. A great "moooo" nearly startled her out of her wits. She hurried down the aisle, picking up a small stool she spotted along the way and quickly found three milk cows standing side by side in one large stall.

Melanie smiled at the cows. "Morning, ladies." She leaned her rifle against the outside of the large stall and leaned under a wood rail that kept the cows in with the stool in hand. To the left were neatly stacked buckets. She picked one off the top and settled in next to the first cow and began milking.

By the time Melanie got to the third cow, her wrists and forearms ached and her fingers were cramped. She accidentally tugged too hard on an udder and the cow sidestepped. Melanie quickly grabbed the bucket to prevent the milk from spilling. "Sorry, girl, guess I'm out of practice." The cow looked back at her and Melanie laughed. "I said sorry!"

Once finished with milking, Melanie started to carefully tuck the buckets up against a wall where they'd be safe from being tripped over. As she leaned over to carefully place another bucket down, another bucket appeared at her side. She startled, but at the sound of Pappy's laugh she immediately relaxed.

"Morning, Little Missy. Thought you'd get a head start today, huh?"

Melanie wiped a stray curl off her forehead with the back of her wrist. "I figured I'd need an early start to get everything done before we set out to see the property."

Pappy leaned over to pick up the last bucket and transport it to the wall. "You know, you don't have to do this on your own. I'm here to help, and once the boys get back there'll be plenty of help to go around."

"It's my ranch, Pappy, so it's my job."

"And I'm your hired hand, so it's my job too." Before Melanie could argue further Pappy started issuing orders, as if this were his ranch and she were the hired hand. "There are leftover eggs from yesterday. Go get started on that breakfast you promised me. I'll finish tending the animals."

Melanie placed her hands firmly on her hips. "Well I'd like to see my animals and ..."

Pappy picked up her rifle, thrust it into her hands, twirled her around, and gave her a shove toward the barn door. "Go on, I'm hungry."

Melanie huffed, but decided you don't argue with a man when he's hungry, so she strode out of the barn and headed for the house. As she entered the large kitchen—her kitchen—she sighed. It would be a pleasure cooking in here, even if it was for fifteen men. After several minutes of opening and closing cupboards and drawers, Melanie was beginning to get a feel for where things were located. Everything except where they kept the apron. She found the flour she had purchased yesterday in the pantry at the back of the stairs and tossed a generous amount onto the work table. She added lard, a dash of milk, sugar, salt, and an egg. One of the few things she remembered of her parents was her mama's recipe for never-fail biscuits. She kneaded the dough together and smiled at the memory of the first time her mama had allowed her to make these biscuits. True to their name, even her inexperienced five-year-old self couldn't make these biscuits fail.

With the oven already heated, another one of Pappy's thoughtful gestures, she popped the biscuits in to bake. Next she scooped coffee into the coffee pot and added water before placing it on the top of the large stove. Then she placed a large cast iron skillet there as well and added a generous slice of butter and whisked eggs while the pan warmed. Once the eggs were done, she spooned them out equally onto two impractical china plates. She added a touch more butter to the skillet and placed two large ham steaks in the hot skillet. By the time the ham steaks were browned and steaming, the biscuits were ready to come out of the oven. She put a ham steak on each plate and then walked around the work table to set the plates on the small table she and Pappy had shared last night. When she looked up, she noticed a large triangle hanging outside just to the right of the back door. With a smile on her lips, she marched outside and rang the triangle with all her might.

Back inside, she placed the tin of biscuits in the center of the table with the crock of butter, filled two cups of coffee, found a small jar of jam which she placed next to the biscuits and grabbed forks and napkins from a drawer. When she saw Pappy walking across the yard toward the house, she hurried to the door and hollered. "Don't you even think of coming into my clean kitchen until you wash properly."

She saw Pappy look down at his hands and clothes. "I'm not all that dirty."

She grinned, realizing this was one way to get him back for his bossy attitude in the barn. "Do you want breakfast or not?"

Pappy shook his head as he marched off toward a pump at the back of the house. Obviously, the old coot wasn't used to washing before his meals. Melanie placed her hands on her hips and nodded resolutely. Well, he'd just have to learn to do so or no meals for him.

It only took Pappy a couple of minutes to return to the house with hands scrubbed and face washed. He took his hat off as he sat at the table and hooked it over his knee under the table. Just as he did last night, he grabbed her hand and said grace over their meal. Melanie allowed him to do so, too scared to interfere with a man and his prayers. Once he raised his head again, he grabbed his fork and took a timid bite of the eggs Melanie had dished out on his plate. A low growl-like sound emitted from his throat and he began shoveling the eggs into his mouth. He put his fork down long enough to grab a biscuit, rip it in half and smother it in butter before taking a large bite out of it.

Melanie stared. "I take it, it's good?"

Pappy's face turned beet red. He wiped his mouth with his napkin and chewed his mouth full of biscuit before responding. When he was free to talk he pointed his fork down at his plate. "We haven't had cooking this good since … well, since I can't remember. The boys are gonna love this."

Melanie tried to keep her smile in place at Pappy's mention of "the boys," but she was afraid she was making a futile attempt, so she quickly covered her lips with her coffee cup. "I'm glad you like it." Melanie looked down the front of her dress that was now dusted with flour and speckled with popped grease. "Although an apron would be handy."

Pappy was too busy wolfing down his food to respond. Melanie dug into her own food. She'd better hurry if she wanted to see her property today. Once they both finished, Pappy pushed back from the table and headed for the door.

Melanie cleared her throat. He turned. "I said thank you."

Melanie tapped her foot. She looked down at the table where he had left his plate and empty coffee cup. She looked back up at Pappy, her foot still tapping. Pappy scratched his head.

Melanie rolled her eyes. Men! You have to direct them like children. "After each meal, I'd like for you to scrape your leftovers into the slop bucket and place your dishes in the sink."

Pappy looked from her to his dishes he had left for her to clean up and then to the slop bucket. He shrugged his shoulders and slowly trudged back to the table. He scraped the last bit of eggs into the bucket before placing his plate, fork, and cup in the sink. He turned back to her and stared as if waiting to receive his next instructions.

She hesitated. She didn't want to come across as bossing the kind old man around. "Thank you. Now if you'd please saddle two horses, I'd like to see the property today. I'll pack a dinner sack and then we can be on our way."

Pappy nodded and headed out toward the barn. Melanie hustled around the kitchen cleaning up the breakfast dishes and wiping down the counters. She split open the remaining biscuits and buttered each half, then sprinkled sugar over each one before reassembling the biscuits. She pulled out a clean dish towel and wrapped the biscuits, then carefully slid them into a burlap sack. She opened the pantry door and surveyed the shelves. She found jerky wrapped in brown paper and added that to the sack. She located the cans of fruit she had purchased in town and selected a can of peaches. As she came out of the pantry, she placed their dinner sack on top of the work table and surveyed the land outside those impractical, yet beautiful windows. The land seemed to go on forever. She was bundling their supper together when Pappy came back in.

He scratched his chin. "That's all we're bringing for dinner?

Melanie faced the expansive windows. "I'll make a hearty stew for supper."

"It'll be mighty uncomfortable, riding all day."

Melanie turned to face Pappy. "I didn't always sleep in plush feather beds and laze about until nearly noon. I did grow up on a farm." Melanie lifted the burlap sack over her shoulder and picked up her Winchester with her other hand. "Are we ready?"

Pappy turned and led the way to their waiting horses. Melanie stuffed the dinner sack into a saddle bag and slid her rifle into the scabbard. By the time she mounted the gentle strawberry roan mare, she noticed Pappy was already seated upon a majestic bay stallion with three skins of water looped over his saddle horn.

Pappy smiled. "Ready?" At her nod he led the way out of the yard and they headed south.

By twilight they rode back into the yard. Pappy had shown her about half the land and Melanie's head swam at the idea of managing all of this land. She dismounted her horse and patted the animal's shoulder. The horse turned its head and nuzzled her shoulder in return, causing her to laugh and stroke down the white blaze on its face.

Pappy unsaddled his horse in the stall next to her. "Brooks bought her just for you."

Melanie turned to him, surprised. "What?"

Pappy nodded and stretched out his hand to scratch the mare's muzzle. "Mmm-hmm. He thought you might like having your own horse to go riding on. It took him nearly three years to find the perfect mount."

Melanie raised an eyebrow. "Three years? The livery boy said a farm not far off breeds horses for sale. Why didn't he just go there?"

Pappy chuckled. "Oh, he did. But he wanted you to have a mare. A gentle mare, one that he could be sure would never throw you. But he also wanted it to be pretty."

Now Melanie laughed. "Pretty? He said those words?"

CHAPTER 6

Pappy rubbed his face and nodded. "Yup. He said a pretty gal deserved a pretty horse. Then one day he heard some old rancher's wife say she thought strawberry roans were the prettiest horses she had ever seen. So, of course, then the horse had to be a strawberry roan." Pappy sighed. "Your great-uncle put so many stipulations and requirements on what he wanted in your horse he nearly drove every horse breeder in the state crazy."

Melanie laughed at the tale of her great-uncle and for the first time in over eight years felt the light of true happiness spark in her heart. She looked to the west. The sun was setting and cast the land in a brilliant orange hue. She thought that just maybe, if she worked hard and kept the ranch hands at a distance, she could find a piece of happiness here.

Chapter 7

PAPPY TILTED BACK his china cup and drained the last of his coffee. The girl surely was something. She'd ridden all day without a complaint, told *him* they'd better get a move on fixing a downed fence, and then told him *how* to go about fixing it. On their way out, she set a snare using little more than her boot strings and sticks *and* actually caught a dang rabbit which she cleaned and skinned herself, then made a tasty, rib-sticking stew, as promised. Pappy shook his head and smiled. Yup, she surely was something.

He looked over at Melanie as she stood at the sink washing their dishes, occasionally pausing to stare at the stars. She sure was a quiet one. Usually women wanted to yammer about every little thing that popped into their heads. He furrowed his brow and wondered if he should be worried that she didn't talk his ear off.

He cleared his throat. "So, whatcha think of the land so far?"

The little lady didn't turn around, her eyes fixed on the stars. "It's a lot of land to care for."

Pappy thought she sounded a bit nervous. "Yup, it is. But you know, you don't have to do it all alone. You've got plenty of men working here and each one does more than his fair share." Pappy laughed. "And I'm sure once they taste your cooking they'll be obliged to work even harder."

His last comment made Melanie laugh and the sound was music to his ears. It stopped all too soon though and she turned around to face him. "Pappy, how much do the men know?"

Her question confused him. "About ranching? Well quite a bit. Brooks wouldn't have hired them otherwise."

She pushed away from the counter and sat across from him. "No, not about ranching." She stared down at the table. "About me?"

Suddenly he understood what she meant. "They know you're Brooks' niece and that he loved you without ever setting eyes on you and searched the last ten years of his life to bring you home."

It may have been his ears or the gust of wind that howled outside, but Pappy was almost certain her voice wavered as she spoke. "So they don't know about the brothel?"

Pappy's heart filled with compassion. "No, darlin', never saw it as their business to tell them, and it'll remain that way unless you tell them yourself. This can be a new start for you, Little Missy."

Melanie nodded. "That's exactly what I thought when I got your telegram." She sighed. "Pappy, I promise you and Great-Uncle Brooks that I'll do my best to deserve this land and everything Great-Uncle Brooks built up on it." With that she stood and returned to washing dishes at the sink.

Pappy stood up and took his coffee cup to the sink, then stepped outside. As he looked up at the stars he whispered to himself, "I know you will, Little Missy. But the thing is, you already deserve it."

Melanie awoke just as the sun began to crest the horizon. She yawned and stretched out her limbs. Yesterday they had ridden through grassy meadows and two creeks and had climbed several rocky hills. The land her great-uncle had built on was vast and the soil rich. She garnered that if she had the inclination to take up farming, the land would produce a good crop. The idea of trying something new, like running cattle, enticed her and she decided before even seeing the ranch that she would stick with cattle and not try to convert the place into a farm.

Melanie rolled out of bed and quickly pulled on her dress and boots and crept downstairs to build the fire back up for hot coffee. She filled the battered coffee pot with water and grounds, then set it to boil. By the time Pappy came down, she had a batter for johnnycakes mixed together and was dropping dollops of the batter into the heated and greased skillet.

Pappy smiled. "How is it you're always one step ahead of me?"

Melanie returned his smile. The old coot had really begun growing on her. And she rather liked calling him Pappy. "I told you, Pappy, that'd I'd try real hard to earn all of this."

Pappy reached around her to pull down plates and cups. "I think we'll be able to see the rest of the land and be back in a couple of hours."

Melanie flipped the johnnycakes to cook on the other side. "Really? So soon? I thought there was more land than that."

Pappy laughed. "Well we rode pretty hard yesterday."

Melanie stared at the cooking johnnycakes while contemplating what he said. They *had* ridden pretty hard. Maybe she should have taken more time to really *see* the land. Her eyes were so fixed on broken fences, what kind of game lived nearby and how deep the creeks were that she hadn't really focused on the land itself. "Maybe we should go back and take a second look."

Pappy shook his head. "No, no, Little Missy. We'll ride hard again this morning and see the rest of the land. Then we've got to get back to chores."

Melanie quirked an eyebrow. "Why's that, boss?" She smiled so he'd know she was joking.

Pappy chuckled. "Because, Little Missy, with the boys gone there's a lot to do for just the two of us."

Melanie's eyes rounded and she felt the heat rise up in her neck. Melanie tried to swallow the lump that always formed when Pappy mentioned "the boys."

"Oh, of course."

"There's a lot more to do than just mend fences." Pappy held up his hand and began ticking off chores. "We've got to restock the wood pile, water and feed the animals, churn butter, and tend the vegetable garden."

Melanie held up her hands. "I know, I know." She shrugged. "I just wanted to see my land."

Pappy was probably right though. There were plenty of chores to be done here first. She cursed herself silently for being so dimwitted. She hadn't even poked around to see what other animals resided at the ranch. She saw the muddy pig pen. And obviously they had horses, but how many? Of course there were hens; she ate the proof for breakfast yesterday. Melanie removed the cooked johnnycakes to a plate. She picked up the coffee pot full of steaming hot coffee and poured Pappy a cup.

"Thanks Little Missy."

Melanie turned back to the stove and grabbed the plate heaping with johnnycakes. She got the butter and a glass jar of maple syrup from the pantry and joined Pappy at the table. "Pappy, after breakfast we'll tend the animals then head out again. I want to see what else lies to the south today."

Pappy smiled. "Yes, boss."

Melanie poured syrup over her johnnycakes. "We'll venture to the north later."

Pappy nodded at her then turned his full attention to his johnnycakes.

With the breakfast dishes cleaned and the animals tended to, Melanie was ready to go see the rest of the south side of her land. She grabbed the front hem of her dress while she placed one foot in a stirrup and swung up onto her horse with the practiced ease of an old farm hand.

She leaned forward and patted her strawberry roan's neck. The roan side-stepped excitedly. "I'm eager too, Brooke."

Pappy had just swung up into his saddle. "Brooke?"

Melanie shrugged. "I couldn't think of a better name."

Pappy chuckled. "I think 'Brooke' is just fine."

They set a rigorous pace riding out over the rest of the south side of the land. Melanie mentally noted more downed fencing and an old rotted-out tree that needed to be removed. Pappy pointed out a large pond where the herd watered and the men swam. Following the fence line home, they came across another creek.

"This one is part of the creek we saw yesterday." He pointed toward the west. "Further north, a third creek connects to this one. All three feed into the pond we saw earlier."

CHAPTER 7

"No wonder the land is so lush."

Pappy nodded. "Old Brooks was mighty particular about the land he staked out."

They picked up their pace and Pappy led them in a more direct route home. Melanie was pleased to see that they arrived home not long after supper. As they rode down their lane toward the house, Melanie didn't stop in the yard. She rode Brooke straight to the barn, hopped down to open the door, and led her sweating horse in by its reins.

"Woo-wee, Little Missy that sure was a jarring ride."

Melanie turned to see Pappy shaking out his legs and she smiled. "Well, I had to get back to my responsibilities."

"The place wouldn't have crumbled away in one afternoon, you know."

Melanie smiled and shrugged then led into her stall while Pappy led his mount to a stall further down. She un-cinched the saddle and heaved the heavy leather to the side panel of the stall. She used a small towel to wipe down Brooke and talked to her in low tones. As she began brushing out Brooke's coat, her thoughts began wandering down the path she had strayed and the years she had wasted with Jonathan. She sighed, wondering what her life would have been like if she hadn't gotten tangled up with a man liked that.

Pappy startled at the loud sigh coming a few stalls down where Melanie was rubbing down her horse. His brow furrowed as he wondered what could possibly distress the girl so much. He cleared his throat. "You upset about something?"

"Hmm? Oh, no."

"Well are you tired?"

She laughed and Pappy smiled at the sound of her musical laughter. "No, Pappy."

"Well then, why the big sigh?"

She sighed again and Pappy wasn't sure if it was annoyance at his constant questions, or if she really was just tired. "I was just thinking about Jonathan."

Pappy stopped brushing his mount and straightened his shoulders. "Jonathan?"

He could hear the sadness in her voice. "He was my fiancé."

Pappy gulped. "Fiancé?"

"Hello? Anyone here?"

Pappy heard Melanie gasp then whisper, "Winchester."

He peered over the stalls separating them. Did she rename her horse Winchester or was she looking for her rifle? Pappy stepped out of the stall, and when he did he noticed Melanie was already in the middle of the long aisle that ran down the barn and had her hands braced on her hips.

"And just who might you be, stranger?"

"Rick Darrel, ma'am. Are you Old Brooks' niece?"

Pappy hurried down the aisle and stood behind Melanie. He knew once the men of Sterling Canyon heard there was a new *eligible* female in town they'd start showing up looking to court Melanie. He glanced heavenward and shook his head at Old Brooks.

CHAPTER 7

So it had already begun. Melanie took a steadying breath. She had already determined that she would never marry, but she had proven time and again in the past that she was an easy target for low-life scum only looking for a good time. Melanie allowed memories of her past to flood her mind so she could harden her heart against any pretty words or lusty gazes this young fellow might throw her way.

She took a step forward. "I am. What do you need?"

She saw the man's throat convulse as if he were gulping. Good, let him sweat. "Uh—did I hear Pappy there say you have a fiancé?"

Melanie slowly shook her head once. "Had. Now what do you need?"

Her answer seemed to release some tension in the young man's shoulders for he stood straighter and strode right toward her. "I'd be real pleased if you'd take a stroll with me, Miss Brooks."

Melanie wanted to step away from the handsome young man, but she didn't dare. She needed to stand strong and appear unbending. She wanted this young fellow to run back to town spreading gossip about the cruel, cold-hearted niece of Old Brooks. "Not happening. Now get off my property."

His eyes widened with surprise and Melanie rejoiced inside. Surely he'd leave now. He surprised her though by taking another step forward and grabbing her hand. "Please, Miss Brooks, won't you at least consider?"

Melanie tried to pull her hand from his grasp, but when she did he reached for her again and his strong hand clasped around her wrist. She fought to control the panic that began to rise in her throat at this young man's grip. She looked from side to side. Where had she put that darn rifle? The young man took another step forward and grabbed her other wrist before gently tugging her toward him. They were so close she could feel the heat emitting from his body.

Suddenly the storm of panic that had been churning in her stomach stilled and from it rose a red-hot anger. She lifted her eyes to meet the young man's and glared with all the pain and hate she felt in her heart. She spoke in clear, clipped words. "Let. Me. Go."

She saw the determination flare in the young man's eyes. "What about dinner at the diner in town?"

Melanie pulled her wrists free then placed her hands on the man's shoulders, hooked her leg behind his knees and forced him to the ground. He laid flat on the ground as she hefted a bucket of fresh milk from this morning and poured it over him, dousing his entire body in warm, sticky milk. As she marched down the barn aisle she called back over her shoulder. "If you're still here by the time I find my Winchester you'll be going home with a hole in your middle."

Just as she ripped the front door open, Pappy had caught up to her. She marched inside and once she heard the door click shut behind them, she whirled around to face him. "Thanks for the help back there!"

Pappy's mouth moved up and down as if he were lost for words. He rubbed the back of his neck. "Sorry?"

Melanie closed her eyes and took a deep breath. "I want any other callers with the mind of courting thrown off the property immediately."

"There aren't a whole lot of women out here. There's bound to be a long line of suitors, Little Missy."

CHAPTER 7

Melanie shook her head vehemently. "And I want each one thrown off the property."

"OK." Pappy stroked his thick, white beard. "On one condition." She nodded. "Why?"

Melanie glared at the old man but her hard façade quickly crumbled at the kindness in the old man's eyes. She sighed. "I have no interest in marriage." There, that should suffice.

Pappy quirked an eyebrow. "A strong, pretty, young woman like you? So you don't ever want to have little babies running around? Or grow old with some good, God-fearing man?"

Tears filled Melanie's eyes. Of course she did. She wanted to fall madly in love, marry, fill her Great-Uncle's house with babies and grow old watching the sunset with her husband. But what good, God fearing man would want a tainted woman like her? She was spoiled goods. She was all used up.

She shook her head slowly. "What would I have to offer any man?" She turned her back to Pappy so he wouldn't see the first of her tears roll slowly down her cheeks. "Pappy, please, on this one thing, please just listen to me. If any more men come around, stand by my decision to see them off the property."

She jumped when he placed a gentle hand on her shoulder. His voice was low and comforting. "I can see how deep this hurts you, so OK, I'll make sure they know they're not welcome to come courtin'."

The kindness in this man seemed limitless. Melanie turned on impulse and wrapped her arms around his waist. She felt a deep connection with Pappy and she could easily allow herself to love him like family. She was comfortable with him and felt safe. So much so, she didn't even think twice about soaking his shirt with her tears.

Pappy gently stroked her head and she barely heard him whisper, "But I'll never stop praying God opens your heart to the man He has set aside for you."

Chapter 8

"THREE WEEKS AND twenty-five men." Pappy shook his head as he marched back toward the barn, the most recent suitor riding off with his tail tucked between his legs. That little spitfire nearly ran each of them off single-handedly too. Although he stuck to his word, he'd come running as soon as he heard the ruckus of a would-be suitor being run off, but usually by the time he showed up the little lady had the situation handled. It was the same scenario each time. The young buck would ride up, tall and proud and hopeful in his saddle, and by the time Melanie was done tongue lashing him he'd ride away with shoulders slumped and head down. And Lord help the fellow that dared compliment her. Being called pretty only seemed to rile her all the more.

One young man in particular, Johnny Gray, had heard the stories of the fierce Brooks girl and her apparent dislike for compliments. He rode up; a smug smile plastered across his face, looked Melanie up and down then declared her the homeliest girl he'd ever laid eyes on. Melanie had responded by shooting him off the property. She got him once in the backside and half a day later the sheriff rode in saying young Gray accused her of attempted murder. Melanie didn't even flinch at the charges. She placed her hands on her hips and told the sheriff she had warned the boy he was trespassing and he'd better leave or else. Thank God that and some fresh biscuits were enough to pacify the sheriff. Pappy had been sweating, wondering what he'd do if she got dragged off to jail.

Pappy glanced back over his shoulder as he entered the barn to see Melanie drop to her knees and resume weeding the large vegetable garden she had insisted on expanding. He smiled to himself and shook his head again. She was full of life and spark. He was sure she'd make some man awfully happy; and probably keep him on his toes, too.

As Pappy settled back into his work, his mind wandered to the many nights he had heard her crying in her room. Concern for his young ward had followed him since the first night he overheard her sobs and what he thought was praying. She repeatedly apologized through gasping sobs and promised to do better. She broke his heart each time she told God she understood she didn't deserve a husband and that she was reaping the consequences of her actions. Someone had taught that girl a lot about punishment and fear, but not so much about God's forgiveness and love. Pappy silently prayed God would show him a way to gently minister to this lost and hurting soiled dove.

CHAPTER 8

Melanie ripped the weeds out of the ground. She glanced up periodically to make sure that foolish boy wasn't coming back. He had the gall to say he knew she'd like him over all the others because he could spit the farthest. Men! She rolled her eyes and shook her head.

"It's definitely going to be easy to stay single if these are the men that come my way." She snorted, "Spits the farthest." She looked up and glared at the trail the boy had taken back to town. "As if that's what I would really want in a husband." She gestured her hands wildly in the air as she pulled weeds and spoke to her growing vegetable plants. "Oh, of course! Just forget honesty and good manners. Throw intelligence right out the window. And who needs a man who can provide and protect his family? Don't you know all a girl needs is a man that can spit real far?" Melanie snorted at the boy's way of thinking.

The nerve of all these men. She had hoped one of them would return with a tale so wildly woven about how cold and distant and ugly she was that it discouraged the others from coming out. Apparently, though, it just challenged them all the more. She was sure after she shot the one in the hind quarters that it would put a stop to it all. Instead she got one day of respite and then the following day four men rode in, one right after the other! Pappy declared he had a headache after the final one finally rode off.

After agonizing over the last three weeks about the fifteen men living on her property, she had finally come up with a good reason for having all those men around. As her employees, she could order them to turn any would-be suitors right around and send them on home. Having fifteen extra men to help with that job would save her a lot of time during the day.

Melanie arched her back to stretch and glanced up at the sun. Pappy would want his noon meal soon. She grabbed the bucket of weeds and strode over to the compost pile and mixed the freshly uprooted weeds in with the decomposing soil. She stopped at the pump and washed up, a requirement she already enforced with Pappy and resolved to enforce with every other man she employed. No man would be allowed entrance into her house without scrubbing his face and hands clean, dusting off his pants, and stomping away any mud on his boots. She checked her nails and, satisfied that they were clean, walked in to her expansive kitchen. She could never hold back the smile that spread across her lips every time she saw this kitchen. Made just for her, as Pappy often reminded her.

She had the stove heated in no time and soon the thick stew from last night was bubbling. She uncovered a loaf of bread and sliced several thick slices, then placed them on a plate. She grabbed two bowls and two spoons and began setting the little work table where she and Pappy preferred to eat. She looked at the long table on the other side of the room and nearly cringed. Soon that table would be full of rowdy men. She much preferred Pappy's and her quiet meals, but she didn't want to put an end to the privilege Great-Uncle Brooks had started with his men by allowing them to eat inside.

Melanie stepped outside and rang the large triangle. Pappy must have already been on his way in because he stepped outside before the bell was even done echoing its ring. He quickly washed and dusted off before coming inside. They seated themselves and he doffed his hat, held her hand as he said grace, then dug in with all the gusto of a starving man.

CHAPTER 8

Melanie glanced back at the long, empty table where her employees would be taking their meals and shivered. She cleared her throat softly to get Pappy's attention. "Pappy?"

Pappy had just buttered a thick slice of bread and was now dipping it in his stew. He smiled. "Yes, Little Missy?"

Melanie grinned at the nickname he had taken to calling her. Any other man dare call her Little Missy and she'd put a bullet in him like she had with the fellow that called her homely. Melanie took a deep breath. "I was just wondering ... what are they like?"

Pappy looked over at the long table she was staring at. "The boys? Oh they're a good bunch." He shoved his bread in his mouth. "Hard workers."

"Any of them drink?"

Pappy thought while he chewed his bread. Finally he nodded. "A couple. But only on their day off."

"Any of them coyote around?"

A deep 'v' formed between Pappy's eyebrows. He pointed his fork at her. "You don't have to worry about those boys coming after you." He buttered another slice of bread. "Besides, if I ever saw one of them take a second look at you I'd throw him off the land myself."

Melanie tried to swallow a bite of potato, but it was hard to get it down around the lump in her throat. "It's a matter of time before someone finds out. Maybe I should just tell them."

Pappy was wiping his bowl with the crust of his bread. "About the brothel?"

"Well, yeah. I was there for five years, that's a lot of time to—*get to know* a lot of men. What if one of these boys," she gestured toward the long empty table, "knows someone I know. Christ Almighty, what if one of these boys *is* someone I *know*!"

Pappy dropped his spoon and it clattered against the china bowl. He pointed a work worn finger in her face. "How many times do I have to tell you about using the Lord's name in vain? I won't tolerate it." He shook his head. "All of these boys have been here for several years and none of them are from Wisconsin."

Melanie breathed a sigh of relief. That was reassuring. She wanted to change the subject from brothels and lusty men's appetites. "Once they return, I want you to show me the rest of the land."

"You know, it's not too long of a ride, we could do it before they come back. In fact, I'll go saddle the horses while you put away these dishes and we'll go right now."

Melanie stacked her bowl on top of Pappy's and picked up the bread plate in her other hand, then deposited them in the sink. "I don't know, Pappy. What about the animals? And supper?"

Pappy shook his head. "If we stop this chatter we can be there and back by nightfall. I don't mind having that stew again for supper." Without waiting for a response, Pappy strode out the back door and toward the barn.

Chapter 9

MELANIE HURRIED TO clean their two bowls and the bread plate, then laid them on a clean towel to dry. She used a clean rag to scrub at a stain on her dress from where the stew splattered. She really needed to purchase an apron from the general store the next time she went to town. Her cheeks flushed a slight red at the thought of her last visit. She had gone, a week after arriving as promised, to fetch her new wagon. It had taken nearly running over a fellow to break through the small crowd of men that came out to gawk as she passed by. She had been so flustered she plumb forgot about picking up supplies at the general store.

As she hurried out the back door she was surprised to see Pappy hadn't saddled their horses but instead had hitched the geldings she had purchased from the livery to the wagon. "I thought we were riding. This will take much too long."

Pappy grinned and patted the seat next to him. "Just climb up here."

Pleased with himself for thinking to bring the wagon and a couple of empty buckets, Pappy grinned the whole way to the small orchard. Old Brooks had planted the trees specifically for his pleasure of fruit pies, but the construction of the orchard was for his niece's delight. Pappy and a few of the other boys had tried their hands at making a fruit pie for the old boss, but each attempt was far less than edible.

Hopefully some of the fruit would be ripe enough for a pie or two and then all he had to do was coax Melanie into baking dessert. Pappy slapped the reins across the horses' backs to urge them on faster. Once they rounded a large formation of rock, the orchard and nearby forest would come into view. Pappy was eager to see the look on her face when she first spotted the rows of trees.

They had barely driven for ten minutes, but Melanie was already sure she would have bruises on her backside from Pappy's excessively fast driving. She looked over at the old man and grimaced as her words clattered out. "C-can't we slow d-d-down just a little? We're not in *this* b-big of a hu-r-r-ry."

Pappy merely looked down at her and smiled. As they rounded a large rock formation he looked over her shoulder and his smile seemed to broaden. He nodded his head toward whatever lay back there. She eyed him suspiciously, but at the twinkle in his eye curiosity had no chance of losing.

Melanie swiveled around to look behind her and gasped. There was a large hedge of rose bushes. She straightened her spine and arched her neck. What were those trees just beyond the bushes? She reached over absentmindedly and patted Pappy's knee. "Hurry, Pappy, I want to see it closer."

Pappy merely laughed. "Go slower. Hurry up." Melanie glanced at him from the corner of her eye to see him shaking his head and smiling. Her own smile spread across her face and she clutched her hands tightly in her lap, eager to see what this tall wall of roses was all about.

As soon as Pappy pulled the wagon to a stop, Melanie jumped down like a rambunctious young girl and hurried over to the hedge. When she reached the roses, or what from a distance she thought were roses, she stopped short. The leaves were smaller than those on a rose bush and the flowers were almost thinner than paper and ranged in colors from deep purples, pinks, and reds to white. In fact these bushes looked more like trees than a bush. Instead of allowing the branches to grow freely, someone had patiently woven each branch through a trellis so the beautiful branches and their flowers created a hedge. She turned to find Pappy and cocked her head to one side. "These aren't roses."

Pappy strode up next to her and plucked a small stem of flowers and sniffed them. "Nope, it's called "crape myrtle." First, old Brooks planted roses." Pappy chuckled. "That old coot planted six different types of flowers, but none liked Texas soil. Most were too delicate and needed to be watered every day." He motioned toward the crape myrtles. "Then he heard about a man who sold these and how they could survive hot weather once their roots dug in deep." Pappy laughed. "He hired a boy to come out here every day and water them for three months and weave the young branches through that trellis. The boys gave him a hard time, but he wanted you to have something special."

Melanie gently fingered the beautiful red and pink flowers nearest her. "But he had already done so much. The house was more than enough." She sighed deeply. She already felt the weight of the ranch heavily on her shoulders. So far she had done a mediocre job of living up to her promise to deserve this land, but now with this beautiful gift before her she felt her efforts even more inadequately.

Pappy gently grasped her elbow. "Well, when you see what's inside, you may not feel the flowers were so much a gift, but more of a bribe."

Melanie raised an eyebrow and looked at him curiously. She opened her mouth to speak, but Pappy chuckled and shook his head. "I'm not telling you."

He led her around the great wall of crape myrtles to a small opening the long branches were obviously trying to close. Pappy ducked under a branch and stepped to one side and Melanie picked up her dress hem as she leaned down and quickly followed after him. Once she had stepped through, she allowed her hem to drop to the ground and stood straight. There, inside the beautiful wall of flowers, was row after row of fruit trees.

Melanie placed her fingers over her mouth and stepped toward the nearest tree. "Apples!"

Pappy stepped next to her and gestured out toward the other trees. "Apples. Peaches. Pears. Plums. Your uncle planted two rows of five apple trees and one row of five for the other kinds of fruit trees. Apple pie was his favorite. He was hoping you'd be so pleased with the flowers you'd be willing to bake him apple pies."

A slight sorrow entered Melanie's heart. Her great-uncle had done so much with her comfort and happiness in mind. She closed her eyes to will away the tears that threatened to come at the thought of never being able to meet such a wonderful, thoughtful man. She sniffed. "I'll never be able to thank him."

Pappy's strong arm circled her shoulders and he gave her a slight squeeze. "He knows you're thankful." He released her and headed for the small opening. "I'll be right back; I forgot something in the wagon."

Melanie saw the mischievous glint in his eyes and knew he was up to something sneaky. She smiled and began venturing further into the enclosed orchard. As she approached the farthest part of the orchard, she realized there was no hedge of flowers enclosing the orchard on the back side, but rather, the orchard opened into a forest. She walked into the forest toward the sound of a bubbling creek. As she stepped further into the forest she was delighted to see blackberry bushes. The branches hung heavy with large, ripe berries. She plucked a berry from one of the branches and popped the fruit into her mouth. The tangy sweetness made her smile and she decided to return with buckets so she could harvest the berries and make jam.

She could hear Pappy whistling happily. She decided to head back and find him. She burst into a fit of laughter at the sight of Pappy quickly filling two empty buckets with ripe apples.

He turned at her laughter and shrugged. "Apple pie is my favorite too."

$\mathscr{C}$hapter 10

$\mathscr{T}$HAT NIGHT, AFTER supper and the most delicious apple pie Pappy had ever eaten, they sat in the large sitting room with the rock fireplace. Pappy whittled away in his large arm chair while Melanie sat in the rocking chair Old Brooks had made for her and mended some of Pappy's socks. The girl's brow was all puckered, a sure sign, Pappy had come to understand, that something bothersome was on her mind.

With his knife firmly in hand, he carefully ran the sharp blade down the wood, causing another curly piece of wood to fall to the floor. "What's on your mind?"

Out of the corner of his eye Pappy saw the sock she was currently mending lower to her lap. She sighed. "Jonathan."

Pappy remembered the man she had named as her former fiancé the morning the first of the town's men came in to convince Melanie to go courting. He glanced up and saw her staring at the large, unlit fireplace. He didn't want to ruin this opportunity for her to open up about her past by seeming nosy, so he tried to remain impassive.

"Mmm." His sharp blade ran across the wood in his hands. His brow furrowed. Was that too impassive? He silently prayed that God would guide him in helping this young woman.

She sighed again. "I really loved him. It went against everything in my heart, but still, I followed after him."

Pappy heard her sniff and looked up. She was wiping a tear from her cheek. His heart nearly broke at the sight of her tears. He cleared his throat gently. "Why did you?"

Her voice cracked. "Because he had convinced me that he loved me. He said he wanted to love me like a hu-hu-hu …," her voice gave way and a deep sob broke through her lips.

Pappy didn't need to hear her say the word. He knew what she was getting at. Anger boiled through his veins at the young man who had lied to her like that. "What happened then?"

Usually she clammed up whenever Pappy tried to ask questions about her past, but her distress had melted the fortress she had built around herself and she oozed with details. She swiped at her nose with the sock she was mending. "Right after, he said he had second thoughts on 'that whole love thing.'" She rolled her eyes. "I felt as if I had spiraled down into this pit and couldn't escape. I became determined to make him marry me." Her shoulders slumped forward. "But I was so stupid, Pappy. I allowed him to convince me that since the deed was already done it didn't matter if we kept on sharing a bed."

Pappy was staring at her with his full attention now, but when her face flushed bright red at the mention of sharing a bed with a man he looked away. Before he could respond she continued. "I became obsessed with marriage. I thought if we could just get married everything would be OK. I thought then maybe I wouldn't feel so dirty." She sniffed again. "But he would never commit further than saying 'one day'."

Disgust and bile rose in Pappy's throat. He mumbled between clenched teeth, "That no-account liar."

Melanie hiccupped. "You can say that again."

Pappy leaned forward. "Then what happened?"

She took a deep breath and sighed slowly. "For three years we played this game of love and hate. The more fake promises he made to me, the more lies I told him about men constantly approaching me, wanting me. I was convinced that if he thought other men saw something desirous in me, he would finally make good on his promises, not wanting any other man to have me." Melanie tried to catch her breath as a fresh wave of sobs assailed her.

Pappy leaned forward to grasp her hand but she pulled away, shaking her head. "Several times he tried to leave, but each time I convinced him to stay by taking him to bed." Her voice rose, "I was so stupid, Pappy! I should have just let him leave!"

Pappy pulled a handkerchief from his shirt pocket and slipped it into her hand. She wiped her eyes and blew her nose. He couldn't help but ask, "Why didn't you?"

She looked up at him with a dark anger clouding her eyes. "Because the longer I followed after him, the more convinced I became that no other man would have me. I was used goods. It was him or no one." She took a shuddering breath. "The morning I discovered he had finally left me and took all of our money with him, my neighbor, Charlotte, took me in."

A fresh wave of anger stole through Pappy's body. "He took all of your money when he left?"

She nodded. "I didn't care at first. I just wanted to cry on that floor until I died." She sniffed and wiped her nose again. A wobbly smile spread across her lips. "But Charlotte wouldn't let me. She's my dearest friend even to this day."

He urged her on. "What happened after you moved in with your neighbor?"

A shadow crossed her face. "She thought that if I met a good, decent man I'd forget all about Jonathan. She thought I had forgotten what it was like to be courted by a man with manners, who respected me as a woman and showed me courtesies." She ran his handkerchief through her fingers. "So she introduced me to a friend of hers, Tom." A dim smile lit her face. "She was right, at first. He was very gentlemanly and it filled my heart with the upmost happiness that a man would treat me with such kindness." Her voice dropped nearly to a whisper. "I hadn't felt so special in such a long time."

"But he didn't turn out to be the man you thought he was."

Melanie didn't take her eyes off of her lap as she shook her head. Pappy's heart dropped and he steeled himself for what she may say next.

"Although he never said or did anything inappropriate, I always had a sick feeling when I was around him. My stomach would twist into knots, and I could scarcely eat for fear I'd be sick in front of him. I should have listened to my instincts." She took a deep breath. "One night we happened to be alone and he—well he, I didn't want to but he—"

Pappy stopped her rambling and held up a hand. His heart sank down into his stomach with a hollow thud. He knew what she was getting at. "It's OK; you don't have to explain that part."

She nodded. "After he left in the morning, I found Charlotte sleeping in the hallway. She had a black eye." Melanie touched a hand to her own eye. "Her pa had finally found her. She had been working at the textile factory." Melanie shook her head. "From everything Charlotte ever told me, he was a mean old devil. She slapped him when he tried to drag her out of the factory, and he hit her back. Her boss threw her pa out, then fired her."

Pappy's hands clenched into fists. What was the world coming to when men tricked women into their beds, beat them, and forced them to do unspeakable acts, and other men beat their daughters? He shook his head as Melanie continued talking.

"We didn't have much savings. I had lost my job a couple of weeks after Jonathan left, so we had already been dipping into the few dollars Charlotte had set aside to escape her pa." Melanie's voice began to waiver and Pappy reached forward to pat her hand. "I had offered to leave, but Charlotte refused to let me go. She said we were family and family didn't just stop caring when times got hard." Melanie swiped her eyes as tears began rolling down her cheeks.

Pappy patted her hand again. "She sounds like a good friend."

Melanie beamed. "Oh, yes. The best."

"So, did either of you find work?"

She shook her head. "No, and when we couldn't make rent, the landlord threw us out. We were huddled under a stairway in an alley during a rain storm when Minnie found us."

The name struck familiar. "Minnie? Minnie's Dollhouse?"

Melanie nodded. "She's the owner of the brothel. She took us both in, instructed the other girls to prepare us a hot bath and then warmed us some leftover supper." Melanie smiled up at Pappy. "She's such a nice lady. She allowed us to stay at the brothel rent free while we looked for jobs." Melanie dropped her head. "But we never did find anything."

Pappy sighed. "And that's how you came to work for the brothel?"

"Sort of. Minnie heard me singing in the kitchen one day and said her clients would absolutely love to hear me sing while they waited for their girls down in the parlor. I agreed to sing, and not long after I had been singing in the parlor, a man offered Minnie quite a generous sum for me. She relayed the offer to me but insisted I didn't have to accept. I refused at first, but eventually more men were making offers, most two, three, four and sometimes five times as much as the original offer. It seemed the more I refused the higher amount they were willing to pay."

Pappy was confused. She seemed so disgusted by the work she had done, yet it didn't quite seem like she had been forced into the position. "So what changed your mind about refusing offers?"

"Charlotte." She swallowed. "Minnie had hired her to serve drinks to the men while they watched me sing. One night her pa found her at the brothel and made a scene. He attacked her, but Amos, the man who protects the girls, immediately pried him off of her and threw him out. That same night I told Minnie to accept the highest offer she received for me. I thought if I saved enough money I could buy us a new future." She shrugged. "We dreamed about where we could go and what we would do once we were there."

Admiration and pride filled Pappy's chest. This woman was a wonder. To save a friend she had thrown herself in the midst of the lion's den. He wondered at the scars that may have been left behind after being sold to the highest bidder like a piece of meat.

Melanie blew her nose. "Charlotte thought that if I was willing to stoop to that work she should too, because after all it was for our future. I argued with her that I was already ruined, whereas she still had something to offer a husband." Melanie's face crumpled. "A few nights later I found out there had been a virgin auction while I was with a customer. Charlotte's vibrant blonde hair got her the name Daisy. Many men had bid to pluck that flower." Melanie seemed to flinch at her own crude statement. She looked up at Pappy apologetically. "Sorry."

Pappy merely nodded. "So why didn't Charlotte come out here with you?"

Tears rimmed Melanie's eyes again and Pappy briefly regretted asking. She sighed. "Her pa. She's scared he'll kill her if she leaves the protection she receives from Minnie's." Iron determination crept into her voice. "But I'll never stop trying to get her to move out here. Never."

Pappy glanced at the clock on the mantel. It was nearly midnight. They'd both get few precious hours of sleep before having to rise in the morning. He sighed. It was worth it to hear the detailed story of Melanie's past, as painful as it was. The girl had definitely found a place in his heart over the last few weeks, and a fierce protectiveness crept up within as he determined never to allow a man to come close and hurt Melanie again. Now he fully understood her resistance to allowing a man near her. He silently wondered if her few questions about the boys had been asked out of fear for her wellbeing. He puffed his chest out. Let one of those boys think about hurting her, and he'd acquaint them with the barrel of his rifle.

Melanie rose from her rocking chair. "I didn't realize it was so late. Sorry for keeping you up, Pappy."

Pappy immediately stood and gripped her shoulders. He peered down to look into her red, swollen eyes. "Don't be sorry. I'm thankful you shared your story. It helps me understand the reasoning behind some decisions you've made recently." He shook her shoulders slightly to make sure she was paying attention. "And just know if you ever feel uncomfortable around one of the boys or if one of them does or says something untoward, you've just got to tell Pappy. You hear me, Little Missy?"

A smile stole across her face and she lunged forward to hug him tightly. "I love you Pappy."

Tears clogged Pappy's throat. He bent to kiss the top of her head and whispered back, "I love you too, Little Missy."

Melanie quickly wrote a letter to Charlotte. She was eager to relay the details of tonight and the feeling of love and acceptance she felt when Pappy pledged his protection. She truly did love the old man and looked to him as a grandfather as well as a friend. She was nearly finished with the letter when she remembered the beautiful crape myrtles surrounding the orchard and added a detailed description of both. Before signing her name, she again invited Charlotte to move in with her.

Once she signed her name, she gently blew across the ink, then folded the letter and placed it in an envelope. She addressed the envelope and placed it atop her vanity. She had planned to ask Pappy to go to town tomorrow to fetch canning jars and she hoped while he was in town he could mail her letter.

Melanie stretched as she rose from her vanity chair and sat atop her bed to unbutton her boots. Too exhausted to undress, she laid on her bed without even turning down the blankets and quickly fell into a deep, peaceful sleep.

Pappy stretched across the top of his bed fully awake while he tried to digest everything Melanie had told him tonight. The poor girl had been tricked into sharing a bed, then afterward had been stripped of all self-esteem and confidence as she followed the low-life Jonathan around, hungry for his attention. Then she was introduced to a creature even lower and more rotten than the first. And finally, to help save her friend, she had freely given of herself to every wolf that could pay the price.

No wonder she was so leery of men. The only experience she had with them was of a lustful and deceitful nature. Pappy breathed a prayer of thankfulness that she had slowly warmed up to him over the last several weeks. His heart stirred at the memory of her sturdy arms wrapped around him earlier this evening. The warmth that spread through his heart was the same love he felt for his nephew.

At the thought of his nephew, he silently prayed for protection and a safe journey home as the boys worked their way back from selling the cattle. Just a couple more weeks and they should be home. Pappy looked forward to seeing all the boys again, but remembered all too clearly the promise he had made to protect the little woman who slept down the hall.

Chapter 11

ELANIE HURRIED TO make sure breakfast was ready by the time Pappy came downstairs. When she heard his boots stomping down the staircase, she poured his coffee and placed his plate on the table so it was hot and ready when he came into the kitchen.

Pappy was pulling his suspenders up over his shoulders as he entered the kitchen. "Breakfast before chores?"

Melanie smiled. "Chores are done. I let you sleep after I yammered your ear off last night."

Pappy sat down at his usual place. "My ears are always open."

As Melanie passed by Pappy to her seat she impulsively leaned down and kissed his forehead. "I appreciate it." When she sat down she noticed the skin under all his white whiskers was beet red.

He cleared his throat and reached for her hand. He said a quick grace over the food, then dug in. "I can't believe I slept so late."

"You were tired."

Pappy guffawed. "And you weren't?"

Melanie smiled and shook her head. "I thought I would be, but I had the most beautiful rest last night."

Pappy smiled and reached across the table to pat her hand. "I'm glad, Little Missy."

She cleared her throat. "I do have a chore for you to do today, though."

Pappy looked up from buttering his bread and quirked an eyebrow. "Oh?"

Melanie laughed. "Don't look so suspicious." She sipped her coffee. "I was just wondering if you could go into town today. I'd like you to get a few canning jars so I can make jams and preserves." She withdrew the letter she had written to Charlotte from her dress collar. "And mail this, please." She slid her hand to the other side of her collar and removed a small wad of bills and slid them across the table to Pappy. "This should cover everything."

Pappy's eyes widened when she pulled the letter and money from her dress collar. "Why in tarnation are you keeping stuff in there?"

She shrugged. "My dress doesn't have pockets, and I don't have an apron."

Pappy's eyebrows nearly touched his hair line. He merely grunted and went back to devouring his breakfast.

"Oh, we should also stock up on more supplies before the boys come home. I want to make sure I have provisions to make good meals for them."

Pappy nodded while chewing eggs and bacon. He pointed his fork at her, "Those boys sure can eat. I'm sure their appetites will increase once they taste the fare you put out."

Melanie laughed. "My cooking is really all that good?"

His eyes widened. "Good? Good doesn't begin to describe it." He chewed another piece of bacon. "And if you ever want to punish one of them, send them out without some of that apple pie."

Melanie laughed and stood to retrieve the coffee pot. She refilled Pappy's cup then placed the pot back on the stove. She sat down and noticed a piece of bacon was missing from her plate.

She looked at Pappy with one eyebrow quirked. "Pappy?"

A rueful smile stole across his lips and his eyes danced with mirth. "Hmm?"

She eyed him suspiciously. "Did you steal my bacon?"

Pappy's cheeks were increasingly turning red. He shrugged. Melanie tilted her head back and laughed.

Pappy would steal bacon from her plate every morning if it meant it would make Melanie laugh with such abandon as she did this morning. The girl was much too serious most of the time; although now he couldn't say he blamed her. He prayed that God would continue to provide opportunities for him to speak to his young ward about God, and how she did deserve what Old Brooks had left her and then some.

After breakfast, Pappy tucked the money and the letter Melanie had given him into his pants pocket. He went out to the barn and hitched the geldings to the wagon. By the time he brought the team out into the yard, Melanie was waiting for him on the porch.

She hurried toward him and handed over a dinner sack. "I packed enough for a day's ride." Next she handed him a list. "This is everything we'll be needing."

Pappy looked down at the list. Most of it was basic staples like flour, sugar, and coffee. The last item caught his eye. "Six dozen canning jars?" He looked up at her bewildered.

Melanie simply smiled and nodded. "There's a lot of ripe fruit out there. It'll make a lot of pie filling, jam, preserves …"

Pappy waved for her to stop. "You had me at 'pie filling'."

He couldn't help but smile as her musical laughter filled the yard. She stood on her tiptoes and quickly kissed his cheek. "Just have a safe trip."

Pappy chucked her under the chin with his knuckle. "You've got it, Little Missy."

He quickly jumped up to the wagon seat and took the reins in his hands. He smiled down at Melanie and gave her a final nod. As he rode out of the yard he felt every bit the proud Pappy.

With Pappy gone, Melanie set out on Brooke toward the hidden orchard. She easily navigated the way Pappy had taken her and in under fifteen minutes was rounding the rock formation and guiding Brooke to the entrance of the orchard. She slid down off her saddle and guided Brooke through the small entrance. She tied the reins to one of the apple trees, pulled her Winchester from its sheath and laid down under an apple tree.

The sun was brilliant—so bright that she shut her eyes against it and basked in its warmth. Even with the constant flow of suitors, life had been good here in Sterling Canyon. She valued the bond she had developed with Pappy, and after last night she felt more assured than ever that he would help protect her from the lustful advances of the men that came from town and the neighboring ranches.

When she had first arrived, she cried herself to sleep nearly every night after first chastising herself for her many sins. Now she scarcely cried herself to sleep. She still felt dirty and used and she still firmly believed that she would never be worthy of this land or of a man's love. But now there was another feeling—one she tried in vain to push down and ignore. Something deep and unrelenting had settled itself into her very soul. Something that contradicted every vile name she could think to call herself and disarmed her thoughts of doubt and unworthiness.

She fought this new, awkward feeling every waking moment. It was exhausting work, and she was scared that one day it would wear her down, but the thought of this new feeling taking over and allowing hope to bloom in her heart was only asking for trouble. If she allowed such hope to take root, she would only be more disappointed and hurt in the end. She didn't want to spend her days dreaming of a husband who would never come, children that she'd never have, and essentially a sense of wholeness that she would never be able to possess.

Melanie breathed deeply of the fragrant apples hanging above her head and the crape myrtles surrounding her wonderful little orchard. This land, this orchard, and the beautiful flowers her Great-Uncle Brooks labored over finding, planting, and caring for, the magnificent house he tried to perfect to a lady's taste—it would be enough to keep her happy.

She sighed. "Thank you, God."

Melanie's eyes snapped open and she bolted upright. She placed her hand over her mouth, her eyes as wide as saucers.

Where had that come from? She hadn't spoken to God on her own accord in a long time. She shuddered to think what He would do to a girl like her. Slowly, she lay back under her apple tree. She closed her eyes and tried to focus her mind on all of the many things she could make using the fruit from the trees and bushes.

A twig snapped and Melanie bolted upright, her hand on her Winchester, ready to pull it into action. Her heart hammered within her chest as she scanned the enclosed orchard unable to locate a single soul. Finally she called out, "Who's there?"

A man's voice came from her right. "It is only Me." She spun up onto her knees and picked her rifle up. There was a simply dressed man sitting on a rock in the right corner of the orchard. His face was covered by shadows.

"Who are you?"

"Be not afraid, child, for I am your Father."

All reasoning told Melanie that this man was most certainly not her pa. Her pa had died long ago in an influenza epidemic. Despite this irrefutable fact, she dropped her Winchester and went to the man.

He placed His hand on her shoulder. "Why do you torment yourself so?"

She looked at Him, baffled. "I don't torment myself."

"Surely you do, for you always say you are unworthy. Who are you to judge which of My children are unworthy, and which are not?"

Melanie stammered for something to say. "But, I've done horrible things. I disgraced myself. I worked in a brothel." Tears began to rim her eyes.

The man nodded His head. "Indeed you have sinned, but so has all of mankind. Is that not why My Son was sent to die?" The man squeezed her shoulder. "Repent and follow Christ, then sin no more."

Brooke nudged Melanie's cheek with her soft, moist muzzle. Melanie sat up and looked around for the stranger sitting on the rock. A dream. It was only a dream. Melanie felt a bead of sweat drip down her temple and realized she was panting and her heart was beating as wildly as if she had been running. She took a deep, steadying breath. She tilted her head back and looked up through the branches of the apple tree. The sun was beginning to set in the east. She quickly mounted Brooke. She took one last look at the place where she had napped, and then toward the corner where the stranger had sat in her dream. She shuddered.

"Let's go home, Brooke."

The suggestion seemed to please her mount, for the mare began moving toward home on her own.

Chapter 12

PAPPY RETURNED HOME late the next morning. When Melanie heard the jingle of the harness and reins she rushed out to greet him. He pulled the wagon to a stop in front of the house. Melanie could see from the porch that the back of the wagon was loaded with all of the supplies she had requested, including the six dozen canning jars.

She smiled to Pappy. "How was your trip?"

Pappy grinned. "Uneventful." He swung down from the wagon seat and walked toward the back of the wagon.

Melanie met him there and together they began lifting items out of the wagon and hefting them into the kitchen. When there was only one box of canning jars left, Melanie allowed Pappy to fetch it while she began putting away all of the staples.

Pappy stomped up the front steps and down the hallway that led to the kitchen. "Where should we stack all of these jars?"

Melanie pointed to the floor space beside the counter next to the stove. "There. That way they'll be handy when I start canning."

CHAPTER 12

Pappy removed a brown-paper-wrapped package from the top of the crate he had just brought in and set it on top of the small work table they took their meals at together. "What's that?"

Pappy didn't answer her; he just set about stacking the boxes of canning jars where she had indicated. When he was done, he smacked his hands together. "Alright, Little Missy, I got to thinking. You got awfully dirty making that pie the other night and I reckon jam making is just as messy. So I got you this." Pappy picked up the brown-paper-wrapped package and thrust it at her.

Melanie's lips puckered in thought. She looked at the package Pappy had thrust into her hands, then looked back up to Pappy. "Well, what is it?"

Pappy shrugged nonchalantly. "Open it and see."

Melanie smiled and quickly untied the string holding the package together. She turned the package over and unfolded the thick brown paper. Inside was a crisp, white apron. She pulled the apron from its wrappings and held it up against her gray calico. She squealed with delight and quickly looped the bib neck over her head and tied the strings around her thick waist.

She flung her arms around Pappy's neck. "Thank you, Pappy!" She stood back from him and looked down at the apron covering the front of her dress. "Oh, thank you!"

Pappy pointed to her midsection. "I made sure it had pockets."

Melanie looked down again and found three pockets sewn side by side. She looked up at Pappy and saw his cheeks were tainted pink. "You're so thoughtful, Pappy."

He shrugged as if the gift meant nothing, but his pink cheeks and the glisten in his eyes were all the proof Melanie needed to know he was pleased she liked his gift.

Together they made short work of the daily chores. Then Melanie convinced Pappy they should drive out again and fill buckets of fruit for canning. As they entered the secret orchard, Melanie's eyes landed on the rock in the corner where the stranger had sat in her dream.

She must have stood there staring for several minutes, for Pappy had to nudge her. "You OK, Little Missy?"

"Hmm?" Melanie spun around to see Pappy with a bucket already half full of apples in his hand. "Oh, I was just thinking." She leaned down and picked up an empty bucket, then started picking fruit from the plum tree.

"Care to share?"

Melanie sighed as she tried to think of the best way to word her thoughts. She had experienced the same dream again the night before and it had stirred something awake inside of her. She wasn't quite sure what it was, but it startled her nonetheless.

She started off slowly. "Do you think God loves us?" She rolled her eyes. The question sounded even more stupid out loud than it did in her head. She was always taught that God was jealous and punished those who sinned against Him.

"Of course I do! And I thank Him every day for that love."

His answered surprised her. "What!"

Pappy stopped picking his apples and walked over to where Melanie was harvesting plums. "Didn't anyone ever tell you, Little Missy? God is a loving, caring God and He sent His Son to die for each and every single one of us, so that we may not die but have everlasting life in Heaven with Him."

Melanie was shocked silent. She stammered to reply. "B-but, I was always taught He's jealous and we have to please Him with good works."

Pappy's eyes seemed to soften. "Oh, Melanie, honey, whoever taught you that was wrong. God can be a jealous God but that is not all He is. He loves you and desires you to follow after Him with your whole heart."

Melanie turned her back to Pappy and began pulling more ripe plums from the tree. Tears rimmed her eyes and she fought to block Pappy's words from penetrating her heart. She didn't want to believe that God loved her. If she believed that, then who knew what she'd believe next?

Pappy rested his hand on her shoulder. "Little Missy, you can avoid other men, but you can't run from Him forever. He's one man that will never stop fighting for you."

Melanie bit back a sob. Unable to respond, she just nodded her head. When Pappy's hand lifted from her shoulder she glanced back to see he had resumed picking apples.

Pappy praised God with all his heart. It wasn't much, but it was a beginning. He had been so surprised to hear Melanie ask a question about God. He didn't know what happened while he was in town, but whatever it was it made him itch to head out again.

It took them an hour to fill the buckets they had brought along and on the ride home to lighten the mood, he tried to ask questions about what she'd make with all the fruit. When they returned home, he helped her unload the buckets of fruit, then led the geldings to the barn to unharness them.

When he returned to the kitchen for his dinner, she ended up wrangling him into helping prepare the jars for canning.

Melanie washed, sliced, and pitted the plums, then added them to a large pot with sugar. She set the large pot on the stove and began stirring the mixture. Pappy was in charge of setting another large pot filled with water to boil, and then he was to dip each jar into the boiling water.

An hour later Melanie declared they were ready to start canning the preserves. She demonstrated how far to fill each jar and how to use the handle of a wooden spoon to get out all the air pockets. Pappy filled each jar just as she had demonstrated, then handed the jar over to Melanie to be boiled and sealed. They made short work of the tedious task and Pappy was delighted to see that somewhere along the way Melanie had baked a plum tart without him noticing.

They sat at the small table eating a simple supper of bread, cheese, and ham while Pappy's stomach grumbled for dessert. Pappy thought of the hard work they had spent that day harvesting, cleaning, preparing, and canning the preserves. He chuckled. "That was nearly as tedious as working the cattle."

Melanie smiled. "Consider us lucky. If Great-Uncle Brooks hadn't insisted on so many windows, the kitchen would have been steaming."

Pappy shook his head while he picked up another biscuit and ham sandwich. "Well one thing is for sure, I'll never take my jam for granted again."

Chapter 13

OVER THE NEXT several days Melanie and Pappy worked side by side harvesting fruit from the orchard and forest and turning it all into jam, preserves, and Pappy's favorite: pie filling. They reserved some of the fruit and canned it whole, so that they would have fruit throughout the winter. Toward the end of the week they had formed a companionable silence while working. One would turn or motion and the other would instinctively know what was being requested or required.

Melanie smiled as she stirred a large pot of apple pie filling. She used the back of her wrist to push a stray curl off her forehead. How long had it been since she had felt so happy and free?

"How fine this morning early, all was sunshine clear and bright. So late I loved you dearly, tho' lost now each fond delight." Melanie heard the song and recognized it. Slowly her hips swayed from side to side. "The clouds seem big with showers, sunny beams no more are seen. Farewell ye happy hours, your falsehood has chang'd the scene."

Pappy cleared his throat. "That seems like a mighty sad song."

"Hmm?"

"That song you were singing. It seemed awfully sad."

Melanie's brow crumpled and she focused on stirring the apple pie filling so it wouldn't burn. She had been singing? "I was singing?"

Pappy looked at her from the corner of her eye. "You didn't know you were singing?"

"I haven't sung since I left the brothel."

"Well you were singing just now." Pappy cleared his throat. "You have a real pretty voice, Little Missy. Do you know any other songs?"

Melanie was still trying to grasp that she had been singing unconsciously. "O-other songs? Whatever for?"

"Well, I imagine the boys might like hearing you sing Sunday mornings."

Melanie rolled her eyes. Every Sunday Pappy had invited her to join him for his own Bible study, and every Sunday she had politely refused. Finally, during a conversation about the men employed on her ranch, Pappy had convinced her she ought to begin joining him when the boys returned. He argued that some of them might not be too keen on working for an employer who at least didn't try to appear interested in God. Melanie doubted his argument and instead believed the old man was just trying to get her to listen to him read the Bible. She had decided, though, that if it meant that much to Pappy she'd at least see what their Bible study entailed.

Before she could respond to Pappy's outrageous idea of her singing for her hired hands, a dog barked in the distance. Melanie shoved the heavy pot filled with apple pie filling toward the back of the stove so it wouldn't burn. She grabbed her Winchester that she always kept an arm's length away and strode for the front door.

Pappy was hot on her heels. "I was wondering if we had seen the last of those suitors of yours."

Melanie shot a heated glare over her shoulder. "They're not *my* suitors."

They stepped out onto the porch together and the dog they had heard barking ran right up to the porch and started jumping up on Pappy's leg. He chuckled and reached down to scratch the dog's ears. "Well, hello there, Sam."

Melanie didn't bother looking at Pappy; she was too busy scanning the tree line for the dog's owner. "You know this dog, Pappy?"

Pappy chuckled again. "Sure do. Melanie Brooks, meet your dog, Sam."

Melanie quickly turned to Pappy. "My dog? I have a dog?"

Pappy nodded and patted the dog's head. "Sure do." Pappy squinted into the distance. "The boys ought to be following behind any minute."

Melanie gasped and put a hand to her hair. "But I'm not ready." She looked down at her stained apron. She had wanted to be starched and pristine when she met her employees. Not a frazzled mess. Melanie bit her lower lip.

Pappy grabbed her arm to get her attention. She looked up into his soft, gray eyes. "You look fine, Little Missy. The boys will like you."

Melanie batted the tears out of her eyes. "What if they don't listen to me?"

89

Pappy shook his head firmly once. "We've pretty much talked over all that needs to be talked over. I agree with your decisions and reasoning. If they don't listen to you, I'll help enforce your orders. My nephew, Nicholas, will too."

Pappy hadn't shared too much about his nephew. In fact, this was the first time he had even said his name. But from what Pappy had said, she could tell he deeply loved the boy he had raised and respected the man he had become.

Melanie reached for Pappy's hand and gave it a quick squeeze. "Thanks Pappy."

In a swoop of hoots and hollers, fifteen men rode fast and hard into the front yard. They rode right up to the front porch, calling howdy to Pappy and riding their horses in circles, kicking up dust all the while. Pappy chuckled at their antics, but Melanie was too nervous to be amused.

A dusty cowboy wearing a red flannel shirt and brown hat was the first to notice Melanie. He reared his horse back in his surprise and shouted, "There's a lady!"

The rest followed suit.

"A lady?"

"Where's a lady?"

"On the porch with Pappy!"

One cowboy in a blue shirt and a black Stetson rode up to the porch. He quickly dismounted and looped his reins over the porch post. He took the stairs two at a time and enthusiastically pumped hands with Pappy. She had always considered Pappy to be a tall man but this stranger in the blue shirt towered over even Pappy. His shirt sleeves were taunt with muscle and Melanie thought his neck was nearly as thick as his horse's. She gulped.

Whistles and shouts went up. Melanie's stomach turned. Not even at the brothel did she ever feel like such a slab of meat.

Here she stood on the porch in front of fifteen dirty men who probably hadn't seen a woman in weeks, maybe months, and right now she felt like each one was probably scheming for a way to get a piece of her. The ice went up in her heart and she stepped forward, aimed her rifle toward the sky and fired a shot.

Silence immediately fell amongst the men. Pappy stepped up next to her side, one hand on his six-shooter and the other resting gently against the small of her back. His touch was a reminder of his pledge to stand beside her.

"I'm Melanie Brooks."

Soft murmurs quickly spread amongst the men.

"Melanie Brooks?"

"Old Brooks' niece?"

"The new boss!"

Melanie kept her expression somber and reserved. She didn't want a single one of them to catch a whiff of the terror she felt growing inside of her. She squeezed her hands into tight fists so at least if they saw her hands shaking they'd think it was out of rage and not fear. The key to handling men was to make them think you had it all together.

She took another step forward so she was standing near the edge of the top step. "Do you treat every woman you meet like this?"

A few men hung their heads. Another man dismounted and kicked an imaginary pebble. One man, still mounted on his horse, removed his hat and spoke. "Sorry, Miss Brooks. We just haven't seen a lady in quite a while."

Melanie snorted. "And that's reason enough to shout and whistle as if I were a dog?"

The man hung his head. "No ma'am."

Melanie eyed the group carefully before nodding. She'd deal with this the way Pappy advised her. "Go wash up. Supper will be ready in an hour. Then you can all start your day off early."

A shout of joy and celebration rose up and the boys raced toward the barn to stable their mounts and hopefully wash up as she had advised. Once the last cowboy had exited the yard, Melanie turned and raced inside. She flew down the hallway to the kitchen, knelt in front of the slop bucket, and retched up the contents of her stomach.

Chapter 14

PAPPY GRIPPED HER shoulder. "Easy now."

Melanie sobbed as she hung her head in the bucket. Pappy was kneeling at her side and slid his handkerchief into her hand. She dabbed at the corners of her mouth.

"Oh Pappy," she sobbed, "I haven't felt so disgusting since I worked at the …" Melanie looked up at Pappy and saw the cowboy in the blue shirt and black Stetson standing behind Pappy's shoulder, looking down at her with concern and confusion etched across his face. Melanie immediately schooled her expression. She brushed her tears away as if they were mere smudges of dirt and shoved up to her feet.

She tucked Pappy's soiled handkerchief into her apron pocket. "Thank you, Pappy."

Pappy leaned close to her ear. "It's OK. Nicholas won't say a word."

All Melanie could do was nod. Pappy stood back and smiled broadly at his nephew. "Melanie Brooks, may I introduce you to my nephew, Nicholas Henderson."

Melanie appreciated the easy manner in which Pappy continued on as if nothing was amiss. It helped Melanie smile brilliantly at Pappy's nephew. She extended her hand and watched it be engulfed by the man's large, beefy paw. "Nicholas, so nice to meet you."

Nicholas Henderson nodded solemnly while he shook her hand. "Likewise, Miss Brooks."

She smiled again. "Please call me Melanie."

He quirked a black eyebrow. "Melanie?"

She nodded. "Yes, please."

Pappy chuckled. "If I were you, I'd do as she says."

Nicholas smiled at his uncle, then nodded toward Melanie. "Yes, ma'am."

"Now if you don't mind, please go wash up. As I said, supper will be ready in an hour."

Nicholas turned toward his uncle with raised eyebrows as if he were questioning her authority. His audacity struck a chord with her. Pappy chuckled again. "Like I said, son, I advise doing as the *boss* says."

Obviously, the clear reminder that she was not some strange woman but rather his employer did the trick. Nicholas tipped his Stetson, turned on his heel, and strode through the front door to collect his horse.

Once he was out of sight Melanie began scrambling around the kitchen. "Pappy I'll need your help tonight."

"My help?"

"Please, Pappy! They're expecting supper in an hour and I'm not ready."

Pappy chuckled. "OK, Little Missy, tell me what to do."

Melanie instructed Pappy to dump the great bin of washed green beans she was planning on canning tomorrow into a roasting pan. She instructed him on how to season them while she quickly mixed together biscuit dough. Once the dough was rolled out, she handed over the task of cutting out biscuits and laying them in a tin for baking to Pappy. She mixed together another dough, this one for pie crusts. Once the biscuits were baking in the oven, she assigned Pappy the task of frying thick ham steaks. She quickly filled three pies with the apple pie filling she had been mixing on the stove.

The oven was full to capacity with a large roasting pan of green beans and biscuits. The pies would have to wait to bake until something was ready to come out. Melanie pulled the large pot of water they were going to use to can the apple pie filling to a warmer spot on the stove. She checked on Pappy, who was successfully frying ham steaks and stacking the cooked ones on a plate toward the back of the oven to stay warm. Satisfied Pappy wasn't burning anything, Melanie hustled outside to her vegetable garden.

"Please, God, let the corn be ready."

Melanie rolled her eyes and shoved down her irritation at catching herself talking to God again. She walked to the far side of the garden where the corn was. She had been so delighted to find such a large crop of green beans ready to be harvested that she hadn't paid any attention to any other part of the garden. To her relief, some of the corn looked ready to eat. She held the front folds of her apron in one hand and used the other to harvest ears of corn. When her apron became heavy she assumed she had enough and hurried back inside.

She dumped the ears of corn into the bin where the green beans had been. "Pappy, how are the ham steaks?"

"Just finished the last one."

Melanie blew a sigh of relief. "Good. Get over here and shuck some corn."

Melanie scuttled over to the stove, grabbed a towel, and opened the oven door. Her biscuits were nicely browned. She quickly removed both tins of biscuits and set them on the counter. She reached for a fork and jabbed at the green beans. They were almost done. She moved the large roasting pan of green beans around and made room for her three apple pies. The coffee pot caught the corner of her eye.

"Ugh, the coffee!"

She thought Pappy may have said something in response but she wasn't sure. She quickly filled the coffee pot with fresh grounds and water, then set it on the stove to boil. She turned to help Pappy shuck the corn when the two tins of biscuits caught her eye. She stared at them. Pappy could eat a whole tin of biscuits on his own. Melanie bit her lower lip. Were two tins of biscuits enough? She whirled back toward the counter and grabbed their last loaf of bread and began slicing off thick pieces. She piled the bread slices on two plates and hurried to place one plate on either end of the long table, then went back for the cooled tin of biscuits. She picked up the crock of butter and rushed to place it on the long table as well. Her stomach flip-flopped. She would have to eat with them at this table. She looked longingly at the small table she and Pappy shared.

"Put that plum jam we made on the table, they'll like that."

Melanie didn't argue. She rushed to the pantry and grabbed the opened jar of plum jam and paired it with a crock of butter. She wiped her hands across her apron front as she hurried back to the small table where Pappy stood shucking corn. She grabbed the ears he had already shucked clean and began breaking them in half and adding them to the boiling water on the stove. She opened the oven door with her apron and jabbed at the green beans again. Done to her likeness, she grabbed a towel and used it to pull the green beans out of the oven. She rushed over to the table and scooped a dollop of butter out, then rushed back to her roasting pan of green beans and tossed them in the melting butter.

Melanie turned and reached to pull down a pretty serving bowl she had discovered while working in the kitchen. She firmly grasped hold of the roasting pan and poured the green beans into the serving bowl. A loud ruckus made her lean forward and look out the window.

"They're coming!"

Pappy added the last ears of corn to the boiling water. "Well, it's been near an hour."

She reached above the counter and opened a cupboard. She pulled out a stack of plates and thrust them at Pappy. "Start setting the table."

She fetched both plates piled high with ham steaks and carried them to the table. She returned and grabbed the large serving dish of green beans as Pappy began setting the silverware out. The coffee was boiling violently so she pushed it back to a cooler part of the stove. She handed Pappy coffee cups, then carried as many as she could over to the table. She placed them in one large heap and rushed back to fetch napkins. The first of the men stomped up the back stairs just as Melanie was placing napkins at each place.

Chapter 15

"OY IT SURE does smell good in here!"

She hissed at Pappy. "Finish the table!"

She hurried to the door to stop the first man from coming in. "Just one minute! Hold out your hands."

He looked at her baffled. Melanie swore she heard Pappy snicker in the background. She arched her eyebrow. "Well?"

Slowly, the man held out his hands. Melanie shook her head at the dirt embedded in his nails. By now the rest of the boys were standing behind this fellow and some were holding back laughs and grins.

She looked out over all of them. "I told you boys to wash up before you came in for supper. No one is allowed into my kitchen without first scrubbing their hands and faces, dusting off their pants, and stomping the mud from their boots."

The group of men emitted a low grumble. Melanie slammed her fists firmly on her hips. From the kitchen behind her Pappy was laughing. "I'd hurry if I was you boys, or she'll let your food get cold."

That seemed to motivate the men, for they quickly hurried off toward the water pump, fighting each other to be the first to use it. Nicholas Henderson stood at the back of the group. He allowed each man to hurry over to the water pump before stepping toward the back steps.

He held up his hands and a smile glistened in his green eyes. "Do I pass your inspection, Melanie?"

Melanie startled at hearing her name rumble like a gentle drumming off this man's lips. She dug her thumbnail into the flesh of her pointer finger to drive out the all-too-familiar pull of a handsome man. *Do not be moved. Do not be moved. Do not be moved.* She took a deep breath and looked down to survey his hands. To her surprise they were scrubbed clean. She looked up at his face and noticed not a speck of dust remained. In fact, the stubble he rode in with no long remained either. Her eyes widened in surprise as she took in his entire appearance. His thick black hair was neatly combed under his Stetson, his crusty blue shirt had been traded for a clean green one, and his boots were free of any traces of mud.

She stared at him with eyes wide open to prevent herself from dropping her lashes into the seductive look that never failed to charm a man. She stepped back into the kitchen and held the door for Nicholas. "Thank you. Please be seated for supper."

A quick glance at the table told her Pappy had taken care of setting the rest of the table. She turned her attention to the men trekking back toward the kitchen. One by one they held out their hands and lifted their faces for her inspection. Each one was permitted inside, and when she turned to seat herself she was surprised to see each man standing behind his chair. Pappy caught her eye and winked. The chair at the head of the table remained empty and Pappy tilted his head ever so slightly to indicate that was where she should sit. When she approached her chair, Pappy stepped around the corner of the table and pulled her seat out for her. She looked at him a bit dumbfounded, as he hadn't attempted to pull a chair out for her since their first dinner together.

Pappy leaned forward and whispered in her ear, "Old Brooks always wanted to make gentlemen out of them."

Melanie suppressed a giggle and nodded her head. Before she sat she smiled at each freshly scrubbed man. "I suspect none of you will have to be told to wash up before entering my kitchen again, correct?"

A low grumble of chuckles filled the room as each man answered at once.

"Yes ma'am."

"Absolutely, Miss Brooks."

"Never make that mistake again, Miss Brooks."

Melanie nodded. "Good. And please, call me Melanie."

A chorus of, "Yes, Melanie," went up and Melanie smiled. She sat in her chair and the men followed suit. Each man routinely grasped his neighbor's hand in preparation to say grace and, as they had discussed in the weeks prior to the boys' return, Pappy led the group in saying the meal prayer. At Pappy's "Amen" hands all around the table shot out toward the meal she and Pappy had rushed to put together. Grumbles of appreciation filtered through the air and jabs at Pappy's cooking sparked laughter.

Melanie raised her voice above the dim banter. "Would anyone like coffee?"

"Yes, please."

"I wouldn't mind a cup."

"Did Pappy make it?"

Laughter exploded into the large kitchen. Melanie couldn't help but be swept away by it. Put food in front of these men and they scarcely paid attention to her. Maybe living in such close quarters with them wouldn't be so bad ... so long as she kept their bellies full.

Melanie stood and retrieved the coffee pot from the stove and began filling the outstretched cups with steaming hot coffee. She came to what looked like the youngest cowhand at the table. "Coffee?"

The young man smiled up at her. "No, thank you. If it's no trouble I'd appreciate some milk, though."

The men around him began laughing and making jokes that milk was for babies. Melanie shamed each one into silence with her meanest-looking scowl. She turned a brilliant smile to the young cowhand. "I'll go get that milk for you."

Melanie filled a pitcher from the milk bucket they kept in the kitchen and returned to fill the young man's cup. She looked around and, satisfied that every man had a full cup of coffee, she returned to her seat where she promptly filled her own cup with milk as well.

Pappy drained his coffee and held out his cup. "That milk does look mighty thirst quenching."

Melanie beamed a thankful smile at the old man. She looked down the long table and was horrified to see that nearly every morsel of food had been devoured. Her stomach rumbled to remind her that she hadn't yet filled her plate to eat.

Melanie rose once again from her chair. "I hope you have room for pie."

Fifteen ruddy faces turned her way, eyes glistening with expectancy as all the men called together, "Pie?"

Melanie couldn't help but laugh. "Yes, apple, I hope that's OK."

Pappy patted his stomach. "More than OK with me."

A series of whoops and calls rose up. Melanie chuckled and turned to Pappy. "Mind helping me serve?"

When Pappy nodded, she once again rose and hurried over to the small work table. She expertly sliced the three apple pies into as equal portions as possible, then turned to deliver instructions to Pappy. She nearly shrieked at the sight of Nicholas standing directly behind her. He towered over her with his tall, muscular stature. Melanie's stomach clenched at having such a handsome man stand so close to her.

Nicholas smiled and dimples framed his lips. "I told Paps I'd help you."

She sniffed. "Please have the men scrape their leftovers into the slop bucket and stack their dinner plates by the sink."

She turned toward the cupboard and retrieved a stack of dessert dishes. She placed them on the work table and began dishing out slices of pie. The men picked up a plate of pie after they had scraped and stacked their dinner plates. When the younger cowhand who had asked for milk approached the work table she offered him a particularly thick slice.

He smiled brightly at her. "Thank you, ma'am."

Once all of the men had their plate of pie, she picked up the coffee pot and began refilling cups. When she came to Pappy she bent to kiss his forehead.

The old man smiled up at her. "Thanks, Little Missy."

When Melanie looked up Nicholas was still standing by the work table, his mouth slightly gaping open. She rolled her eyes and silently huffed. Let him think what he wants.

Once each man had his fill of pie and coffee Melanie resumed her position at the head of the table. "Did you all enjoy your pie?"

"Oh, yes ma'am!"

"It was the best apple pie I've ever had."

"That was better than my ma's pie!"

Melanie held back her smile. She stood at the head of the table with her hands primly folded in front of her. "I'm so glad you all enjoyed it. Please keep in mind then if I ever see or hear of any Brooks' employees calling out to a woman like you all greeted me today; there will be no dessert for that employee for a month."

A low groan rose up in the kitchen, followed by profuse apologies.

"We're sorry, Melanie."

"Don't take away our pie; we didn't mean any harm."

Melanie held up her hand to bring back silence. "In the future keep in mind you are to treat *all* women with due respect." Melanie arched an eyebrow. "Understood?"

The men chorused, "Yes, ma'am."

Melanie smiled. "Good. As I promised earlier you may have the rest of the day off and I believe Pappy informed me that tomorrow is your regularly scheduled day off. If any of you plan on going to town to enjoy the services of the saloon that is your business, but please do not come back until you are well and sober." Melanie unclasped her hands. "With that, I wish you all a good rest and enjoy your time off."

The men stood, and much to her delight took their dessert plates with them to scrape any leftover bits into the slop bucket before stacking their dirty plates by the sink. Melanie smiled inwardly. Men *can* be taught new tricks. While they meandered out, they offered her more thanks and compliments on the meal.

The young man who had requested milk stayed behind. "Miss Melanie?"

Melanie sighed. "Just Melanie, please."

The young man's cheeks tinted red and he nodded. "Melanie. I was wondering if you would like some help doing the dishes."

Melanie glanced down the long table at the many forks, knives, cups, and serving dishes. If she lingered in the kitchen cleaning she'd have an excuse to stay inside. She had felt rather comfortable with the men while they ate. In fact, she rather enjoyed hustling back and forth to fetch them whatever it was they needed. She wasn't so sure, however, that she'd feel that same comfortable contentment outside in the dimming light.

She smiled at the young man. "What was your name?"

"Douglas Spells, ma'am."

"I appreciate your offer, Douglas, but I can manage. I would, however, appreciate it if you could empty the slop bucket."

He nodded vigorously. "Yes, ma'am!" He picked up the slop bucket and quickly headed out the kitchen door.

Melanie called over her shoulder, "Good night."

Pappy still sat at the table sipping his coffee, and Melanie took up the seat at the head of the table to sit with him before she started cleaning the kitchen.

"Well?"

She smiled at Pappy and rolled her eyes heavenward. "That was a whirlwind."

Pappy chuckled. "Yup, I told you those boys would appreciate your cooking."

Melanie wrung her hands under the table. "It was a bit unnerving at first. But then," she shrugged, "it didn't seem so bad."

Pappy leaned over and patted her hands. "You did good, Little Missy."

"Am I interrupting something?"

Melanie's head snapped up. There in the doorway leading to the hall stood Nicholas. Pappy chuckled his good natured laugh. "Not at all, son. Let me top off my coffee and we'll have a talk in the big sitting room."

Nicholas was staring at Melanie with his piercing green eyes while he talked to Pappy. "What about the boss? She should hear about the cattle run too."

She didn't like the way this man was staring at her, and she definitely didn't like how her stomach somersaulted every time he spoke. She forced herself to think of Tom and the night he drugged her. A fresh layer of ice surrounded her heart and fortified her strength to resist any charm or flowery words this handsome man might possess. She glared back at Nicholas.

In short, clipped words she responded for Pappy. "I have a kitchen to clean."

He leaned against the entry way. "I'd think the boss would be interested in how much her cattle sold for and what problems we may have run into."

Pappy was at the stove refilling his cup with coffee. He strode up to his nephew. "What did you call her, son?"

Nicholas looked at him quizzically. "Boss?"

Pappy nodded. "So, are you now telling your *boss* what to do?"

Nicholas glanced at Melanie from the corner of his eye. "No, sir."

Pappy grinned. "Good. Then let's go talk and when Melanie is done here, she can join us." Pappy smiled in her direction. "If that's OK with you."

Melanie smiled her gratitude. If it weren't for the old man she'd surely have throttled his nephew. Fortunately, Pappy had a subtle way of handling certain situations. "I'll be there shortly."

Melanie dismissed them both by turning her back to them and began attacking the mound of dirty dishes.

Chapter 16

ELANIE PUSHED ALL thoughts of Pappy's handsome nephew and a ranch full of men aside. She enjoyed working in the spacious kitchen her uncle had built for her, and she didn't want thoughts of her worst fears and weaknesses tainting the joy of moving about her kitchen. She hummed softly while she poured hot water into the sink and began scrubbing each dish clean. She washed, rinsed, dried, and put away every dish much faster than she had expected. She wiped down the long table, her smaller work table, and each counter. She carefully covered the remaining slices of apple pie and set the tin out of the way. She stepped back and surveyed her kitchen. Satisfied everything was righted back to its former order, she untied her apron and hung it on the peg by the hall doorway.

As Melanie walked down the hall toward the large sitting room, she ran her hands down to smooth out her dress and tucked a few stray curls behind her ear. She stopped short at the terse, whispered words spilling from the room.

"I don't want to hear about making jam. I want to know what's between you and that woman."

Pappy's voice took on a hardness she had only heard the day she called herself a whore. "Son, has it occurred to you that it may be none of your business?"

She heard Nicholas sigh. "Yes, sir. I just never thought you'd take up with a woman."

Melanie winced. The familiar shame flared in her heart and spread throughout her body with every heartbeat. She placed a hand over her stomach and listened for a response.

Pappy nearly growled back. "Melanie is a good girl and she deserves the respect of every man on this ranch. To insinuate that she would *take up* with a man is not giving her that respect."

"Pappy, I didn't mean to insinuate anything. I just thought," Melanie heard him sigh again. "From what I've seen so far I just thought the two of you ..."

Pappy cut him off short. "Well, you thought wrong! That girl has shown more grit, determination, and spirit than all the boys put together. She's a good girl with a caring heart and tender feelings."

Melanie heard a masculine grunt. "Doesn't seem so tender to me."

"This is your last warning, son. I will not tolerate foul talk regarding Melanie." Pappy's voice seemed to soften. "We don't always know what a person has gone through to make them the way they are. And we shouldn't judge what we don't know."

"Well, what has she gone through?"

CHAPTER 16

Melanie held her breath. She knew Pappy was faithful to standing by her but she wasn't sure he wouldn't confide in his nephew. She held her breath as she waited in the hall for his reply.

Pappy chuckled. "Not for me to say."

Relief flooded Melanie's heart. The answer was good enough for her. She cleared her throat and quickly entered the doorway to the sitting room. "So, Nicholas, are you ready to give your report of the cattle drive?"

Nick glanced back over his shoulder on his way to the bunkhouse. He wasn't quite sure what to make of Old Brooks' spitfire of a niece. She was a sturdy-looking woman, the kind of woman a man as big as Nick wouldn't have to worry about hurting with his size. She had pretty eyes, too. He couldn't help but notice how they nearly turned to gold in the soft lamp light of the sitting room. He liked the way her curly hair broke loose from her bun and framed her face. He thought it made her look gentle and beautiful, like a soft-spoken angel. Her sharp tongue and icy glares had proven otherwise rather quickly though. Her rude behavior thoroughly confused him.

What was even more baffling was the odd relationship that had developed between his uncle and the fiery woman while the cowhands ran the cattle to market. He scratched his jaw. Maybe it wasn't the unseemly type of relationship he was picturing in his mind. He glanced back over his shoulder.

"Then why is Paps staying the night alone in that house with her?"

Nick shook his head. Nothing seemed to make sense. When they all rode up he knew immediately that the girl standing on the porch clutching her rifle was Old Brooks' niece. The old boss would have gotten a hoot out of seeing her put all those men in their places. Nick smiled. He sure had anyways.

He kicked a rock as he neared the bunkhouse. After the incident in the kitchen, Nick had been eager to please her by following her first orders as boss. He scrubbed his hands and face, shaved, changed his shirt, brushed his boots clean, and combed his hair like he was going to Sunday service. He had pictured a smile spreading clear across her round cheeks as she praised him for his cleanliness. Instead, the little minx fixed him with the coldest of glares and merely permitted him entrance into her kitchen—the kitchen he had spent an entire summer building! Nick huffed. Just what was going on here? She seemed warm and comfortable with Pappy, but the minute he spoke or so much as looked her way, she'd turned cold as ice.

"Paps has never lied to me. Surely if there was something going on he'd just tell me." Nick shook his head. "Then again, if he was too ashamed …"

Nick stopped talking to himself as he pushed open the door to the bunkhouse and stepped in. He meandered over to his cot and dressed down for bed. He laid with his arms tucked up under his head. Pappy was being too protective of this woman, and it was cause for there to be secrets between them. Since Paps had taken him in as a boy, they had shared everything with each other. Good, bad, or worse they never held anything back.

He thought back to the episode in the kitchen when they had first gotten home. She said she hadn't felt like such a piece of meat since … since when? And after dinner, he overheard her tell Pappy how she felt overwhelmed serving the men at first. Nick shrugged that thought aside. What woman *wouldn't* be overwhelmed serving fifteen ravenous men for the first time?

Nick closed his eyes as he thought of the few times he had interrupted Pappy and Old Brooks' pretty little niece in what had appeared to be an intimate conversation.

Pappy.

Pappy!

She called him *Pappy!* What woman would call her man Pappy? Nick breathed a sigh of relief. Pappy did warn him that people become who they are through the circumstances they have lived through. Maybe they were nothing more than a young woman and an old man who had formed an odd friendship. Nick frowned. But then why did she kiss Pappy's forehead so affectionately at supper? Pappy didn't even flush, and she had leaned down so naturally without any hesitation, it looked like a regular routine of theirs. Nick tossed to his side and punched down his pillow. None of this sat well with him.

Chapter 17

ELANIE ROSE EARLY the next morning as usual. To her surprise Pappy was inching his door closed, obviously trying to be as quiet as possible. She waited with a smile on her face for him to turn around. When he did she was sure he'd jump clear out of his shoes.

He chuckled. "You nearly scared me to death, Little Missy."

Melanie grinned. "I wanted to wake up early and make breakfast for any of the boys still around."

Pappy shook his head. "You always wake up at this hour." He grabbed hold of her elbow and began escorting her down the stairs.

Melanie enjoyed how comfortable she was with Pappy. Even when he grabbed her elbow or rested his hand over hers on the table she felt no feelings of shame or disgust. She simply felt protected and safe. Sometimes, when the dark clouds of her past weren't hovering so close around her, she could even feel a slight bit loved.

She smiled up at him. "How about I feed the chickens and get the eggs, and you milk the cows? If Douglas is around this morning I'll have him slop the pigs after breakfast."

Pappy squeezed her elbow. "Sounds like a plan, boss." He winked.

Melanie quickly finished her chore, then hurried back to the kitchen to begin breakfast. She looped her apron over her head and tied the strings in the back. She was pleased to see a small flame still flickered inside the large cast iron stove. She added a log and patiently waited for it to catch fire. Once the log was fully consumed by flames she added several more logs to get the stove hot. She filled the coffee pot with fresh grounds and water, then set it on the stove. She fetched a side of ham from the pantry cellar that her great-uncle had so cleverly designed as a place to store perishable food, and sliced thick slices of bacon. She placed several strips of bacon in her large cast iron skillet and turned to her work table to mix together some pancake batter. She whisked the remaining eggs into a frothy frenzy and set them aside.

Pappy came in with a fresh bucket of milk. "Where you want this, Little Missy?"

Melanie nodded to her work table. "Up here, please." She twirled around to the cupboard where she kept her pitcher and brought it down. She placed it down in front of Pappy. "Mind filling that?"

Pappy silently obeyed and placed the pitcher on the table. She smiled as the old man began pulling down plates and opening drawers to retrieve silverware and napkins. Melanie turned back to her sizzling bacon and forked the crispy strips out onto a plate, then carefully laid down more in the hot grease to cook. Melanie looked over the food she was starting to prepare. She worried her lower lip. Last night those men wolfed down everything she prepared in a matter of minutes. Some even had double portions of pie, surely that meant they had still been hungry.

Melanie hurried over to the pantry and lifted the heavy wooden bucket where they had been storing their potatoes. She looked over at Pappy as she thumped the bucket on top of the work table. The old man was laying down the last place setting.

"Pappy, can you help me cut potatoes?"

He nodded. "Be right there."

Melanie got two knives, placed one on the table for Pappy, and got to work dicing the potatoes. She switched between cutting potatoes and flipping bacon. When the bacon was all cooked, she dumped the diced potatoes into the spitting hot grease left from the bacon.

Pappy looked over her shoulder. "Those won't cook in time."

Melanie opened a cupboard and pulled out a large plate. "This is a trick Ma taught me." She poured a half glass of water into the pan and quickly slid the plate over top the skillet.

Pappy's white eyebrows rose. "Won't they be mushy?"

Melanie grabbed the bowl of pancake batter and began spooning out batter onto another hot skillet. "Trust me Pappy, they'll be delicious."

Melanie reached for a strip of bacon and chomped on it while she piled a large serving platter high with pancakes. Pappy brought her a biscuit that was somehow overlooked from last night. "I noticed you didn't get much to eat last night."

She laughed. Melanie grabbed another strip of bacon and sandwiched it in her biscuit. "Much? Try nothing at all. I put my plate right back in the cupboard."

Pappy huffed.

Melanie grinned. "It's OK, Pappy, I have enough padding. I won't be wasting away any time soon."

Pappy growled. "Don't talk like that."

The coffee began to boil, so she grabbed a towel to push it to the back of the stove. She heard the potatoes sizzling and lifted the plate to make sure the water hadn't cooked away yet. As she lifted the plate, a large pocket of fat popped out and sprayed across her forearm. She dropped the plate, causing it to clatter back on top of the potatoes and called out in pain.

Pappy was at her side in a heartbeat. He was gently holding her forearm in his hands to inspect for burns. "Are you OK, Little Missy?"

The back door opened and in walked Nicholas. His eyebrows rose so high Melanie was sure they'd come back around to form a mustache under his nose. "I seem to have the most peculiar timing."

Melanie rolled her eyes. "Fat from the bacon popped on me."

Nicholas strode over in two long strides. "Are you burnt?"

Pappy released her arm and lifted his head. "Just small burns where the grease hit her. Nothing serious."

Melanie turned back to the stove and lifted a pancake before it burned. She stirred the potatoes and seasoned them with pepper and salt. All the while she tried to ignore the large handsome man she was sure was staring at the back of her head. She also tried to ignore the fact that she kept referring to him as handsome in her thoughts. A bead of sweat dripped down her spine and made her twitch. What was it about that man that put her on edge?

"Oh, Melanie?"

His voice was clear and strong and masculine. Melanie felt the goose bumps rise over the flesh of her arms. She gripped the handle of the skillet. "Yes, Nicholas?"

"I forgot to mention last night, I found a man I think could be an asset to the ranch."

She furrowed her brow. She thought all of the men at supper were her employees. "And you didn't introduce him last night at supper?"

Melanie tasted a potato to see if it was done. When the potato easily mashed between her tongue and the roof of her mouth, she poured the skillet full of potatoes onto a large serving plate. She whisked the eggs one last time and threw them into the pan the potatoes had just vacated. She quickly stirred them around, watching carefully as clumps of cooked eggs built up in the soggy mess.

"I couldn't. He preferred to stay the night in town." He paused when Pappy reached past her to grab the tall plate of pancakes. He cleared his throat. "Anyways, he helped on the run and proved to be quite useful. I told him to ride out early this morning. He should be here before sunset if he rides hard."

Melanie nodded while she cooked the rest of the moisture out of the eggs. "Sounds fine. Thank you for telling me."

Pappy returned and Melanie handed him the dish of fried potatoes. He plucked one off the top and tossed it in his mouth. "Mmm, you were right. Those are good."

Melanie smiled sweetly at the old man. "Told you so."

Melanie poured the eggs onto another large plate. She glanced up at the table and noticed Pappy forgot to set out cups. "Oh Pappy, cups."

The old man nodded. "Sorry, Little Missy."

CHAPTER 17

Melanie glanced at Nicholas. He was wringing his beefy hands like an uncomfortable school boy. Melanie nearly grunted. What does he have to be so uncomfortable about?

"If you're going to stand in my kitchen, then make yourself useful." She thrust the plate of eggs into his hands then quickly turned toward the pantry for the crock of butter and jug of maple syrup.

She approached the long table and surveyed the piles of pancakes, bacon, eggs, and potatoes. "Do you think it'll be enough Pappy?"

He laughed his endearing chuckle. "I think you put out quite a feast."

"Looks mighty good, Melanie."

Melanie stomped past Nicholas and his phony compliment to go ring the triangle.

Chapter 18

ICK WAS SLIGHTLY amused and slightly irritated. He tried to give the girl a compliment, one he had genuinely meant, and she didn't even have the grace to say thank you. She just marched right past him to call the boys for breakfast. He rather liked her spunk but wished she wasn't using it against him.

He had awakened this morning with the good intentions of putting all suspicious thoughts of Pappy and Melanie aside. Even when he walked in on them in close proximity of each other, Pappy holding her arm, he pushed away the feeling that something was amiss. He saw the red blotchy burns on her arm and figured Pappy was just being his usual caring self, but then he saw how they worked together.

It was like an orchestrated dance. One moved to grab something, the other leaned out of the way without so much as a glance. One pointed to something and the other knew which of the many seasoning canisters, serving plates, or silverware was being requested. They worked in absolute companionable silence, a thing he had only seen once before in his lifetime, and that was between his mother and father. Nick scowled. This behavior was not like Pappy at all.

Everyone joined hands as Pappy said grace over the delicious looking breakfast Melanie and Pappy had prepared. Immediately after the "Amen," the boys reached for the nearest platter and began filling their plates. Murmurs of profuse compliments floated up toward the head of the table where the new boss sat. Her cheeks seemed to warm at all of the praise and Nick wondered what the difference was between his earlier compliment and the compliments the boys were offering now.

Nick observed that once again, Melanie barely sat during the meal. She would no sooner sit, then shoot right back out of her chair to fetch something for one of the boys. He was nearly tempted to ask for something just to see if she would get up for him too, but he couldn't think of a single thing that he might possibly need that wasn't already on the table.

At the end of the meal each man scraped his plate and stacked it next to the sink. Nick fought to hold back the grin that twitched at the corners of his lips. She had less than three hours of interaction with the men and already she had trained them to do exactly what she wanted. Nick shoveled another fork full of potatoes into his mouth. He didn't blame a single one of them. Her cooking wasn't just good, it was the absolute best he'd had in years. If she sold her meals, she'd easily put the hotel diner in town out of business.

Nick purposely made sure he would be the last man to leave. He noticed that, like last night, Melanie's plate stayed completely clean. He reached over and picked her plate up. There was a bit of eggs left and a slice of bacon. He had a pancake left on his plate and glanced up to make sure she wasn't looking, then quickly slid the pancake to her plate. Pappy was bringing over the coffee pot and winked at Nick while he filled Melanie's cup with the steaming liquid.

Pappy whispered, "That's mighty nice of you, son."

Nick smiled. He hadn't liked Pappy's stern admonishment to speak kindly about the new boss last night. It had made him feel like a small child. This appreciative Pappy was much more to his liking. When the last of the men had scraped and stacked their plates and Melanie had wished them a good day off, she turned to face the mess awaiting her. Nick grinned as her eyes settled upon him.

"Thanks for breakfast, Melanie."

She nodded pertly and began gathering dishes from the table. Pappy cleared his throat. "Little Missy, Nicholas saved you some breakfast."

Her head shot up and she looked at Nick. She hesitantly shifted her gaze to Pappy. Out of the corner of his eye Nick saw Pappy nod toward the table as if telling her to sit. He glanced at Melanie in time to catch her subtly shake her head. Pappy slowly nodded his head toward the table again. Melanie fixed her coldest glare on Pappy and triumph rose up in Nick's chest to know she could look that coolly at Pappy too.

Pappy nodded at the table again. "Most of the boys are going into town, so it's just us for Bible study today."

Melanie's jaw nearly hit the table. "That's *today?*"

Nick looked at her quizzically. "Well, it *is* Sunday."

Her eyes widened and her lower lip immediately disappeared between her teeth. "Oh, Lord, already?"

Nick wasn't quite sure what the problem was. He lost track of what day it was too sometimes, but he didn't react in such a worried way. Maybe this was just how women were. He didn't have much experience with women, growing up on a ranch full of men.

He leaned across the table to whisper at Pappy. "Are all women like this?"

Whack!

Nick didn't think she could hear him whisper, but the stinging on the back of his neck where she had slapped him with a wooden serving spoon was proof she had. Nick sat up straight in his chair, ready to apologize or fend off more attacks, whichever proved to be more necessary. He had expected to see her hands fisted onto her round hips and her face red with fury. Instead her shoulders seemed slumped forward and tears rimmed her eyes, making Nick instantly regret his comment. He had the sudden urge to reach out and pull the sullen looking woman into his lap.

"You men are all the same. You leech out every last drop a woman's got to give and then you wonder why we're a little skeptical or vulnerable. You just can't seem to figure out why women are so ..." she rolled her eyes and motioned with her hand. She shook her head violently. Nick suspected she was trying to hold her tears at bay. "Men are idiots!"

She ran to the back door, flung it open, and ran across the yard to the barn. Nick rose to follow after her. He wasn't quite sure what to say, but he felt the proper thing to do would be to follow after her and at least apologize for his whispered question to Pappy.

Pappy rose and gripped his arm, restraining him from following after her. "Stay here, son. She needs to be alone." Pappy strode toward the door.

"Well where are you going?"

Pappy pointed toward the barn. "After her."

Nick sighed, exasperated. "But you just said she needs to be alone."

Pappy gestured wildly toward the table. "I understand what that was all about. You don't."

Nick stepped forward. "Then tell me so I can understand."

Pappy shook his head. "I already told you, not for me to tell."

Nick shrugged, defeated. "Then what am I supposed to do?"

Pappy grabbed Melanie's Winchester that was leaning against the counter. "You could start by cleaning the kitchen." Pappy's chuckle followed him out the door.

As Nick watched Pappy cross the yard toward the barn, Melanie nearly flew across the yard on her strawberry roan. Her hair easily unraveled from her bun and flew in a wave behind her. Nick was about to turn away, but then she rode out from under the shade of the yard and into the sunlight where her brown hair suddenly seemed to sparkle magnificent shades of red, brown, and blonde. His fingers twitched to touch the long curly strands. Nick shook himself mentally. Touch his boss's hair? Why was he thinking such absurd thoughts? He turned away from the windows and began cleaning the kitchen while he tried not to think of all those luscious curls and the fiery woman beneath them.

Chapter 19

BROOKE SKIDDED AS Melanie pulled hard on the reins to make her mare turn a hard right around the rock formation that shielded her private orchard. She raced her horse up to the small entrance created by the beautiful crape myrtles and crashed through the overgrowth. Melanie pulled up on her reins and Brooke finally came to a stop halfway down an aisle of the apple trees. Melanie gasped for a breath of fresh air, but none would come. She moved to dismount, but looking down made her unbearably dizzy. She slumped forward on her horse, hugging Brooke's neck while she tried to calm her breathing. Tears smarted her eyes.

"That stupid man with his stupid comments and his stupid, handsome face."

"I hope you're not talking about me."

A small shriek escaped Melanie's lips as she startled upright, smacked her head on an apple tree branch and went tumbling down to the ground. Rough hands were running down her arms, but she couldn't see her attacker because darkness shrouded around her. She flailed her hands in the air to fend off whoever was attacking her.

"I was just making sure you didn't break a bone. Calm down, Little Missy, it's me." One of her flailing hands made contact with a scruffy beard. An iron clasp latched onto her wrists.

"It's *Pappy.*"

It was then that Melanie realized she had squeezed her eyes tightly shut. She opened her eyes to see Pappy kneeling beside her, concern and fear etched across his features. She took a deep gasping breath and lunged forward to wrap her arms around his neck.

"Oh, Pappy, I feel so horrible."

"Well, running out like that was a mite rude."

She shook her head vigorously against his shoulder. A wave of nausea followed. She clutched tighter to the old man's neck. "Not about that. All the time. I feel horrible all the time."

Melanie suddenly pushed Pappy back, crawled a short distance from him and vomited the biscuit she had eaten earlier. She heaved again but nothing came up this time. Her stomach roiled and she heaved a third time. The acidic taste of vomit rose in her throat and burned the back of her mouth but her stomach had nothing else to rid itself of. Her arms began to shake from holding her weight and she allowed herself to fall over. She laid there with her eyes closed.

She felt so low and so miserable she barely had the strength to whisper. "Pappy, the world is spinning."

"Shh, you just lay there, Little Missy. I'll be right back."

She heard him rustling around in his saddlebags, then hurriedly walk away. Her stomach clenched and she thought she might be sick again but no energy remained to prop herself up. She tightly closed her eyes against the harsh, brutal, spinning world. Why did Nicholas Henderson have to be so handsome? And why did she have to feel that old, shameful burning attraction? His dark hair, pure green eyes, broad shoulders, thick arms, dimpled smile, long legs.

Melanie shuddered despite the sweat breaking across her forehead. She positively hated herself for feeling the jittery excitement in her stomach each time Nicholas was near. She downright loathed herself for being so weak as to even entertain the idea of what life might be like next to a man like him. She dug deep for the old memories of Jonathan and Tom and encouraged the icy fear of being wronged again to encase her heart. She needed to be strong, and the only way she knew how was to steel herself with the anger she felt toward those two men and the fear she felt toward all other men.

She felt like centuries had passed by the time Pappy returned. He knelt beside her and wrapped an arm around her shoulders. "Here, rinse your mouth then drink some real slow."

Cool, fresh water rolled past her lips. He must have gone to the creek to fetch water. She rinsed her mouth as Pappy had advised and then took a tentative sip. Her stomach growled. She looked up at Pappy, "I think I'm sick."

Pappy shook his head. The girl was sick alright. Staying up half the night every night repeating how unworthy and dirty she was, then waking before the sun rose to begin making breakfast, which now entailed making a large feast to feed all of the men. Pappy knew from experience that feeding all those men was a task, and so was cleaning up after them. She didn't even get to enjoy the meals she prepared, for as soon as she sat she was up again to retrieve more coffee for one fellow or sugar for another. Pappy shook his head. Besides the biscuit this morning she hadn't eaten since supper yesterday afternoon.

He gently gripped her shoulder. "Melanie, girl, you need to slow down."

Fear flashed through her eyes. "I can't! I promised I'd earn this ranch."

He shook his head again. "Don't you see? Look around you! Look at this flower-enclosed orchard. Go take a good long look at that large yellow house covered in windows. This was all yours long before Old Brooks passed on. There's no need to *earn* it."

Pain clouded Melanie's eyes and Pappy's heart broke at the sight of her. He gathered her up in his arms and gently rocked her in the middle of the orchard. She sobbed her heartache into his shirt and Pappy prayed that God was touching her heart so she could begin the process of healing.

She used her apron to blow her nose. "Why me, Pappy? Why is it always me?"

Pappy wasn't quite sure what she meant. He furrowed his brow as he tried to figure out what she meant. Maybe he was as perplexed about women as was his nephew.

She coughed through her tears. "Is it because I'm ugly? Do I look as stupid as I act?" She buried her face against his shoulder as a fresh wave of sobs stole through her throat. Pappy almost didn't hear her say, "Why do men always hurt *me*?"

He held her tighter. He didn't know why she was abandoned by a man she thought would one day be her husband. Nor did he know why another man would take advantage of a woman as he had. Melanie obviously made some poor choices, but Pappy doubted it was from stupidity. To his way of thinking her bad decisions were mostly made out of the absence of her parents and a lack of self-confidence. From the way she told her story, it sounded more like she just wanted someone to love her.

Pappy didn't love her like a husband, but that didn't mean he had no love to offer her at all. In the weeks they had lived and worked together he had grown to deeply respect, admire, and love this young woman. It was easy to think of the girl as part of his family. And obviously something about his other family, Nicholas, upset her terribly. Pappy suspected Melanie might be a tad smitten with his nephew, but he wasn't sure, nor did he want to mention it to her. At least not right now. He would, however, have a talk with Nicholas.

Pappy squeezed Melanie and kissed her forehead. Her sobbing had eased into sniffles. "Let's get home, Little Missy."

Melanie hiccupped. "I don't think I can ride back."

Together they rose to their feet. "We can ride double."

He was surprised when she didn't resist. Pappy looped her mare's reins over one hand while he cradled her in his arms, her head resting against his shoulder. He rode slowly home, taking about twice as long as usual. The slow swaying of the saddle lulled Melanie to sleep almost instantly. His heart ached to see her twitch as she gently murmured, "No, please. Please. No."

Pappy prayed that whatever nightmare she was having would cease so the girl could get some peaceful rest. He also prayed that God would touch her heart and heal her wounds. "Open her eyes, Father. Show her not all men are as evil as the ones she's encountered."

Nicholas met Pappy in the yard behind the house. Pappy thought his eyes shone with concern. "Is she hurt?"

Pappy lowered his voice so he wouldn't wake her. "Just worn out. Help me."

Pappy lowered Melanie into Nicholas's arms. She snuggled her head against his nephew's shoulder and Pappy saw the quick smile that flashed across Nicholas's lips. Pappy raised an eyebrow. Could it be Nicholas felt attracted to Melanie also? That might explain why his nephew was so accusatory about the kinship between him and Melanie.

Pappy allowed Nicholas to carry Melanie into the house and up the stairs, but outside her bedroom door, he gathered her back into his arms and instructed his nephew to bring together any men who hadn't gone to town. Pappy entered her room alone and carefully laid her down on the bed.

A soft sob broke through her lips as Pappy pulled away and she softly murmured, "Keep them all away or I'll never be clean."

Tears sprang into Pappy's eyes. The only times he had ever cried was when his brother died years ago and young Nicholas sobbed he had no one to love him. The brokenness of this young woman ripped his heart out. If he could, he'd hunt down every man who had so much as looked at her wrong and wring their necks. Of course, he couldn't do that, but he could do as she asked. He could keep them all away.

Pappy quietly shut her door and crept downstairs. He stepped out onto the front porch and was surprised to see not a single man had gone to town for a day off. He placed his hands on his hips and stepped forward to address them.

"You haven't been home long enough to witness this for yourselves, but that young lady up there," he jerked his thumb toward the second story, "has been working with the energy and strength of all of you put together. Now she's plumb wore out." Pappy laid down the new rules during meal time. They were to behave in an orderly and quiet manner. If they needed something they were to help themselves so that Melanie could sit and enjoy the meal with them.

"And since I have you all here," Pappy stepped down from the porch into the throng of men so he wouldn't have to shout, "if any of you see a feller on the land, you're to immediately show him off the property."

"What if he's here for business?"

"Then bring him to me."

"Shouldn't he talk to the boss about business?"

Pappy glared in the direction the question came from. "Men have been riding out ever since she got to town. She's not interested in courting, but those knot heads don't seem to grasp that. If I determine they truly are here for business, then I'll show them the way to the boss."

"Is it true she shot a man?"

Pappy scanned the men. "Who said that?"

A stranger stepped forward. Pappy's hand immediately went to his six-shooter. The man held his hands up. "Hey, I was invited!"

Nicholas stepped forward. "This is the man I was telling you about. He left town last night, so he arrived just a bit ago."

The man extended his hand. "Mike Groover. As your nephew just said, I just came from town. While I was there I heard she had shot a man for calling her homely."

Pappy was pleased to hear some grumbled remarks in Melanie's defense. It meant the men liked her. He shook the man's hand. "Pappy Henderson. And yes, it's true."

Eyebrows shot up to hairlines and mouths gaped open. Pappy nodded. "Young Johnny Gray showed up one day. He heard rumors Melanie didn't take to compliments all that well, so he figured he'd insult the girl into marrying him. She warned him he was trespassing, but he didn't heed that warning. She started shooting and he took off. She got him once in the backside."

"Oooo," sounded throughout the small crowd of men followed by a few chuckles.

"I mean it though, boys. If anyone shows up to bother Melanie you're to turn him right back around to where he came from. That girl has had a hard life, she works hard, she's a fair boss, and she cooks fine fare." The men shared their agreement about her cooking. "I think the least we can do is see to this one thing for her. Don't you agree?"

Douglas Spells, the youngest cowhand on the ranch, stepped forward. "I don't mind throwing some men off the property for the boss."

Nicholas nodded. "I'd be glad to keep them away too."

Pappy arched an eyebrow. He had a growing suspicion he knew why Nick would be glad to keep men from coming to court Melanie. If she took a liking to one of them, then Nick would have competition. After the rest of the men agreed to adhere to this new rule, Pappy ushered Nick inside.

Chapter 20

*N*ICK DIDN'T WASTE time cutting to the chase. "What happened out there?" He was pointing in the direction of the orchard.

Pappy eased himself down into his armchair and shook his head. "Nicky boy, I probably shouldn't be telling you this, but I can see it's the only way to make you understand."

Nick sat down in the adjacent armchair, his chest tight with foreboding. "Tell me what?"

Pappy pinched the bridge of his nose and sighed. "She's had some *hardships* in her life and they've resulted in deep, wounding scars. No matter how hard she works or how good she tries to be, she never feels good enough." He motioned around the room. "She doesn't feel worthy of all this."

"But Old Brooks built this *for* her."

"I know, I know. But when I try to explain that to her, she just falls to pieces." Pappy leaned forward and rubbed his face with his hands. "She also hasn't had the best experience with men. That's why she comes across so ..."

Nick snorted. "Cold? Unfriendly? Rude? Distant?"

Pappy fixed him with an angry glare. "I've warned you son, and now here I am betraying her confidence to help you understand." He shook his head and rose to leave.

Nick shot up and grabbed his arm. "I'm sorry, Paps. It's just I haven't been home two days yet and already that woman has me fired up under the collar."

Pappy leaned close, his nose almost touching Nick's. His face began to flush with anger and he gritted his teeth while he spoke. "Well she's had much worse done to her than a less-than-warm greeting. So, if she appears a bit cold or distant or rude, then believe me when I say the girl has earned the right to act as such. It's a wonder she doesn't just shoot every man she meets!" Pappy turned to leave, then immediately turned back around to face Nick. "And another thing, did it ever occur to you that she might act like that as a form of defense? Underneath all that spit and anger she's a frightened little girl."

That little fireball ... a scared little girl? Nick nearly guffawed. "Has she told you she's scared?"

"Some things don't need to be said, son. I've spent close to two months alone with her. We've worked side by side, taken meals together, talked into the late of evening ... day after day it was like that. She's gotten to know me and trust me, and I her."

The spark of irritation he had been feeling since Nick saw how close Pappy and Melanie were burst into a full flame. Just what was Pappy revealing here? That they did have a relationship of questionable intentions?

Nick gritted his teeth. "Just what is going on between the two of you?"

Pappy's features hardened then quickly softened. "The girl is like family to me. And she's expressed how I'm family to her." Pappy slapped him on the shoulder and chuckled. "Don't worry, son, you have no competition in me."

Nick's brow formed a deep 'v' and he wondered just what Pappy meant. Why would Pappy be competition for him? He had no interest in the brooding, cold, distant woman even if she was a good cook or had long, curly auburn hair that nearly shimmered in the sunlight, and well rounded hips to carry all of those sons he'd always desired, and full lips he was sure were soft and sweet …

Nick shook his head. What was he thinking? He had no interest in the woman and that was that. He turned on his heel and strode out the front door.

Melanie quietly stood up from her stoop on the stairs. She had been awakened by her employees' excited calls and was coming down to investigate. Before she could completely descend the stairs, Pappy and Nick's heavy footsteps were banging down the hall toward the large sitting room. She knew she should be angry at Pappy for sharing so much about her with his nephew, but her mind, body, and heart ached too much to scrounge up an effort to be mad at him.

She had just witnessed Nick stop Pappy at the threshold and exchange a few last words. She wasn't quite sure why Pappy called himself no competition for Nick. What would relatives be competing for? The only competition she could think of was that of an adverse nature. Melanie shuddered. She was positively certain that Pappy would never compete for her in that manner. Nicholas, however, was a stranger to her still. After Pappy chuckled all the way down the hall toward the kitchen, Nick had stood there staring at nothing. At first his face had been clouded and brooding, but then slowly the clouds parted and his eyes brightened as a slow grin spread across his face. He seemed to have caught himself, though, because he gave himself a literal shake, and then stormed down the hall and out the front door.

Melanie silently crept back up the stairs and returned to her bedroom. She lay down on her soft bed and pulled her knees up to her chest. She slowly rocked back and forth, trying to lull herself to sleep while she pushed all thoughts of men and *their* lustful ways aside. Tears flooded her eyes and she nearly snorted at the irony of her thought. Men and their lustful ways? What about her and her lecherous activities? She pulled her pillow over her face and released her sorrow, pain, and shame in great, gasping sobs.

Chapter 21

THE NEXT MORNING Melanie rose and fixed breakfast as usual. She used the iron triangle to call the men in and was quite perplexed when each one filed in quietly and in an orderly fashion. She had only fed them two meals, but so far they had shown up rowdy to each one. They each stood behind their chairs until Pappy pulled her chair out to help her sit. Her dog, Sam, nosed his way into the kitchen and trotted over to plop himself at her feet. Pappy led grace and instead of the usual grabbing and fighting for the nearest dish, Pappy handed her the closest platter piled high with sausage. She looked skeptically at him, but he nodded his encouragement so she forked sausage onto her plate then passed it to Nicholas who had taken his usual seat to her right. As she passed the dish on, the other men picked up the platter closest to them, filled their plates, and passed the platter on. It gave Melanie the sense of a serene family having a quiet breakfast.

Melanie tried a wobbly smile. "My, we're all so quiet this morning. Did something happen that I should be aware of?"

Douglas Spells spoke up. "Nothing, but Pappy opening our eyes to how valuable you are." He ducked his head. "We're sorry for being so demanding at meal time."

Another man spoke up. "Next time we do something wrong just threaten Pappy's cooking and we'll straighten up."

The men laughed, but a stern look from Pappy quieted them instantly. She covered his hand with her own. "I rather like their rowdy laughter." She turned her attention to the men watching them. "But I also like this organized way of serving."

The men chuckled and Melanie smiled. She truly did like it when the men were talking and laughing, but this way of passing dishes was much cleaner for her table than the barbaric method of grabbing and fighting for food off the closest platter. The normal banter took up once Melanie began to eat.

Pappy leaned over to whisper close to her ear. "How are you feeling today?"

Melanie tried to smile. "Empty."

Pappy frowned and patted her hand. "I'm here to talk."

Melanie diverted her attention from Pappy to the back door when she heard someone knocking. She rose to answer the door, but one of the cowhands waved her back and he rose to answer it. In walked a stocky man of medium height with a shock of wheat blonde hair and a handlebar mustache. Melanie's heart stilled. Something about the man seemed familiar. He looked her directly in the eye and she saw recognition flash across his face, confirming they had met somewhere. Melanie knew there was only one way she knew this man. He must have been a former customer.

The man swaggered up to the table. "My, oh my, Miss Melanie Brooks."

Melanie swallowed. At least he hadn't used her brothel name, Rosie. He walked around the table to where she sat and Pappy pushed out his chair, his hand resting leisurely on the back of it, his hip cocked to show off his six-shooter. The rest of the men immediately stopped eating and sat at attention.

Melanie put on her sweetest smile and stood. "Mr. …?"

The man chuckled. "You don't remember? Mr. Groover, Mr. Mike Groover."

Inside her chest her heart raced. She definitely remembered Mr. Mike Groover. He was one of her customers who had gotten too rowdy and Amos had to throw him out before she ever even gave him what he paid for. He came back the following morning and tried to demand his money back but Minnie had refused.

Melanie squinted as if trying to determine if she'd ever met him before. "Hmm, I'm sorry, Mr. Groover. I don't remember ever making your acquaintance."

Red crept up Mr. Groover's neck and Melanie wondered if he took what she said as a reference to her having never slept with him. He took a step closer and tucked his thumbs in his belt loops. "Well, I definitely remember you. As a matter of fact, if I recall correctly, you owe me a night's wage."

Pappy stood so fast his chair clattered backwards. He grabbed Melanie's elbow and pulled her away from Mr. Groover and stood between them. Sam stood and growled at Mr. Groover. Fifteen chairs scraped across the wood floor as every man she employed stood, hands resting on their six-shooters.

Nicholas grabbed Mr. Groover by the arm and turned him around. He pushed the man in the back to make him walk. "On second thought, Mr. Groover, I don't think we'll have need for another cowhand. Thank you so much for your time."

The cowhand who had opened the door to allow the man in now opened the door so Nick could throw him out. It was the first time Melanie had been grateful Nicholas Henderson was such a large, intimidating man. Once Mr. Groover was out the door and riding back toward town Melanie sagged back into her chair.

Pappy's heart raced at the sound of a dull thump behind him. Did the girl faint dead away? He spun around quickly to see Melanie slumped in her chair. Her face was a sickly pale gray and her hands shook in her lap.

Pappy knelt down in front of her and grabbed her hands. "Little Missy?" He squeezed her hands and she looked up into his eyes, her expression completely void of emotion. "Melanie? Are you OK, Little Missy?"

Her lower lip quivered and she moved her mouth to talk but no audible words would come. Tears filled her eyes and made Pappy's heart clench. He should have interviewed the man first. He should have inquired where the man had come from. Pappy scolded himself for his neglect.

Melanie's thumb rubbed against the back of Pappy's hand and he looked up at her. She whispered, "Will I ever be free?"

"He's gone and we'll make sure he never steps foot on this land again. Him and any other man." Pappy squeezed her hands again. "Do you hear me? You'll never see him again, Melanie, never!"

Nicholas moved to stand at Pappy's shoulder. "What's wrong with her, Paps?"

Pappy looked up to see the rest of the boys crowding around their side of the table. Douglas Spells stepped forward. "What can we do to help you, boss?"

Melanie looked out at the boys. She motioned toward the table. "Please sit. We need to talk."

Pappy looked at her skeptically. "You don't have to tell them anything. It's none of their business."

Melanie shook her head. "Didn't you see how they all reached for their guns?"

Pappy shrugged. "They're paid to work and protect the ranch."

"Well they have a right to know what they're protecting. And possibly from whom."

Pappy squeezed her hands again. "Little Missy, it's none of their business. They would have fought today to protect you from that man." A murmur of agreement rose up behind him.

She shook her head sadly. "Don't you see Pappy? What if he had a gun? One of them could have died today because of my past." She nodded toward Nicholas. "Would you have felt so congenial if it were your nephew who was killed?"

Chapter 22

MELANIE PUSHED UP in her chair to address her employees. She folded her hands neatly in her lap so the men couldn't see them shaking. She wanted to keep the past in the past and avoid the embarrassment and judgment that would surely come once people knew. But after this morning, seeing each one rise with their hands ready to pull and fire their guns in her defense, she knew she had to tell them. She would never forgive herself if one of them was killed or injured while trying to defend her from someone in her past.

She stared at the table, unable to meet their questioning eyes. Pappy reached over and grasped her hand under the table. She looked at him and breathed a heavy sigh. Whatever would she do without this old man in her life? He had become her friend and confidant and ultimately her family. She squeezed his hand and looked up to meet the eyes of her cowhands.

She cleared her throat so it wouldn't wobble. "That man, Mr. Groover, he was a former customer of mine."

"Were you a seamstress?"

"I bet she was a cook."

Mumbled agreement followed the remark.

Melanie closed her eyes. Each one thought the best of her. She hated to dash their good opinion of her. "I wish I had been something as respectable as that. I worked in a place called Minnie's Dollhouse."

From her right, Nicholas barely whispered, "A brothel?"

Melanie nodded. "A brothel. I worked there for the last five years. When I got Pappy's telegram, I thought I could make a new life here. Today was proof that I obviously can't. I would never forgive myself if one of you boys got hurt on account of my sinful past."

Douglas Spells softly asked, "Why'd ya have to work there, Miss Melanie?"

Pappy scowled at the young man. "Hasn't she told you enough?"

She smiled sadly at Pappy. "It's an honest question, deserving an honest answer." Melanie dug her thumbnail into the soft flesh of her palm, hoping the physical pain would distract her from the turmoil raging inside. "My roommate's pa beat her at work and she lost her job because of it. I had lost my job several weeks earlier. We couldn't pay rent so we were kicked out." Melanie tried to smile but her lips began to quiver and her voice began to shake. "One night during a rainstorm Minnie found us huddled in an alleyway. She took us in and we were there ever since."

She thought tears shone in Douglas's eyes. "Why didn't your friend come to Texas with you?"

Melanie looked down at the forgotten food all across the table. "She's scared her pa will come for her if she leaves the brothel, but I keep inviting her." Melanie blew out a deep breath and shrugged her shoulders. "Anyways, Mr. Groover was a former customer. He was very aggressive though, so I had him thrown out before anything …" She stopped short, embarrassed she had said so much.

She looked around the table and met each one's eyes. "I will understand that if after hearing all of this any of you decide to leave. Pappy tells me you're all believers in Christ, so I understand if you don't want to work for a …" she paused and glanced at Pappy, "a *fallen woman.* And don't worry about your wages; I can pay anyone who leaves today for the entire season."

Silence thickened the air in the kitchen. Every man was looking down. Some pushed their forgotten breakfast across their plates. Melanie's heart beat erratically in her chest. What if they all decided to leave? She'd be left with no help to run the ranch.

Finally Douglas stood and slammed his hat onto his head. "Well, *boss,* those fences you want fixed won't mend themselves. If I see any sign of that Groover fellow I'll be sure to send him home the same way you did Johnny Gray."

His reference to the man she shot in the backside caused the other men to chuckle and they began standing to their feet. Each one made eye contact with her and nodded. She knew a lot was being said in that nod. She knew it was their unspoken agreement to stay and work for her, a former brothel girl.

"Let me know if you need anything boss."

"Yeah, me too, boss."

"Hope you're making supper this afternoon boss. Pappy can't hold a candle to your cooking."

The remaining men laughed while they exited the kitchen. No one had forgotten to scrape their plates clean and stack them by the sink. Melanie slowly shook her head. These were definitely a good bunch of men.

Melanie looked over at Nicholas, still sitting to her right. "Nicholas, would you mind giving me some privacy with Pappy?"

He nodded, his expression solemn. "Yes ma'am." He stood with his plate, scraped it clean then picked up the slop bucket and headed out toward the pigpen.

Melanie looked over at Pappy and smiled. "I can't believe they're all staying."

Pappy nodded. "They're good men."

"I want to show them my gratitude. I'll have a lot of work ahead of me to get ready. Can you go hunting today and pick more apples from the orchard?"

Pappy smiled. "They would like that." He leaned closer. "But are you sure you'll be OK by yourself?"

Melanie surprised herself by actually giggling. "After this morning, I feel a lot better about a lot of things."

Pappy squeezed her hand. "I'm glad to hear that, Little Missy." He rose and covered his thick, white hair with his Stetson. "I'll be back."

Nick tossed the remnants of breakfast into the trough for the pigs to enjoy. A brothel? He shook his head in disbelief. A *brothel*? His new boss came from a brothel?

"Then why is she so scared of men?"

"Say something, son?"

Nick whirled around to see Paps standing behind him. "Just talking to myself, Pappy."

"I was just coming to let you know I'll be going hunting. I want you to stay close to the house and keep an eye on things."

Nick turned and pretended to knock out the last bit of food scraps into the pig trough. "Yes, sir."

"If Melanie needs help with something I want you to see to helping her."

Nick nodded, "Don't worry, I'll help the boss."

Pappy sighed. "Son, try to remember it wasn't a life she had willingly chosen, but she had to survive somehow." He turned to head inside the barn before Nick could reply.

Nick wasn't quite sure that was a good enough explanation. Weren't there churches or charity houses where she could have sought shelter? He cringed at the thought of strangers going to her bed on a nightly basis after paying the required fee. He felt sick to his stomach.

When he was a young boy becoming a man, Pappy had taken him aside and talked with him about the sinfulness of tom-cattin' around. He explained that the closeness two people can experience should only be shared within a marriage bed. That night, in the privacy of his own heart, he had vowed to God to withhold from intimacy with women until he was lawfully wed. He had kept that vow for the last thirteen years and he was determined to keep it until he put a ring on his bride's finger.

He glanced back at the house. He was almost disappointed that woman would never be Melanie Brooks. He shuddered at the thought of taking up with her after half the country had. No sir, he would never think of touching that woman's hair again. Or kissing her full lips. Or wondering how many sons those wide hips of hers could bare. He'd no longer admire the strength of her thick arms or the speed at which her thicker frame could move. He'd never again hope her eyes would twinkle at him the way they did when she looked at Pappy or hoped she'd kiss *his* forehead as she passed by. And he most certainly would never wonder if she was the future Mrs. Henderson ever again.

Nick stood ramrod straight. Just where had all of *that* come from? He clenched his hands into tight fists. "Lord, forgive me. I know I'm better than that. I know somewhere You have a pretty little wife for me who has stayed whole and pure."

He glanced over his shoulder on his way to the barn and saw Melanie descending the back porch with a large metal bin in her arms. She walked over to the garden and knelt down in the soil as she dug with her hands. Nick turned to watch as the sun transformed her brown curls into the vibrant shades of red, blonde, and brown. He realized he was holding his breath when his chest began to ache. He rolled his eyes and stormed into the shelter of the barn.

Chapter 23

APPY RETURNED FROM doing Melanie's bidding shortly after supper. She regaled him with how she had bravely faced the men without him at her side for the first time during supper and how she hadn't felt a bit of tension or unease during the entire meal. Pappy seemed to be real pleased by this bit of news and he kissed her cheek in congratulations.

Melanie quickly set a place for Pappy at the small table and served him a plate of food she had reserved for him. "Well, Little Missy, what do you have planned for that deer I felled?"

She grinned knowing her answer would please Pappy. "Venison steaks."

He smacked his lips together. "Mmm-mmm-mmm! I'll be sure to work up an appetite."

Melanie rose and began peeling the apples Pappy had brought home. Once they were peeled, she cored and sliced each one. By the time she had tossed the sliced apples with sugar and cinnamon Pappy had finished his supper and was heading back into the yard.

"I'll go skin and butcher that deer."

Melanie merely nodded while she mixed together dough for her pie crusts. She lined three pie tins with crust then filled each one with the cinnamon-sugar coated apples. She rolled out the top crusts for her pies, pinched and tucked the edges, then placed the pies in the oven to bake.

She formed another ball of dough, this one for bread. She was hoping she had her timing figured correctly. If she set her dough to rise now, then she should be pulling it out of the oven just in time for dinner. Fresh bread hot out of the oven was always a favorite of hers. She hoped the men found it to be a treat as well. She made enough dough to form three loaves. She covered them with a clean towel and set them aside.

Next she needed to prepare the potatoes she had dug up earlier this morning. She had already rinsed them clean outside, so now she just needed to peel and quarter them. She placed the skinned potatoes in a pot of water so when it was almost time for supper she'd just have to move the pot over to the stove. She picked up two large bowls, one filled to the brim with pea pods, and sat at the work table. She made quick work of shelling the peas, then emptied them into one of the smaller roasting pans.

Satisfied that all of the preparation work for dinner was complete, Melanie removed her apron and headed back outside to weed the vegetable garden. The sun was shining brightly and it seemed to warm her through to her very soul. She couldn't help but smile as she pulled weed after weed from the vegetable garden. She had shared one of her most heinous secrets with a room full of men, and to her complete surprise not a one had made an unseemly remark or refused to continue working for her.

Sam came running around the corner of the house and headed straight for her. She laughed as he jumped up and placed his front paws on her shoulders, causing her to fly backwards. The large dog pinned her down with his paws on her shoulders as he lapped at her face. Melanie giggled and squealed. For the first time in nearly ten years she felt like a carefree girl.

Nick was heading back inside the barn to retrieve a hammer and nails when feminine laughter stopped him in his tracks. He spotted Melanie pinned down by Sam in the vegetable garden. The dog was licking her face and she was laughing and squealing at his antics. This was the first time he had heard her laugh. The musical sound seemed completely contrary to her usual icy exterior.

"Oh, Sam, stop you big goose!"

Nick grinned. Sam was now standing with his front paws on her shoulders and his back paws on her stomach, his tail wildly whipping back and forth. She giggled again as Sam nuzzled her shoulder and playfully growled. Nick crossed his arms across his chest as he watched. Sam jumped off Melanie and barked sharply twice. She laughed as she rolled onto her hands and knees and barked back at the dog. Sam lowered his head so it was almost touching the ground while his backside and tail remained high in the air. Melanie mimicked Sam and growled playfully. She reached a "paw" out and swiped at Sam's paw. The dog jumped to the side and barked again, then lunged forward and nipped at the curls framing Melanie's face. Melanie squealed and Nick chuckled out loud.

Pappy appeared by his side. "It's good to see her having fun."

Nick realized he was grinning from ear to ear and quickly schooled his expression. "Sure, a girl deserves some fun after working hard."

"I haven't seen her laugh like this the whole time she's been here. She's had a heavy heart and carries an even heavier burden."

Nick scowled. "Well she did work in a brothel, Paps."

"Yup, I reckon being forced to work in a place like that would scar anyone's heart."

Pappy obviously mistook his meaning. Nick had meant she ought to feel burdened by her sins. Instead Pappy thought he meant she was burdened by the things she was supposedly forced to do. Nick glanced back across the yard to where Melanie and Sam still played. Melanie was teasing the dog with a thick stick, obviously working him up to a game of fetch.

She threw the stick across the garden. "Go get it, Sam!"

The dog took off running and barking after the stick. Nick looked back at Melanie in time to see a brilliant smile break across her face. Her eyes shone with what he thought was happiness. Nick grinned. If she wasn't a fallen woman he bet he'd find ways to make her smile more often. Pappy interrupted his thoughts.

"She deserves a good man, Nicky boy."

Nick couldn't think of a thing to say so he repeated what he said earlier. "Well, she did work in a brothel, Paps."

Pappy squeezed his shoulder. When Nick met his uncle's gaze his heart dropped. He had never seen his uncle look so disappointed. This time Pappy had grasped his meaning.

"I'm sorry that's a problem for you. Truth is, I was thinking you had designs on the girl. Now that I know different, I'll try to discourage her attraction to you."

Nick huffed. "She's not attracted to me, Paps. You've seen how she treats me, she can barely stand me."

Pappy shook his head. "Since when did you stop listening to your old uncle? Didn't I already tell you she acts like that because she's scared?"

Nick held out his hands in front of him. "What's there to be scared about?"

"For one, you're a big man. I'm sure your size intimidates her. She's had to fend off men before and I'm sure she wonders how she would manage to fend off a big man like you."

Nick felt like Pappy had just punched him in the gut. He gritted his teeth together and ground out, "I would never assault a woman!"

Pappy shrugged. "She doesn't know that." Pappy shrugged again and Nick hated seeing disappointment etched into his features. "It doesn't matter anyways. You've already judged her in your heart. Just do me a favor, do *her* a favor, and stay away from her."

Pappy trudged off toward the house, his shoulders slumped. Nick had never felt so low in his life. Paps was right. He had judged her, but he hadn't judged her as anything more than what she had already admitted she was—a tainted woman.

Melanie rushed back upstairs. She wanted to look her best when she expressed her thanks to the men for choosing to remain in her employment. She slipped off her dirty work dress and pulled out the blue calico with the tiny yellow flowers she had worn when she had first arrived at Sterling Canyon. She was surprised when the cloth at her arms fit more loosely and the material at her bosom didn't pull tightly across her chest. She sat at her vanity and smiled to herself. Ranch life was obviously good for her figure. She let down her bun and brushed out her hair, then quickly formed a braid down her back.

She hurried back downstairs to finish cooking supper. Pappy was turned toward the stove, but glanced over his shoulder when he heard her approach. He took a quick second look then turned, his face beaming.

"Why, don't you look lovely tonight, Little Missy."

Melanie felt her cheeks burn. She was sure the old man was just being nice, but she didn't bother to argue. "I wanted to look my best when I thanked the men for staying."

She brushed past him to fork the potatoes before he could make any further embarrassing comments. The potatoes were tender so she slid the lid on and poured the hot water into the sink. Pappy came up behind her with the masher and she moved aside to allow Pappy to mash the potatoes while she added butter, cream, salt, and pepper.

She checked the venison steaks sizzling on top of the stove and turned them to cook on the other side. Then she picked up the bucket of milk and carried it to the table where the roasting pan of peas sat. She ladled the cream off the top of the milk and spooned it over the peas before putting them in the oven.

Nick strode into the kitchen for supper. The scent of cooking venison wafting through the yard had encouraged him to arrive early. He stopped short when he looked up at the table. There were platters of venison steak, mashed potatoes, creamed peas, sliced bread still steaming from the oven, crocks of butter and jam, hot coffee in every cup except Douglas's who preferred milk, and standing at the head of the table was Melanie. She wore a pretty blue calico dress dotted with yellow flowers. Nick liked the way the blue in her dress seemed to brighten her brown eyes.

If it was up to him he'd never allow her to wear those dark work dresses ever again. A long braid flowed over her shoulder, small curls springing out down the full length of it. Nick grinned at her unruly curls.

Pappy cleared his throat. Nick turned and caught a cold glare from his uncle. It was a clear reminder of their earlier conversation out by the barn. Pappy had told him to stay away and Nick knew that was the proper thing to do. He had no desire to make a fallen woman his wife. He pushed away all thoughts of how pretty Melanie looked tonight and focused on the tantalizing smell of supper.

Chapter 24

PAPPY WATCHED AS day after day Melanie earned the respect of her cowhands. When he told them how she shot Johnny Gray she instantly won their admiration, but respect was something a person couldn't earn through a story. The boys watched her weed the vegetable garden, can fruit and vegetables, keep house, do laundry, and still find time to prepare them three meals a day. She surprised them all by adding to her duties learning how to wrangle and brand the calves, ride out to help mend fences, hunt fresh meat, and more than once they witnessed her single-handedly run off a potential suitor.

When the boys first arrived home, Pappy would overhear talk about the good food, but beyond that they were skeptical about their new boss. From what he could hear none of them held the years she worked at the brothel against her, except in the regard that it wasn't ranch work. Each one seemed skeptical of her lack of ranch experience, but her eagerness to learn and her no-quitting attitude had slowly won them over.

Now, several weeks after the boys had been home, Pappy overheard talk of how strong their new boss was, how fast and accurate she had become with her Winchester, how she turned saltier than an old outlaw when suitors came riding in, but could turn instantly sweet when talking to the animals. And Old Brooks' dog, Sam, took an instant shine to her. The dog rarely ever left her side these days, which the boys took as a good sign that she was a lot like her great-uncle.

The best part of all of was Melanie's growing interest during their weekly Bible study. Two weeks ago she had asked how a person got to Heaven. The boys had all become real quiet while Pappy explained about how you accept Christ as your Savior. And just last week, while they were canning vegetables from the garden, she asked if he thought God could forgive her sordid past. He asked if she felt ready to receive Christ as her Savior, and he was sure she was about to say yes when Nicholas walked in and his brooding mood clammed her right up. Pappy had prayed every day since that he'd be given another opportunity to ask her.

Pappy sighed, contented for the moment. Yup, all was finally right on Old Brooks' ranch. Pappy looked heavenward. "I hope you see the good you've done this girl, you old coot."

Pappy leaned against the porch rail sipping his coffee while he looked out over the land. It was a quiet morning. He was waiting for Melanie to get back from checking a fence, then they were to ride out and pick more fruit together. Pappy lifted his cup to his lips for another swallow of coffee when a feminine scream rang through the air. Pappy dropped his coffee cup, his hand immediately going to his six-shooter. He waited to try to determine where the scream had come from. Sam darted out of the barn barking, then turned around and headed back inside. He saw the boys running across the yard to the barn and quickly joined them.

Melanie had sent some men to fix a fence yesterday and, as had become her custom, she rode out to check it once they reported it was finished. She didn't think they took offense to a woman checking their handiwork. In fact she thought they rather respected her for taking such an avid interest in what went on around her ranch. She knew Pappy was waiting for her, so she had ridden hard to get home. When she galloped into the yard she rode right into the barn, unsaddled Brooke, and hitched the geldings to the wagon. She was just about to ride out and pick up Pappy from the house when a soft mewing caught her attention. Nicholas happened to walk in as she was searching for the source of the mewing.

"Lose something?"

Melanie didn't bother turning around. She still felt that horrible burning attraction and was scared that if he saw her face he'd be able to see her every emotion. Thankfully, they both kept so busy there was scarcely any time for her to be bothered by him. A few times she had caught him staring at her with that stupid grin on his face, but other than that they had minimal interaction.

Melanie peered around some buckets. "Don't you hear that?"

"Sounds like a kitten."

She grabbed a large barrel and heaved it away from the wall. Nick appeared instantly at her side.

"You shouldn't be moving that, it's much too heavy for a woman."

Melanie felt the heat rise in her neck. She fisted her hands on her hips and arched an eyebrow. "Do I look like a daisy ready to wilt to you?"

He looked her up and down and it took all of Melanie's will not to twitch at his close inspection. He shook his head. "No, you look like a stubborn calf."

Melanie narrowed her eyes. "If Pappy wasn't your uncle you'd be eating trail dust right now."

The man had the audacity to laugh in her face. Melanie threw her head back and sighed in frustration. She was about to club the arrogant man in his gut when a small, furry ball up in the rafters caught her attention. She side stepped to get a better angle. There, high in the rafters above their heads was the lost little kitten.

"Oh, you poor thing, however did you get way up there?"

Melanie quickly climbed the ladder to the hayloft. She gathered her skirts as she straddled the beam the kitten had somehow managed to crawl out on, but not back.

Nick was still chuckling when he realized the little spitfire was gone. He rubbed the back of his neck as he hoped he hadn't gone too far in teasing her. He had seen her cry on several occasions when she thought she was alone in the orchard or barn. Usually she mumbled unintelligible sentences he could never quite make out. He hoped she wasn't heading toward one of her quiet spots to shed some tears now. He'd feel horrible if he was the reason she cried. If Pappy found out, he'd probably make sure he really was thrown out on his ear.

When he promised Pappy he'd stay away from Melanie, he thought it would be easy, since she was a fallen woman and all. Time and again he was proven wrong. Over the last several weeks she had blossomed into a completely different woman. She smiled every day now, except for when he was around. He always tried to catch her unawares so that he might catch a glimpse of her one dimpled smile. A few times he had overheard her singing in the kitchen while she cooked. She had a melodious voice that Nick thought could soothe the most savage of beasts. Each time Nick saw her riding her horse, he would stare in hopes that her hair would come loose and fly wildly behind her like that day when he had first come home. He was thoroughly surprised when she began to look at ease during their weekly Bible study. She had even asked a few questions about God's love and Jesus' sacrifice.

He tried shaking free of these thoughts though. She was mighty pretty on the outside as well as strong, hardworking, smart, and compassionate. Nick knew that no matter how she acted, she'd always be a fallen woman. Nothing could take away the years she spent selling what was rightfully her husband's to other men. Nick deserved a better woman than that, so he knew he was wasting his time with thoughts of Melanie.

Nick grabbed the reins of the team she had hitched to walk the horses out to the yard for Pappy. He stopped short when hay floated down from above and landed on his outstretched arm. He looked and saw Melanie crawling across a beam.

"You blasted woman!"

Melanie gave a soft shriek as she lost her hold on the thin beam and tumbled over the side. Nick's stomach clenched. He hadn't meant to yell like that. Even though she dangled by her arms, his heart raced. How long could she hold on?

He heard her grunt. "You stupid oaf, you startled me."

Well she still had her grit so she couldn't be in that much danger. "Hold on, I'm coming to get you."

She nearly guffawed. "Don't bother. I've almost reached the kitten." She swung her legs up and wrapped them around the beam.

Nick's hands sweated as he watched her pull herself right side up on the beam again. Sam circled around below her barking. She hollered down to Nick. "Don't go looking up my skirt now."

He shot his gaze up at her and saw her face was flushed bright red. From exertion or embarrassment, he wasn't quite sure which. Nick snorted. "Who knew a brothel girl could be so modest?"

Nick slapped a hand over his mouth, immediately regretting his words. He stood silent for a moment to see if she would respond and prayed she hadn't heard his comment.

A tear splattered across his cheek. He looked up again to see her staring down at him, tears streaking her face. "So is that what you think of me? Just some dirty brothel girl?"

Nick opened his mouth to argue but how could he argue what he so strongly felt in his heart? She nodded once and returned her focus back to fetching the kitten, effectively dismissing his presence completely. He stood there staring, hoping, and praying he'd have the words for a proper apology by the time she came down again.

Suddenly her eyes widened and she gasped. Nick's mind raced to figure out what could possibly be up there to startle her so. Melanie glanced down to an empty stall then lunged forward and grabbed the mewing kitten. At the same time a snake Nick hadn't seen from the ground sprang from its coiled position on the beam. Melanie screamed as she threw herself and the kitten over the side of the beam to avoid being bitten.

"MELANIE!"

Nick rushed to where she had landed. As he opened the door to the stall she fell into, the other cowhands were already rushing inside the barn. Nick hollered over his shoulder, "Over here!"

They rushed to aid their boss. Nick was relieved to see she had landed on a heap of old blankets. The stall with the heap of blankets must have been where she looked right before she threw herself off the beam. Her eyes were closed, but the tears she shed at his harsh words were still fresh on her cheeks. His stomach churned when he saw the unnatural way her arm was twisted. Curled into a shaking ball of fur on her chest, clung the kitten. He heard the distinct rattling of a rattlesnake and froze. He scanned the stall and found the snake coiled in the corner.

The men pushed from behind. "What happened?"

"Why's the boss laying in the stall?"

"Come on, Nick, she needs help!"

Nick shushed them. "She fell. There's a rattler in there with her."

The men immediately stopped shoving from behind and became very quiet. Nick slowly reached for his six-shooter and un-holstered the weapon, never taking his eyes off the deadly snake. He fired one shot and the snake's head separated from its body. Nick exhaled deeply and quickly holstered the gun again, but before he could rush to Melanie's side, Pappy pushed him out of the way.

His uncle's steady hands were shaking as he reached behind her head to feel her neck. He saw relief flood Pappy's features, "Her neck isn't broken."

Nick hadn't realized he was holding his breath until he exhaled. "Thank God."

Pappy wasn't sure what had happened to cause this accident, but he was determined to find out right after he got Melanie to the doctor in town. He removed the frightened kitten from the front of her dress and handed it back to a reaching hand. Pappy gently folded her obviously broken arm across her chest and winced when she moaned. He carefully gathered her in his arms and hoisted her up, then he strode to the hitched wagon and laid her in the back.

Douglas hopped in with her. "I'm coming with you, Paps."

Pappy nodded as he climbed into the front of the wagon. Another cowhand brought the armload of the blankets she had fallen on and jumped in the back. He worked with Douglas to cover her up and make her as comfortable as possible for the long ride to town. Pappy softly clicked to the horses and began a slow walk to the yard. The rest of the cowhands followed silently behind like a sad funeral procession. The thought made Pappy shiver.

Chapter 25

APPY HAD BARELY just cleared the large barn doors when Douglas shouted, "She's waking up!"

Pappy set the brake and hopped over the wagon seat into the back of the wagon. He pushed stray curls out of her face. "Little Missy, can you hear me? It's Pappy."

Her brow furrowed as she squinted her eyes open. "The kitten?"

A cowhand leaned forward with the small ball of fur in his hand. "He's just fine boss."

She tried to reach out with her broken arm and winced. She stated flatly, "It's broken."

Pappy frowned. "Afraid so, Little Missy."

"But we have to finish branding the cattle."

The cowhands were crowded around the wagon bed. "Don't worry, boss, we'll make sure the rest of the calves are branded."

"You just worry about getting better so you can make us pies."

The men chuckled. They each wore their best smile as they offered her encouraging words and well wishes for her health. Pappy made sure she was comfortable, then climbed back over the wagon seat and clicked the geldings into a slow walk.

Nick walked beside the wagon. "I'll catch up on my horse with food supplies."

Pappy looked down at him. "Good, then I want to hear what the heck happened in there."

His nephew bowed his head and nodded, then hurried over to the house. Pappy wasn't sure what had happened, but if Nicholas had anything to do with it, Pappy would be sure the boy was tanned a new backside. As Pappy drove the wagon slowly down the lane two more cowhands rode up on mounts.

Ron, a sure shot with a rifle, announced, "We're coming too, Paps."

Jimmy, a man of few words, explained. "Just in case."

"Thanks boys."

Pappy constantly looked over his shoulder to check on his ward. The girl had grit alright. He heard her softly grunt from time to time but she never complained of her pain. She had Douglas and the other cowhand, Mitch, help her sit up amongst her bed of blankets, and Sam was curled up at her side. From time to time the dog would whine and Pappy thought he must sense her pain.

Melanie scarcely felt the pain shooting up and down her broken arm as she was jostled around in the back of the wagon. The immense ache she felt her in heart far outweighed the pain in her arm. Nicholas's words in the barn were proof that no

162

matter how hard she worked, how good she acted, or how much she prayed she'd still always just be a dirty, tainted woman. No matter where she went, who she tried to become, what façade she put on, she'd always be a brothel girl.

Her head ached so she closed her eyes against the blaring afternoon sun. Sam whined so she rested her hand on his head. Someone shoved a hat onto her head and she opened her eyes.

Douglas's head was bare. He shrugged. "You looked like the sun was bothering you."

Melanie offered him a weak smile. "You're so considerate, Douglas. Thank you."

The young man blushed. He had been timid and shy when Melanie first met him, and the other cowhands teased him unmercifully. Melanie had always tried to discourage their teasing and in the passing weeks she felt they had backed off considerably. Douglas often offered to work alongside her and it was during those long hours of working side by side that she had gotten to know the young man better. Uncle Brooks had taken him in after his Ma died in childbirth. He'd lived on the ranch his entire life.

The other cowhand in the wagon bed, Mitch, had also become a sort of friend to Melanie. At forty-two he was the oldest cowhand she employed, besides Pappy. One day while they mended a fence together he had confessed Uncle Brooks had taken him in as a washed-up drunk. He explained how he used to have his own ranch, but one winter his wife and three children succumbed to an outbreak of cholera. He had started drinking and lost everything he had worked his whole life for. Uncle Brooks found him lying on the side of the road for dead, took him in, and helped him turn his life around.

The two riding sentry to the wagon were loyal men as well. They never failed to help her without being asked. If they were mending fences and she was trying to heave the heavy lumber by herself, they merely grabbed hold of the other end and helped. Never did they make her feel less than by making comments of her being a woman like Nicholas had just earlier this afternoon. She nearly snorted at the memory of his comment. Like being a woman made her weak and helpless.

Ron slowed his horse and looked down at her in the wagon bed. "How are you feeling, boss?"

She tried to smile, but the wagon hit a bump and she winced instead. "Not bad, Ron. Thanks for coming along."

"Wouldn't want those hooligan suitors of yours to be buggin' you."

Melanie tried to laugh but it came out as more of a sigh. "I don't think I'll be able to shoot any of them off the property for quite some time."

Jimmy slowed his horse on the other side of the wagon. He patted the butt of his rifle. "Don't worry."

Melanie looked between the two. She would have never guessed they were brothers what with Ron having thick, curly red hair and Jimmy having straight blonde hair. They insisted that they were though and Pappy had confirmed it. Uncle Brooks adopted them off the orphan train at the ages of seventeen and fifteen. When Uncle Brooks had heard how no one wanted such old boys, he had declared they were exactly what he needed. Shortly after meeting them, Pappy had also confided that her great-uncle had set up savings for both the brothers and Douglas so when they were ready they could set out to start their own ranch. Melanie promised she'd maintain all of Uncle Brooks's former promises. Melanie quit her silent musings when she spotted dust on the trail behind them. She squinted. "Rider."

Ron and Jimmy immediately turned their horses and rode to the back of the wagon, rifles drawn. Douglas pulled his six-shooter and Mitch pulled a rifle from behind him. Sam lifted his head and growled. Melanie nearly grinned at the peaceful feeling resonating throughout her body. These men knew she came from a brothel. Yet here they were, guns drawn, ready to defend her with their lives. No man had ever cared enough about her to protect her so willingly. She felt gifted by their genuine friendship and loyalty.

Sam sniffed the air and immediately stopped his growling. He jumped up onto the tailgate of the wagon and barked, his tail wagging happily.

The rider waved and shouted. Melanie's heart sank in disappointment and dread. The rider was Nicholas Henderson.

Nick galloped to catch up to the wagon. He saw Ron and Jimmy at the back with rifles drawn. Nick waved his hands in the air and shouted. Their rifles lowered, so Nick kicked his horse faster to close the gap between them. Pappy turned on the wagon bench, his usually kind eyes squinted and glowering. In fact, it seemed the only one happy to see him was Sam. Nick rode up to the back of the wagon, then turned in his saddle and untied several sacks he had packed with food stuffs. In his saddle bag was one of the smaller cast iron skillets. He handed everything over to Douglas, the only man who moved to help him.

Pappy looked toward the sun. "We should stop and set up camp."

Melanie sat up straighter and Nick saw her wince with the effort. "Not yet, Pappy, we still have a couple of hours of daylight."

"I don't want you getting worn out, Little Missy."

"What will wear me out is three days of traveling with a broken arm. Let's push and keep it down to two days."

"Stubborn as her uncle." Pappy mumbled, but it was loud enough for even Nick, mounted and riding behind the wagon to hear.

Melanie sniffed. "Stubborn is a fine quality to possess out in the wild west!"

The boys laughed at her remark and Nick caught himself grinning. Melanie must have caught him too, because she lowered a hot glare at him that nearly made his skin burn. He saw her jaw tighten as she clenched her teeth and Nick ducked his head to avoid being burned by the spitfire's scolding stare.

She surprised him by saying his name. "Nicholas."

His head snapped up. "Yes, Melanie."

He thought he saw a fiery arrow shoot from her eyes when he said her name. He gulped. "Head back to the ranch."

The boys grew uncharacteristically quiet. Nick looked around but each one had his head diverted in a different direction pretending to look out over the land. He took a deep breath. "Sorry, boss. I'm coming too."

Pappy clicked the wagon back into action. "Little Missy, if it's OK with you I'd prefer Nicholas stayed." Over his shoulder Pappy sent Nick a fiery glare of his own. "We have a pending conversation that cannot wait."

Melanie turned her head, obviously displeased by the situation. She lifted her good arm in the air and flicked her wrist, effectively dismissing him from her presence. Nick burned under the collar. He kicked his horse into a gallop and rode off ahead of the wagon before he lost his tongue and made the situation worse.

Once he was a good distance away from the wagon he slowed his horse to a walk. He looked up at the sky. "When will I learn to keep my thoughts to myself, God?"

An eagle soared through the sky overhead. It let out a loud cry as it swooped and dipped with the light breeze. Nick shook his head. He had only spoken the truth back in the barn. Wasn't truth something God demanded? So why did she react so horribly when she heard his comment? Granted, it was a mite rude, but it was still the truth. She knew where she came from, so why did she look so hurt? The memory of her tear falling on his cheek sent a shiver down his spine. She looked like the saddest little angel perched up on that beam with tears streaming down her face.

An *angel?* Now he was comparing the brothel girl to an angel? Nick snorted and started surveying the sides of the road for a good place to camp for the night.

Chapter 26

AFTER ANOTHER HOUR of traveling Melanie had to admit defeat. "Pappy?" Her voice cracked from all of the trail dust.

Pappy began to slow the team. "Yes, Little Missy?"

She sighed, she hated being so weak. "I'm ready to stop."

Ron stood in his stirrups. "Looks like Nick cleared a spot for camp just ahead."

Their little party rode slowly to where Nicholas had cleared away the dead brush on the ground and had started a small fire. Once Pappy had stopped the wagon, Douglas and Mitch lowered the tailgate. Sam jumped out and immediately began sniffing around their campsite. Melanie tried not to move her broken arm in the makeshift sling Douglas and Mitch had put together as she used her good arm to help her scoot to the edge of the tailgate. When she reached the edge, Douglas and Mitch reached up and between the two of them they lowered her down without jostling her at all. She smiled gratefully to them for such an uneventful descent.

Jimmy was dusting off a large rock near the fire. He pointed to the rock. "Boss."

Melanie smiled. "Thanks, Jimmy."

Never mind that her dress was already dirty and in need of a good scrubbing. She appreciated that some men still treated her with kindness. In fact, Jimmy brushing off that rock for her to sit on was the most gentlemanly thing a man had done for her in a long while. Melanie felt a stirring in her stomach. To be treated like a lady. What a wonder. She glared at Nicholas. Hadn't she asked for just a small decorum of decency earlier this afternoon? And how did he treat her? By reminding her that she was just a common harlot! Tears threatened to spill from her eyes and she stood abruptly.

"I'm going to turn in, Pappy."

The old man was just now placing the skillet over the fire. "What about dinner? You haven't had anything to eat since breakfast."

"Not hungry." She trudged over to the wagon and was trying to figure out how she'd get in when Nicholas offered her a boost. She ignored him completely and turned toward the campfire. "Jimmy?"

Jimmy hurried over and to her pleasure shouldered right on past the high and mighty Nicholas. He grabbed her securely around the waist and hoisted her up into the wagon. She had planned on scooting back to her bed of blankets but before she could move Jimmy hopped over the side of the wagon and began rearranging her blankets into a nest-like bed. He squatted down by her on the tailgate and lifted her. She could feel his arms shake slightly under her weight and she had to will her cheeks not to turn red so he wouldn't see her embarrassment. He gently placed her down in the little nest of blankets. She was amazed at how much more comfortable the new arrangement was than the blankets all heaped together. He pulled a free blanket up over her and nodded.

She snuggled further down under the blanket. "Thank you, Jimmy."

He placed one hand on the side of the wagon and jumped down. Melanie spotted Nicholas still standing at the tailgate of the wagon. His mouth was set in a grim line as he looked from Melanie to Jimmy and back to her. She rolled her eyes. The lout probably thought she was now having an affair with Jimmy as well as Pappy.

Nick wasn't sure why, but a hot anger was boiling in his belly. Seeing Jimmy place his hands on Melanie's waist to lift her into the wagon had set a rock to dropping in his heart. Seeing Jimmy hoist Melanie up into his arms and lay her down in the little bed of blankets he had made for her set his temper to flaring. Just who did Jimmy think he was?

"Nicky boy, let's have that chat now."

Nick took one last look at Melanie, all snug in the back of the wagon, then headed to where Pappy and the other men sat around the campfire. He had been dreading this conversation at first, but while they had ridden, Nick had considered what he would say and he had finally decided to tell them only the details which directly involved her fall.

Pappy didn't waste any time. "So what happened in the barn today?"

Nick sighed as he sat on the rock Melanie had vacated. "I walked into the barn and she was looking for a lost kitten. I turned my back for one second and she was gone. I started leading the wagon to the yard for you and some hay fell on me from above." Nick shook his head. "The fool woman was crawling out across the beam where the kitten was stuck. I hollered up at her and she startled."

Pappy interrupted. "Well why in tarnation would you yell at a body perched on nothing but a slender beam?"

Nick held up a hand. "That wasn't when she fell. She was maybe a foot or so away from the kitten, and I saw her eyes widen like she was scared. She kept glancing down and before I even knew what was happening she lunged forward and grabbed the kitten, then threw herself off the side of the beam. It wasn't until she started falling that I saw the rattlesnake spring at her, and that's when I knew what must have spooked her."

Pappy sighed and looked back over to the wagon. "What a brave little woman."

Nick snorted. "More like foolish."

Pappy shook his head. "Nope, I say brave. She just wanted to rescue that little kitten. She had no way of knowing there was a rattlesnake up in the rafters."

Ron nodded his agreement. "I say it was right brave, too. It gives me the willies just going up in the hayloft. That kitten would have been snake food if it had to rely on me."

The men chuckled and Pappy began handing out tin cups of beans and rice. Nick took a bite and nearly spit it back out.

The rice wasn't completely cooked. Crunching sounds took up all around the campfire as the men tried to chew their dinner.

Jimmy surprised everyone by speaking up with a question of his own. "So why did she have tears running down her cheeks?"

Nick shrugged. He wasn't completely comfortable telling everyone what he'd said, but he was even more uncomfortable lying to his uncle. He scratched the back of his neck. "I might have said something and she accidentally heard."

The men stopped chewing their crunchy rice. Pappy prompted him. "And you said what exactly?"

Nick gulped, suddenly feeling a heavy guilt burden his shoulders. "She had told me not to look up; she didn't want me to see …"

Pappy waved the end of his sentence away with his fork. "OK, she asked for you to be a decent, respectful man. And you said?"

Heat crept up Nick's neck. Maybe he was wrong to have said what he said. She was just asking for some decorum—surely even a brothel girl was entitled to that. Nick stared at the fire, suddenly too ashamed to meet another man's eyes. "Um, I might have said," he tugged at the bandana around his neck, "I might have said she was awfully modest for a brothel girl."

Nick hadn't seen or heard anyone move. He just felt a sudden blinding pain radiate from his nose across his entire face as he flew onto his backside. His eye sockets burned and his cheeks throbbed. He felt warm liquid running down his nose and dripping from his chin. When he opened his eyes, his vision blurred, but he could still make out Douglas's form standing over him.

CHAPTER 26

The young man was obviously stronger than he looked, for he was able to lift Nick several inches off the ground by his shirt front. "How dare you talk to a good and decent woman such as Melanie like that!"

Nick looked at Douglas bewildered. Words he meant as thoughts only poured from his mouth. "Good and decent? She sold herself to men for money!"

Douglas leaned down low to meet Nick's eyes. "That's right, she did, she most certainly did. But what would you have her do? Starve to death?" Douglas released his hold on Nick's shirt and Nick thudded back to the ground. Douglas pointed over to the wagon. "So you want to condemn her just for fighting to survive?"

Douglas stepped back from him, his chest heaving, and sat down. Nick scrambled to his feet and took the rag Pappy offered him for his nose. When Nick looked around the campfire Ron, Jimmy, Mitch, and even Pappy wore the same angry, disgusted look as Douglas.

Douglas sat with his elbows on his knees and his head bowed. His voice was distant and strained. "Just what would you do to survive? Would you so easily turn your life over to death? I admire her will to live."

Nick had never thought of it as if it were him. He heard someone sniff and looked up to see Pappy with tears in his eyes. He had never seen his uncle cry before. The disappointment clouding Pappy's features was near to unbearable.

Pappy sniffed again and his voice creaked as he spoke. "I thought I raised you better than that." He shook his head and jerked a thumb over his shoulder to the wagon. "I was teaching her that God could forgive her despite what she had done in the past. She was finally starting to believe that God could love her regardless of the years she spent in the brothel." Pappy swiped his wrist across his nose. "I thought I taught you about the same loving, forgiving God."

Nick could barely whisper, his throat was so clogged with shame and guilt. "You did, Paps."

Pappy's eyes turned fiery and his voice steel. "Then why is it so hard to extend that same love and forgiveness to her? What has she done that is so wrong in your eyes she can't be forgiven?"

"Pappy, I do believe God forgives her."

"Then why do you still condemn her?"

Mitch poked a stick in the fire. "Old Brooks saved me from dying on the side of the road. He showed me that I had sinned against God by drinking myself into a stupor and losing all that God had blessed me with." Mitch sighed heavily. "But he also taught me that once I asked God to forgive me it was like none of that had ever happened in God's eyes. Old Brooks called it a clean slate. A fresh start."

Pappy grunted. "That's all she was after, you know. She just wanted a clean start. For her and her friend." Pappy's voice gentled. "In fact, the only reason she started to do more than sing at the brothel was so she could earn enough money to get her friend as far away as possible from her abusive pa."

Nick vaguely recalled Melanie talking about a friend too scared to come to Sterling Canyon because her pa might find her. He had obviously put the information out of his mind. Nick's stomach clenched and he was sure he'd lose the crunchy rice in his stomach in front of all these men. He glanced over at the wagon. She hadn't just been fighting to survive for herself; she threw herself into the lion's den to help save her friend too.

Nick hung his head, the full weight of his guilt pressing down on his shoulders.

"My ma died bringing me into this world." Nick didn't have to look up to know Douglas was talking. He had known the young man since the day Old Brooks brought him to the ranch as an infant. "I've known all of you my entire life. Something you don't know though, something only Old Brooks told Pappy and later on me, was that my ma was a brothel girl."

Nick's head snapped up. Douglas pulled a piece of paper out of his vest and held it up. "Old Brooks gave this to me. It's a letter from my ma. She wrote it to explain why she had worked in a brothel." Douglas tucked the letter back into his vest. "Her man had run out on her, leaving her with no money and no food. She had to walk across the desert to get to town." Douglas sniffed. "She was half dead by the time she stumbled into town. The saloon owner took her in, promised to care for her so long as she cared for a few of his customers. She hadn't known what she was getting herself into until it was too late. Then the saloon owner wouldn't let her leave."

"Nick." Douglas paused until Nick finally looked up at him. "So by your way of thinking, even though my ma was tricked into working at the brothel and then forced to stay, she's still just a harlot?" Douglas swallowed hard. "So in your mind, does that make me a whore's son?"

Nick's eyes widened and he shook his head. "No, no, Douglas you were the best kid growing up and now," Nick gingerly touched the side of his sore nose, "well you've grown into a strong man with a good head on your shoulders."

Douglas nodded, "So the circumstances people are forced into shouldn't be the basis for which we judge them?"

Before Nick could reply, Jimmy surprised them all by speaking up for the second time tonight. "If you hadn't known where she worked prior, what would you think of her?"

Nick couldn't respond out loud even though he knew the answer. He would freely think what he fought his mind not to think already. That Melanie Brooks was the strongest, smartest, prettiest, most caring, wittiest, hardest working, spunkiest woman he had ever laid eyes on. He had been fighting his mind and heart to maintain what he thought was righteousness, but instead he had sorely misjudged a good woman who had done what she deemed necessary to provide a better life for herself and her friend. Nick's heart plummeted, and he prayed God would open the earth and swallow him whole.

Tears ran down his cheeks, but he was too racked with guilt to be embarrassed. He looked up at Pappy. "What have I done?"

Pappy's eyes filled with a sad sympathy. "Why don't you sleep under the wagon tonight?"

Nick didn't respond. He just stood and trudged over to the wagon, then lowered his large frame to the ground and crawled underneath. He covered his face with his arm as tears leaked from the corners of his eyes, down his temples and into his hair.

Chapter 27

ELANIE HAD HEARD the men softly talking from a distance, but didn't bother to try and listen in. Her mind and heart were too consumed with the harsh words Nick had delivered to her earlier that day. His confirmation that she would never be good enough to right her past drove her to unspeakable depths of sadness. She felt darkness creeping in on all sides of the wagon, and finally she closed her eyes and consented to being devoured. It felt like she was tumbling down a bottomless well and she wrapped her good arm protectively around her body.

She whimpered. "I'm too fat, too ugly, too bad. I'm a whore. A harlot. A Jezebel. I'm used goods. Tainted." She croaked but held back her sobs. "No man will ever love me. I will never have a husband. I will never have children. I'm used up. I have nothing left to offer."

Tears began spilling down her cheek and she stuffed her fist in her mouth to stifle her sobs. Her body shook with her silent sobbing and her broken arm ached, but Melanie scarcely felt the pain. Thoughts of Jonathan assailed her and she buried her face in blankets to mute her moan of agony.

"Why Jonathan? I gave you everything." She whispered to the blankets. "And you betrayed me. You took everything I had to give and left me with nothing." Her heart broke anew at the memory. Those had been dark days after he abandoned her. She would have allowed herself to die if it hadn't been for Charlotte. Charlotte had taken her in. Charlotte used up her meager savings to support them both after Melanie lost her job. Charlotte introduced her to Tom.

Melanie's stomach clenched and she grabbed her middle with her good arm. "Oh, God, why? What did I do?" Tears squeezed past her closed eyelids and dampened the blanket she pressed her face against. "Why did Tom have to hurt me?"

She took a deep, shuddering breath. "I'm dirty. I'm bad. I'm used. I'm tainted. I'm ugly. I'm fat. No man will ever love me. No man will marry me. I'm dirty. I'm disgusting." Her voice shook, "I have nothing left to offer."

Nick slowly removed his arm from his face and stared at the bottom of the wagon bed. He had been too consumed with his own tears and guilt to hear any noise coming from the wagon bed until now, when he thought he heard a low moan. He listened intently. There it was again.

Melanie's low moan was full of sadness and pain. Her voice shook as she spoke. "I'm too fat, too ugly, too bad. I'm a whore. A harlot. A Jezebel. I'm used goods. Tainted. No man will ever love me. I will never have a husband. I will never have children. I'm used up. I have nothing left to offer."

Nick winced at every word. Had his comment sparked such a self-loathing tirade? Fresh tears sprang to his eyes at the very thought. He listened quietly as she continued to whisper about a man named Jonathan who had apparently left her. Nick was torn between a fiery anger and a deep sadness when she accused another man named Tom of hurting her. Nick clenched his fists. Who would hurt such a kind woman?

You did.

Nick had to quickly shove his fist in his mouth to stop the groan of agony welling up in his own heart. Here he was ready to fight the man named Tom for hurting Melanie, when he had hurt her too. He had judged her harshly and held himself above her when, in reality, he was probably no better than those fellows she called Jonathan and Tom.

Nick listened for what felt like half the night while she silently chastised and condemned herself. By the time she finally talked herself to sleep, Nick's heart was battered, bruised, and broken. He stared wide awake at the bottom of the wagon and wondered just how badly her heart ached to say all of those things about herself.

As morning dawned Nick realized he hadn't slept at all. He crawled out from under the wagon and was relieved to see Pappy was awake and sitting by the fire by himself.

Pappy looked up when he heard someone approach. He was relieved to see it was Nicholas. He had hoped they'd have some time alone to talk. He poured a cup of coffee and offered it to his nephew.

"Didn't sleep much; did you?"

Nick's eyes were bruised from the wallop Douglas gave him but Pappy suspected they'd have been rimmed with dark shadows anyways. Nick accepted the cup of coffee and sat with a dull thud.

"You knew that she'd ..." Nick gestured toward the wagon.

Pappy nodded. "Yup, like that most every night when she first came. She was doing it less frequently, but I figured after yesterday she'd be up all night telling herself those blasted lies." Pappy rested his elbows on his knees and leaned forward. "I wanted you to see for yourself that she doesn't need any one of us judging her. She's doing a mighty fine job on her own."

"She talked about two men, Jonathan and Tom. Who are they?"

Pappy sighed. He had promised Melanie he wouldn't tell anyone about her past relationships. Now he debated if it would prove to be more helpful for Nicholas to know. Pappy stared at the campfire and pleaded for God's guidance. The other men began to stir and joined them at the campfire. Pappy took it as his sign to keep Melanie's past to himself.

Pappy set his hands to cooking the oats Nicholas had packed, but his mind was focused on Melanie. He knew her heart must be torn raw this morning. Once the oats were cooked he took a tin cup in and scooped up some of the cooked oats. He wiped the side clean, and then walked to the wagon.

Melanie was lying on her back, her eyes wide open and rimmed with red. Pappy's heart sunk at the sight of her. "Brought your breakfast, Little Missy."

The girl didn't move, just shifted her eyes to look at Pappy. He climbed up over the side of the wagon and knelt next to her. "Melanie, honey, sit up and eat."

She looked at him through glassy eyes for a moment, then turned her head and closed her eyes. Pappy rested a hand on her shoulder. "You've got to keep your strength up, Little Missy."

Melanie didn't open her eyes. Pappy sighed, defeated. He climbed back down and strode over to the campfire. He saw Nick look at the tin cup still full of oats, then glance back at the wagon.

"She not awake yet, Paps?"

Pappy shook his head as he stared at the campfire. "She's awake. She just refuses to eat."

Chapter 28

PAPPY WAS GLAD when they finally pulled up in front of the doctor's office a few hours past noon. Douglas had coaxed Melanie into eating a piece of jerky, for which Pappy was profusely thankful, but other than that the girl hadn't eaten, drunk, or even spoken since the day before.

As Pappy set the brake, Dr. Williams strode out onto his porch. "Problem, Paps?"

Pappy nodded toward the back of the wagon where Mitch and Douglas were helping Melanie down. "Boss took a bad tumble and broke her arm."

Dr. Williams hollered over his shoulder to his nurse. "The Brooks girl is here with a broken arm. Ready some bandages."

Dr. Williams held the door open as Mitch assisted Melanie through the door. The few people out walking through the little town of Sterling Canyon stopped to watch. Pappy could already hear the whispers. He should have suspected their arrival in town would cause a stir, especially after all the stories Melanie's hopeful suitors surely brought back with them.

Melanie sat on an exam table and allowed a man with soft, manicured hands who had introduced himself as Dr. Williams to exam her arm.

"Did you sustain any other injuries?"

Melanie thought of the knife Nicholas had thrust in her heart. "I banged my head."

Dr. Williams felt around on her head and she winced when his fingers roved over a large lump.

"Hmm, yes you have quite the goose egg back here." He stooped and looked into her eyes. "Have you had a headache? Blurry vision? Dizziness?"

Her voice was flat when she answered. "None of that."

"Well it's very good the bone of your arm didn't break through your skin. I'm going to have to set your arm. It'll hurt a great deal, but I have some medicine that could help with the pain if you would like."

Melanie stared out the front door. "Just do it."

Dr. Williams motioned toward her loyal cowhands and Nicholas. "You boys get ready to hold her down."

Mitch, Douglas, Ron, and Jimmy stepped forward, ready to do as the doctor instructed. Melanie was relieved Nicholas stood back. She wouldn't want him getting his hands dirty by touching her. Dr. Williams braced one hand on her shoulder and gripped her wrist. On the count of three he pulled on her arm and Melanie felt the bone slide back into place, but she didn't flinch. Her body, mind, and heart were numb to pain.

The doctor looked at her a bit bewildered. She raised an eyebrow. "W-well, I'll just bandage this arm and you can be on your way." As the doctor bandaged her arm in wet strips of gauze, a young woman flew through the door.

She was instantly cooing at Melanie's side. "Oh, you poor dear! When I heard Brooks's niece was in town with a broken arm I just *knew* it was you." Melanie pulled back from the woman. The young woman's forehead wrinkled. "Well, don't you remember me? I'm Reverend Merryweather's wife, Louisa Merryweather."

Melanie shook her head to clear her mind. "Yes, of course. We rode in on the stage together. How could I forget?"

Louisa Merryweather's face bloomed into a brilliant smile. "Yes, yes that's correct! I so desperately wanted to ride out and visit you, but when the Reverend heard it was a full day's ride out he didn't think we could take such a long journey." She tsked, "Oh, but you poor thing. Now I wish I would have insisted upon a visit."

Louisa Merryweather began to wrap her arms around Melanie in a warm embrace. Melanie's eyes widened and her heart began to race. She couldn't let the good preacher's wife touch her. Melanie leaned backward and nearly tumbled off the other side of the exam table.

Melanie couldn't reach out and stop the woman's arms from entwining around her so she used her voice. "Watch out, I'll taint you!"

Her cowhands fell silent, understanding exactly what she had meant. Dr. Williams looked at her quizzically and she was sure he thought she hit her head much harder than she said. Louisa Merryweather, however, planted her hands firmly on her hips and narrowed her eyes.

"Everyone out." Her dainty little foot tapped impatiently as she looked around at the room full of men. "I said *out!*"

Melanie nodded toward her cowhands and each one begrudgingly exited the doctor's office. Dr. Williams seemed ready to argue at first, but a stern look from Reverend Merryweather's pretty little wife had him snap his mouth shut and usher his nurse outside as well.

The reverend's wife turned back to Melanie. "Just how do you think you can taint me?"

Obviously the good preacher's wife didn't recall where they had picked Melanie up. Or maybe she had, and still didn't realize that "Minnie's Dollhouse" was a brothel. Melanie sighed. She might as well just tell the poor woman the truth. "Mrs. Merryweather ..."

The reverend's wife interrupted. "Louisa."

Melanie shook her head. She couldn't bring herself to address this kind woman by her first name like they were the closest of bosom pals. "The place where you picked me up, Minnie's Dollhouse, it's a ..."

Again the reverend's wife interrupted. "I know, it's a brothel."

Melanie gasped and her eyes widened. "You know?"

The good preacher's wife snorted. "Oh, honey, I know." The woman leaned close. "Let me tell you just how well I know."

Melanie sat on the exam table with mouth gaping, completely stunned and amazed, as Louisa Merryweather wove a tale of how she had worked in a brothel since she was eleven years old. Then ten years later her reverend husband spotted her and married her on the spot.

"He just married you? Just like that?"

Louisa nodded. "Yup, said that when he saw me he felt the immediate prompting of God to whisk me away from that place and make me his and only his for the rest of our lives."

Melanie nearly whispered. "Even though you were a *whore*?"

Louisa's eyes filled with tears. "Oh, honey, don't use that word. To me, that word insinuates you *liked* it. That you *wanted* it." She shook her head sadly. "Me and you, we were just too scared to die on the streets."

A friendship nearly as deep as the one Melanie felt toward Charlotte instantly bloomed in her heart. This woman, this reverend's wife, understood. She more than just understood, she had *lived* it. And look at her, she seemed whole. She seemed more than just whole. The woman was radiating with happiness, femininity, and the righteousness befitting a reverend's wife.

The doctor peeked his head inside. "I really should finish bandaging that arm before the plaster sets."

Louisa waved him in and Melanie gripped her new friend's hand to catch her attention. "I promise I'll come along with the boys when they fetch supplies next time."

Louisa smiled. "Be sure to come and visit me when you do. We'll talk more over tea."

Melanie nodded and bid Louisa goodbye. When her cowhands stepped back inside, her heart felt lighter and she managed a small smile for their benefit.

Pappy sent a prayer of thanks up to Heaven. Whatever Mrs. Merryweather said to Melanie he was profusely grateful, for it seemed to have lifted the girl's spirits. The smile she flashed at the cowhands was a bit wobbly, but her eyes shone with a timid happiness. He hoped that whatever was said between the two women sparked a friendship. A reverend's wife was surely a good friend for the girl to have.

Dr. Williams finished bandaging Melanie's arm, then had them all wait for the outermost layers to dry. Pappy was glad they dried quickly and then paid the doctor and promised they'd take real good care of her as the boys ushered her out the door and back to the wagon.

Chapter 29

ELANIE WAS JUST about to climb aboard the wagon with Douglas and Mitch assisting her when a ruckus across the street caught her attention. She pulled away from their grasp and turned to watch. A stout, balding man was standing in front of a saloon yelling at a young woman who appeared to be a few years younger than Melanie.

The man shouted. "Your pa died owing me debt."

Melanie could barely hear the girl's timid response. "But I don't have the money to pay you back."

The man laughed and grabbed the girl's arm. "Then you'll have to work it off."

The girl squirmed, trying to break free of the man's hold. "Let me go! You're hurting me."

Fury rose up in Melanie's chest and her body set itself in motion before she knew what she was doing. She grabbed Douglas's six-shooter off his hip and marched across the street. Thoughts of Jonathan, Tom, Mr. Groover, Minnie's former boss,

Charlotte's abusive pa, and all of the other horrible stories she'd heard from the girls at the brothel fueled her steps. She took a deep breath as Nicholas's words assailed her once more, but this time she didn't allow them to crumble her weak defenses. This time his words transformed the shattered pieces of her heart into an ironclad fortress.

The stout man was so busy trying to pull the helpless girl inside his saloon he didn't even notice Melanie approaching. Her blood ran cold as she lifted the six-shooter and pressed it against the man's temple. Melanie pulled the hammer back. The soft metallic click sounded next to his ear and he instantly stopped pulling the girl, but didn't drop his hold of her.

Melanie spoke slowly through gritted teeth. "Let. Her. Go."

The man looked at her out of the corner of his eye. "Just who do you think you are?"

"My name is Melanie Brooks."

Sweat broke out across the man's forehead. "*The* Melanie Brooks?"

"The one and only." She pressed the six-shooter harder against the man's temple and allowed her voice to drip with all the venom that had been spewed at her over the years. "Now are you going to let her go or do I have to blow another hole in your head so you can hear me?"

The man's hands released the girl and she stumbled backwards. Sam crept forward, low to the ground. The hair on the back of his neck stood straight up and all of his teeth showed as he growled. Melanie saw the man's arm move and she thought he was going for his side arm. Her finger twitched over the trigger. She would gladly kill this man to save the girl.

Several metallic clicks sounded around her and Melanie chanced a glance up. Her loyal cowhands stood in a semi-circle in front of the saloon, their six-shooters and rifles at the ready. Douglas was unarmed, as she had taken his gun, but the young man didn't hesitate in stepping in front of the girl. Her heart rose—there *were* good men in this world.

Melanie's voice was low and menacing. "We've got six guns on you. Even if you were fast enough to pull yours and shoot one of my men, you'd still be dead six times over before you even hit the dirt." A bead of sweat rolled down the man's temple. "Now raise your hands slow and steady."

The man complied, but still tried to argue. "The girl's pa died owing me a debt."

"How much?"

The man thought for a second. "Hundred dollars."

Melanie didn't flinch. "Pappy, pay the man."

Pappy tucked his six-shooter back in his hip holster and stepped forward. "He's probably lying."

"I don't care, pay the man." Melanie pressed the barrel of the gun harder against the stocky man's temple so he'd know she was talking to him. "If you ever so much as look at that girl again, I'll be coming back."

"D-d-don't worry, Miss Br-r-r-ooks, I won't bother her again."

Melanie took a slow step back away from the man, then walked over to the girl clinging to the back of Douglas's shirt. "Do you have a place to live?"

The girl was visibly shaking. She looked at Melanie with red rimmed eyes and shook her head. "I broke my arm and Doc Williams says I've got to take it easy for a while. Can you do any household chores?"

The girl shrugged. "Some. Ma died before she could teach me how to can, but I make real good hot cakes and I can skin just about any animal one of your men hunt down."

Melanie nodded. "If you're interested you've got the job."

Melanie saw the girl fist the back of Douglas's shirt tighter. "Yes ma'am, I'm interested!"

"Good." Melanie handed Douglas his six-shooter and then offered her good arm to the girl. The girl released Douglas and wrapped her arm around Melanie's good arm like a vise. Melanie hollered over her shoulder, "Let's go, boys."

Melanie and the girl climbed into the back of the wagon as the cowhands slowly walked backward, their guns still drawn on the stocky saloon owner. Sam jumped up into the back of the wagon and Mitch and Douglas climbed in after him, their guns aimed across the street. Ron, Jimmy, and Nicholas took turns mounting their horses. Pappy finally climbed up onto the wagon seat and clicked the geldings into action. As the wagon headed out of town Mitch and Douglas knelt in front of Melanie and the girl and Ron, Jimmy and Nicholas stood mount to mount in front of the wagon. Once the wagon had turned down the trail and was out of danger of being shot at, the three mounted men turned their horses and galloped down the trail after the wagon.

Nick's heart raced. He had never seen a woman pull a gun on a man like that before. In fact, he had never even seen a *man* pull a gun on someone like that before. What was that crazy woman thinking? She could have gotten herself killed. Nick took a deep breath as that thought settled deep into his heart. *She could have been killed.*

All to save that girl. Nick shook his head. It seemed that this woman was constantly putting herself in harm's way to help someone else. Nick wondered who had ever tried to help her. From the sorrowful self-loathing he had heard last night, it sounded like a fair share of people had thrown her in harm's way instead of trying to rescue her from it.

Nick's stomach clenched as he counted himself as one of those people. He'd been so busy looking down on her for her past sins, he'd completely neglected to see her glass heart—the one he knew by the look on her face in the barn he had shattered. For the first time in his life he had ignored Pappy's stern warnings and advice, and for the first time in his life he was the cause of a problem, not the handy solution.

Melanie heard the girl sniffle and tipped her head to see a tear roll down the girl's cheek. She wrapped her good arm around the girl's shoulders. "It's over, honey. It's all over."

The girl buried her face against Melanie's shoulder and sobbed. "I was so scared."

Melanie gave the girl a squeeze. "You looked mighty brave to me."

The girl's head snapped up. "Me? Brave?" She shook her head. "No ma'am, you're the one that put the gun to his head and demanded he leave me alone. Not even the men passing by on the boardwalk cared to stop and help me."

"Yeah, but you stood up to him. You told him no. You fought against him."

The girl shook her head. "That doesn't hold a candle to what you did."

Melanie shrugged. "So, what's your name?"

The girl bowed her head and sniffed again. "Pa never saw fit to name me. He just called me 'girl'."

Melanie's face melted into a severe scowl. What kind of pa cared so little for his daughter that he didn't even name her? Melanie didn't want the girl to feel bad, so she quickly plastered a grin across her face. "Well, what did you always dream your name could be?"

The girl's head remained bowed but Melanie could still see the beginnings of a smile pull at the corners of her lips. "Esther. I don't remember much of my ma; I don't even remember what she used to call me." The girl's voice dropped low. "But before she died she told me there was an Esther in the Bible that sought God and was able to do all kinds of things. I've never forgotten that story."

Melanie raised her eyebrows. "You don't say? Well then, I guess we'll call you Esther." Douglas's voice sounded low from beside Melanie. "Esther is a real pretty name."

Esther peeked up at Douglas, and Melanie saw that her cheeks were tinged pink. "Thank you."

"So, *Esther*, you know how to cook?"

Esther nodded. "Yes ma'am. My pa made me cook his meals … when he was awake to eat them."

Melanie nodded knowingly. "Well first off, I prefer being called Melanie. Second, I sure hope you're a good cook because my boys have big appetites."

Esther sat up and turned her head. "Six is a lot more than just pa and me, but I think I can manage."

"Oh, honey, this is just half of them. There's ten more back at the ranch."

Esther's eyes widened. "I've got to feed sixteen cowhands?"

Melanie grinned. "Well, fifteen cowhands and Pappy, making sixteen men. But don't worry, I don't think I'm completely useless."

Esther shook her head and softly whispered to herself. "Sixteen men. I've got to feed sixteen men."

When they stopped that night to camp, Pappy allowed Esther to take over the cooking duties so he could talk to Melanie. He met her at the wagon where she was carefully sliding down over the tailgate. Pappy grasped her elbow and made sure she didn't slip.

"How you feelin', Little Missy?"

She huffed. "A bit tired."

"Well it's been a rough couple of days."

"I've hardly done a thing besides sit in the back of a wagon."

Pappy nodded. "I know, but sometimes sitting can make a body weary." He nudged her with his elbow. "So can crying."

She glared up at him but her voice shook when she spoke. "His words cut deep."

Pappy wrapped an arm around her shoulders. "I know they did, Little Missy."

She turned her head into his shoulder. "Pappy I was just beginning to believe all of the hype you were trying to drum at me. But Nicholas, it was like he was confirming what you were trying to beat out of me, that no matter how hard I worked to become a better person I'd *always* be that girl who worked in the brothel."

Pappy's arm tightened around her shoulders as the anger he felt toward his nephew flared. He was going to have a stern talking to with that boy the minute they got home. He'd built himself up on a pedestal by judging Melanie, and Pappy wasn't going to stand for it. It was time someone knocked him down a few notches.

Pappy leaned down and kissed the top of Melanie's head. "Melanie, honey, you still are worth all the love, mercy, and forgiveness God has to offer. Don't let some blockhead like my nephew convince you otherwise."

Melanie remained quiet so Pappy figured the girl was done talking about Nicholas. He jostled her shoulder to get her attention. "Hey, you know you were pretty impressive today." He chuckled. "Scared me ten years closer to my grave, but you showed more brass than all the men in Sterling Canyon."

Pappy's heart soared when Melanie laughed. "I'm sorry I scared you. I just couldn't watch another girl have the innocence beat out of her by a brothel."

"Hmm, so it looks like you're following in your Great-Uncle Brooks's footsteps, eh?" She looked at him curiously and Pappy chuckled. "By taking wards in, Little Missy. Nearly every man working on your ranch was somehow rescued or adopted by your uncle."

She smiled up at him. "Why yes, I suppose I am then."

Chapter 30

NICK CAREFULLY WATCHED Melanie for any signs of discomfort or pain as they headed home. He hadn't slept again last night. He had lain under the wagon and listened to her muffled cries and self-loathing tirade. His heart had broken anew, hearing all of the horrible names she called herself. Hearing her lowly opinion of herself had almost taken him by surprise, for after talking with that preacher's wife she had seemed to brighten back to the woman she had become before his comment. Obviously, his words had cut much deeper than he had suspected.

He sat straighter in his saddle. Well he'd just have to find a way to make it up to her. Nick silently prayed that God would show him how to fix all the wrong he had bestowed upon that woman—that wonderful, beautiful, spitfire of a woman. As Nick prayed with all the power of his heart, a thought wedged its way into his mind. He needed to stop fighting his heart and allow his affection to grow rather than trying to snuff it out. A grin creased his face and Nick straightened his shoulders with determination and excitement. He was going to court Melanie Brooks.

As their wagon quickly rolled along the trail toward home, they passed a cowhand herding a stray calf. The cowhand was more than happy to see Melanie. He quickly plopped the animal into the back of the wagon and doffed his hat. "Sure glad to see you're doin' just fine, boss."

Melanie tried to smile despite the hollow ache that resumed residence in her chest. "You probably just missed my pie."

The cowhand actually blushed. "You sure do make good pie, but we've all missed you something terrible. Just not the same without your singin' and jokin'."

Nicholas rode up next to the wagon, nearly wedging his horse between the wagon and the cowhand. Melanie thought she detected ice in his words. "Ride ahead and tell the others."

Before Melanie could silence Nicholas with a hot glare and invite the cowhand to ride along, the cowhand slammed his hat back onto his head and raced toward the ranch to alert the others the boss was coming home. By the time they drove into the yard cowhands gathered around the wagon, some hitching their arms over the side board to ride along with her. Their questions and excitement at her return were overwhelming.

"Are you feelin' OK, boss?"

"Can you make supper tonight?"

"So it's really broken?"

"Does it hurt bad?"

"What happened the other day anyways?"

"Glad to see you're back, boss!"

Melanie thought it would be best to show them all just how well she was feeling so she refused any assistance getting out of the back of the wagon. Feet steady on the ground, she firmly grasped Esther's hand and strode to the porch steps so she could see everyone clearly as she addressed them.

She held up a hand to silence their constant inquiries. "*Gentlemen,*" she tried emphasizing the word as much as possible, "thank you for your concern." She made sure to meet each man's eyes. "And thank you even more for running this ranch on your own."

"Aw shucks boss, ain't nothin' but a coupl'a days."

"Yeah, we'd do anything for you, boss."

In spite of the hollow emptiness in her heart, Melanie couldn't help but grin. "While we were in town we picked up a girl to help me in the house." Melanie pulled the girl out from behind her. "This is Esther. I want you to treat her with as much respect and courtesy as you give me. Anything less will not be tolerated."

Melanie tipped her head toward Esther's ear to privately ask the girl a question. "Do you have a beau?"

Esther's big eyes grew even more round. "A b-beau? No ma'am, I mean, Melanie."

Melanie quirked an eyebrow. "Do you *want* one?" Esther averted her gaze to the ground and shook her head. Melanie leaned closer. "I was only asking because once the boys in town hear there's a new girl on my ranch they'll start comin' a callin'. I know from experience. I was just curious if you would want to meet some of them."

This time Esther's gaze flicked over to where Douglas Spells stood. Esther quickly looked back to Melanie and shook her head. "I don't think I want to meet any of them."

The corner of Melanie's mouth wanted to tug upward but she fought it to stay down. She stepped away from Esther again and addressed her cowhands.

"Esther doesn't want to be bothered by any men from *town*," she met Douglas's eye and hoped he got the hint, "so we'll just continue running off any suitors. If she changes her mind and wants to meet with one of these men, you are not to leave her alone with the man. Ever."

Pappy stepped up onto the porch and wrapped his arm protectively around her shoulders. The embrace was comforting and for a split second Melanie could almost imagine what it would feel like to have a husband's arm around her. Protecting her. Encouraging her. Loving her.

Pappy's voice broke through her thoughts. "It's early in the day, everyone get back to work. Melanie needs to rest, doctor's orders."

Melanie whirled toward the front door and hurried in. Pappy's embrace had led to thoughts of a life she knew for certain now would never transpire. She ignored the dizziness that assailed her as she whirled around, her need of a few seconds alone to rein in her emotions and reaffix a stony front being of great importance. No more than halfway down the hall the dizziness begin to take over and Melanie stretched her good arm out hoping to grasp a nearby wall. Instead, arms corded with iron-hard muscle scooped her up and clutched her close to an equally hard chest. Melanie's heart pounded as she struggled to clear the dizziness from her mind and determine in whose arms she was. Pappy's arms didn't feel this thick and his chest wasn't this solid. The only other man on her ranch who had come close enough for her to feel their muscles and strength so intimately was Jimmy and his arms had shook under her weight. These arms remained firm and steady beneath her.

Melanie struggled to be released, but the iron strong arms wouldn't release her. She squinted her eyes open to see her captor, but the slightest bit of light caused a new wave of dizziness to assail her. A soft groan escaped her lips and the man holding her clutched her tighter. Until the dizzy spell passed, she would have to relent to remaining in whoever's arms she was being held so securely.

A gentle jostling and the feel of a man's thick thighs beneath her told her they were now sitting. Before she could push herself off this man's lap and fall ungracefully to the floor, the man tugged her closer still.

His breath was warm against her skin as he leaned closer to her ear and whispered, "I've been a fool." He softly kissed her temple.

Melanie's heart stopped its rapid beating. The high and mighty Nicholas Henderson was holding her? An ice cold sensation ran down her body, causing her fingers and toes to tingle. What was this man up to? Judging her for her past one minute and trying to steal kisses in the kitchen the next? The lure of a brothel girl must have been too much, even for such a righteous man as Nicholas. Her stomach dropped and she clenched her fists. So she wasn't good enough to be treated with decency, but she was good enough to use? An extra layer of rock formed around the iron clad fortress housing her heart.

Nick looked down at the beauty in his arms. He squeezed her tighter when she tried to squirm out of his grip. Boy had he been acting like the biggest fool this side of the Mississippi River. He couldn't resist nuzzling his face against the soft curve of her smooth neck.

"I'm so sorry, Melanie. Please say you forgive me."

The beautiful bundle in his arms snorted as she placed her hands against his chest with a mighty shove. "Forgive *you*?" She huffed. "Forgive you?" She pounded a tightly wound fist into his ribs and he momentarily loosened his grip, surprised at the pain she was able to inflict. She quickly jumped out of his arms and took a defensive stance in front of him, her hands balled into fists at her hips. "Why should I forgive you when you constantly throw in my face that God can't forgive me?"

Nick swiveled in his chair to watch her storm down the hallway. He cringed when he saw Pappy coming in through the front door rushing to Melanie's side. Pappy spoke too softly for Nick to hear what he said but Melanie's response was nearly shouted.

She pointed toward the kitchen with her bandaged arm. "That nephew of yours thinks I'm so despicable for working in a brothel, yet not so much that he feels he can steal kisses."

Nick gulped. Pappy's face turned bright red and he left Melanie in the middle of the hall to march straight for him. Melanie turned on her heel and disappeared up the stairs. Nick stood to face his uncle for the tongue lashing he knew was coming.

Pappy marched straight up to Nick until they were almost nose to nose. His voice was low and menacing. "You kissed her?"

Nick took a deep breath and nodded his head. "Just the side of her head."

Pappy's breath came in great heaving puffs. "What on God's green earth possessed you to do such a thing?"

Nick could do nothing more than shrug. "I was trying to say how sorry I was."

Pappy nearly growled in response. "I thought I told you to stay away from her."

Nick looked Pappy in the eye so his uncle could read all of the sincerity in his eyes. "Yes sir, you did. But recent events have caused the blinders to fall from my eyes, and now I realize what a fool I've been." Nick sighed and ran a hand through his hair. "I've been fighting an attraction to that girl, Pappy. At first I thought there was no way we could be together because of her past and all. But now …" Nick sighed again, his heart filled with doubt and longing, "… now I can't see a possible future without her at my side."

Pappy pulled a chair out and sat across from Nicholas. His heart was lightened by his nephew's confession, but doubt still lingered in the back of his mind. Today Nicholas seemed at peace with Melanie's past, but what if tomorrow he felt differently? Pappy just couldn't risk allowing anymore hurt come to the tenderhearted girl.

"Son, you know I love you and up until recently I've always been proud of you." Nicholas nodded, so Pappy continued. "That young woman has been through the fires of hell a few times already and I'd hate to see her abused any further."

Nicholas's eyes widened. "Surely you know I'd never hurt her!"

Pappy lifted an eyebrow. "Haven't you already?" Pappy recognized the pain in his nephew's eyes and saw regret and shame cloud over his face. Pappy sighed. His heart went out to the two dearest people in his life, his nephew and Melanie.

Nicholas hung his head. "How can I possibly fix this, Pappy?"

Pappy grunted. "Son, have you forgotten all of the lessons I taught you over the years?" Nicholas looked up with a quizzical expression. "When you were a boy and stole a peppermint candy from the general store, what was your punishment?"

Nicholas's brows rose. "I had to apologize?" Pappy raised his brows in response. "You think if I apologize to Melanie she'll forgive me?"

Pappy shrugged. "Just because we apologize doesn't mean the person has to forgive us." Pappy paused. "Or forget what we did."

"If my apology won't win Melanie over, then why bother?"

Pappy's eyes grew wide and he leaned forward. "Just what kind of dust-for-brains nephew did I raise? You should apologize because it's the right thing to do!" Pappy slapped the table top to make sure Nicholas was listening. "Jesus willingly went to the cross knowing that one day a young man would treat a young woman, cruelly simply because she was forced to sell herself in prostitution to survive; yet He said, 'He's still worth it.'"

Pappy shoved away from the table and stormed out the back door. He thought he had raised Nicholas to develop a personal relationship with Christ, but the fact that his nephew had to ask why it was important to apologize was proof enough he hadn't succeeded. His heart ached for his lack of success in raising the nephew for whom he was responsible.

He kept marching across the yard until he was well out of earshot. "God, please forgive me. I failed in raising that young man." Pappy ran his hand down his face. He turned and began pacing as his mind began filling with instances of when he should have used a heavier hand with the boy.

Chapter 31

NICK WATCHED PAPPY pace the yard. He was shaking his head and his hands were flying wildly. Nick could barely make out his lips moving as he spoke. Nick smiled. He was probably talking to God again. Above him, a door squeaked open. Nick looked up and heard the soft shuffling sounds of Melanie walking toward the staircase. He sighed. Pappy's words had cut his heart wide open.

"Jesus willingly went to the cross knowing that one day a young man would treat a young woman cruelly, simply because she was forced to sell herself in prostitution to survive; yet He said, 'He's still worth it.'"

Tears pooled in the corners of his eyes obscuring his vision. He looked up at Pappy, still pacing the yard as he spoke to God. When was the last time he had prayed? Or read his Bible?

"Oh, you're still here."

Nick's head snapped up. Melanie stood in the doorway to the kitchen, her eyes red and swollen. He quickly stood and reached over to pull a chair out for her.

"Will you please sit? I'd like to say something."

Nicholas tried to ignore the sting to his heart from the wary look in her eye. She had every right to be skeptical. As she sat he scooted her chair in, then resumed his seat across from her.

Melanie uncharacteristically propped both elbows on the table and rested her face in her hands. "Well?"

Nick eyed her carefully. She hadn't eaten in close to three days and she had nearly passed dead away when they arrived home. "You haven't eaten."

Melanie tried not to roll her eyes. "Haven't been hungry."

The self-righteous man sitting across from her leaned forward and pressed a hand to her forehead. She immediately sat up and leaned away from his touch. His brow furrowed. "I'm worried you're making yourself sick. How do you feel?"

Melanie shrugged. "A bit dizzy."

The scraping of his chair as he stood rang like thunder in her ears. She heard the opening and closing of cabinets and the soft clink of china. In a few minutes a plate of cheese, bread, and a sliced apple was sitting in front of her.

"Please eat."

Melanie forced her head up to look at him. His eyes were underlined a deep gray and his nose was swollen and red, but none of that masked the pleading she saw in his intense stare. She sighed and picked up a piece of apple. She held it up for him to see, and then bit the piece of apple in half.

A smile creased his sun-tanned face. "Thank you."

She focused on chewing her apple and tried not to think of how much more handsome he looked when he smiled. "What happened to your face?"

His smile turned bashful and he gingerly touched the side of his nose. "Let's just say you have some loyal cowhands."

Melanie raised an eyebrow and nodded. She took another bite of apple and sighed heavily. "So what did you want to say?"

Nicholas immediately became somber and a tight knot formed in her belly. She slipped one hand under the table and clenched it into a tight fist as she readied herself for more of his harsh words.

She was surprised when his voice came out strained and trembling. "I wanted to say," he cleared his throat, "I wanted to say I'm sorry for the way I've been treating you."

Melanie was ready with a tart response, but the sheen of tears in Nicholas's eyes stilled her tongue. The apple Melanie had just swallowed suddenly felt stuck in her throat.

"What's changed your mind?"

Nicholas hunched his shoulders and looked down at his lap. Melanie mused silently to herself that if he wasn't such a large bulk of a man he'd look exactly like a naughty school boy. The thought softened a small corner of her heart and she began picking at the bread and cheese on her plate hoping she looked unaffected.

Nicholas cleared his throat. "I don't think I've had a change of mind." Melanie rolled her eyes. She knew he'd never apologize. Before she could respond he continued. "But rather, I think it's been a change of heart."

Melanie's brow came up in a gathered peak. "What's that supposed to mean?"

Nicholas looked up at her. "Several people have pointed out to me that I've been very, very wrong." He sighed and ran a hand through his hair. "Now I have this constant pain," he pointed to his chest, "in my heart. I feel horrible for the way I've treated you. I feel even worse for what I said in the barn."

Tears stung Melanie's eyes, but she willed them back. She suppressed the warmth trying to break free from the fortress surrounding her heart by reminding herself that men often said things to get what they wanted. The reminder helped her sniff the air haughtily, but instead of her prepared scathing hot words tumbling from her lips, something else came out.

"You know, I used to be treated like a lady. I just wanted to be treated like one once again." She gasped, surprised at the confession and dug her nail into the soft flesh of her palm while she waited for his reaction.

Nicholas's eyes darkened and he lowered his head again. "I realize that now." He lifted his eyes to her face. "Can you please forgive my self-righteous attitude and my horrible treatment of you?"

Melanie dug her nail deeper into her skin hoping the pain would help her remember all the evil men were capable of and not fall for what was surely just a trap. Her mind scrambled for something to say, something ice cold and short. Before she could think of anything, her mouth took on a mind of its own once again.

"You should know why someone does something before you go around condemning them."

Nicholas's head snapped up and his words rushed out in a jumbled fury. "Pappy's been saying the exact same thing. He said something happened, but he wouldn't tell me much more than that. Then he made me sleep under the wagon and I heard you talking. You mentioned two men. What did they do to you?" His last question came out as more of a growl that made Melanie jump.

Her heart began racing as she tried to process everything he had blurted. Just how much had Pappy told him? And if he slept under the wagon and heard her talking about two men, then surely he heard all of the other things she had whispered to the night. Her heart slammed against her ribs and her palms began to sweat. Nicholas continued talking as if he could hear her very thoughts.

"I heard every rotten thing you said about yourself and it nearly tore my heart apart to know I caused some of that pain." He paused for so long Melanie thought he was through talking. She looked up and his intense gaze stared back at her. His voice was thick and low. "Melanie, I'm so sorry."

Her bottom lip began to tremble so she quickly tucked it between her teeth. This man was tearing the fortress from around her heart brick by brick. A sob broke through her lips and she slapped a hand over her mouth and closed her eyes tightly to keep the gathering tears from falling.

Nick sprang out of his chair and knelt at Melanie's side when another ragged sob broke through the hand clasped over her mouth. He had just decided to leave her to contemplate his apology, when the beautiful spitfire began to fall to pieces before his very eyes. Nick reached under the table to grasp her clenched hands.

He tried to speak softly and gently despite the urgent need to know what troubled her. "I'm here if you need to talk." He paused, not quite sure she had heard and then repeated himself. "I'm here for you, Melanie."

The fallen beauty sniffed and looked at him with eyes filled with sorrow and pain. She opened her mouth to speak and her voice croaked with raw pain. "I didn't want to work in a brothel."

Nick squeezed her hands. "I remember you said you were helping a friend."

Melanie closed her eyes as she nodded. "Charlotte. She took me in after Jonathan left me."

"Who's Jonathan?"

"He was my fiancé."

Nicholas tried to hold back the shock, horror, and grief playing across his face as Melanie told her story of heartache and abuse. He clenched his hands at his sides into tight fists when she described how her selfish fiancé left her penniless. He ground his teeth together as she described a man she met soon afterward. Thus far she had described him as a gentleman, a dream come true, but Nicholas knew better. If she was telling him about this man, then he must surely have hurt her. In this instance, Nick hated being correct.

Melanie choked as she tried to describe the night this new gentleman made a flagitious claim to her body, her mind, and her soul. He couldn't bear to watch this beautiful woman relive the night she was violated. Before she could continue with her modest attempt at discreetly describing such an incident, Nick gently squeezed her good hand.

Melanie's shoulders slumped forward and she began weeping. Concern shot through Nick's body when Melanie began quaking with deep, uncontrollable sobs. He slipped his arms around her waist and pulled her into his lap on the floor. She leaned against his chest and tucked her head beneath his chin. Nick wrapped his arms protectively around her and gently rocked from side to side.

"Shh, now. It wasn't your fault. You were just trying to survive." He kissed the top of her head and brushed stray curls from her face. "You were trying to take care of Charlotte the best way you knew how."

As he spoke words of assurance and comfort to Melanie, any lingering shreds of doubt about her character faded away. He fully realized now Melanie hadn't just been trying to live. She had been fighting to protect her friend. As he rocked back and forth with the weeping angel in his arms his heart vowed to always protect her.

After several long minutes Melanie's tears began to abate and she stirred in Nick's arms. Not yet willing to let her go, he pulled her tighter to his chest. She sniffled once and murmured against his chest.

"I never should have come here."

Nick grabbed her tightly and craned his neck so he could peer down into her sodden face. "I'm glad you came here. I'm glad I met you, Melanie Brooks."

Before he could stop himself Nick lowered his mouth to hers. He barely heard her softly gasp in surprise, his need to kiss away all her pain so fervent.

Chapter 32

MELANIE PLACED HER fingertips to her mouth. Nearly three weeks later and her lips still tingled from Nick's sudden kiss. Never had she expected a man's mouth to ever feel so gentle. She felt slightly embarrassed at how she had clutched the front of his shirt, pulling him closer, and holding him there. Yet she wouldn't trade that moment in the kitchen, locked in his embrace, for anything.

A loud clatter sounded from behind and caused Melanie to whirl around. Esther was kneeling on the ground trying to wipe up scrambled eggs.

"Esther, are you OK?"

"Yes, I just lost my grip on the skillet and dropped it." The girl was frantically trying to scrape the eggs off the floor and scoop them back into the cast iron skillet. "I'm so sorry, I didn't think it'd be so heavy."

Melanie chuckled and knelt beside her to help clean up the mess. "Accidents happen. We'll just fry up some extra bacon and pancakes."

Esther wiped her forehead with the back of her hand. "How do you keep up with all these hungry men?"

Melanie gripped the skillet's handle tightly with her good hand and placed it on the countertop, then heaved herself up. "Well, before I had you, there was Pappy. I'm sure if we asked he'd still be agreeable to helping."

Esther sprang back to her feet. "No, ma'am. I promised to help and I'll do whatever you ask. I plan on earning my keep."

Melanie turned back to the stove and removed the cooked pancakes, then spooned out more batter onto the hot griddle. "You're already doing more than enough to help me."

The first of the boys came stomping through the yard to the back door. "Woo-wee, it sure does smell good in there."

Melanie quickly flipped the last of the pancakes and pressed them down with the back of her spatula to help them cook faster. Esther was rustling around in the pantry. "Well, hurry up now; we've got some hungry men headed our way."

Esther popped out with a jar of maple syrup. "Yes, Miss Melanie."

Douglas was the first man in the kitchen. He removed his hat and smiled hello at Esther. Esther paused and smiled bashfully at him before hurrying to the table with the syrup.

Melanie jumped when a work-roughened hand gently cupped her elbow. "Good morning, Melanie." Nick stood so close his breath tickled the stray curls at the nape of her neck.

Melanie swallowed. "Good morning."

Nick released her elbow and strode over to the long table. With Esther now sitting immediately to her right, Nick sat a seat further away from her. She wasn't sure why, but missed having his large frame seated next to her. She pushed the thought away and flipped the last pancakes onto a large serving plate, then hurried over to the table. As always, Pappy said grace and breakfast commenced.

As the last of the pancakes and bacon disappeared, Sam rose from where he had been curled at her feet and growled. The hair on the back of his neck rose and he crept slowly toward the back door. Everyone stopped eating and stared at him.

Melanie rose from the table and grabbed up her Winchester leaning against the doorjamb. "What is it, boy?"

Sam began pawing at the back door. He looked back at Melanie and began to whine. Melanie lifted her Winchester with her good hand and balanced the barrel over her cast. She figured if she had to she'd do alright firing this way. Melanie lowered her rifle and turned back to the table, "Jimmy and Ron, come with me. Pappy, mind helping Esther clean up?"

Esther straightened in her chair. "I don't mind cleaning up by myself."

Nick stood up and absentmindedly laid a hand over the pistol on his hip. "Mind your boss." It was the gentlest thing he could think to say without alarming the girl. Besides, he had bigger problems to think about than hurting the girl's feelings. He didn't want Melanie going outside to take a look around, but he knew it was futile arguing with her. The best way he could protect her was to go with her.

Nick glanced back at Pappy before walking out the back door. Pappy nodded once toward Melanie and Nick knew he was asking him to watch over her. Nick touched the brim of his hat, then followed Melanie and Sam down the back porch.

Back of the house there was mainly flat land. There weren't that many places a man could duck low and creep up on them. Nick began praying fervently that if there was someone or something out there God would protect them all.

Pappy rubbed the sides of his jaw. The rest of the boys still sat silently around the table, their breakfast forgotten, their ears tuned for gunfire, and their fingers itching to reach for their weapons. Pappy cleared his throat. "Boys, go start chores."

He rose from the table and began stacking Melanie and Nicholas's plates atop his own. He scraped off the leftover food into the slop bucket and piled the dishes into the sink. The cowhands followed suit. Esther remained seated at the table, staring out the numerous windows with eyes wide and mouth gaping.

Pappy didn't want her to be frightened and thought it best to busy her mind with work. "Come on, Esther, you've got to help this old man with the kitchen chores." Her eyes remained glued to the windows. "Sam probably just smelled an animal."

She turned her worried gaze to him. "You really think so?"

Pappy nodded. "Yup. Happens all the time. My Little Missy is just a mite jumpy is all."

Douglas approached and leaned close to Pappy as he lowered his dishes into the sink. "Maybe so, but I think I'll help in the kitchen just in case."

Pappy wasn't going to argue with the young man, so he just nodded. When Esther finally stood and began helping clean the aftermath of breakfast, Pappy offered her a bright smile. Besides the occasional murmured exchange of words between Esther and Douglas, the three of them worked in silence.

Pappy was scrubbing a cast iron skillet when a creak on the front porch caught his attention. Any other day he'd think it was one of the boys coming in for a cool glass of lemonade, but a morning like this a man just couldn't be sure. There it was again, the slow creaking of wood from the front porch. Pappy glanced at Douglas and the boy must have heard it too, for he was looking down the hall with his hand already on his six-shooter.

"Douglas, put Esther down in the pantry cellar."

Douglas quickly grabbed Esther's elbow and led her toward the pantry. He lifted the cellar door and helped Esther inside before closing it on top of her and rolling a large barrel over the door.

Together, Pappy and Douglas crept down the long hallway toward the front door. They removed their six-shooters as they each took a side of the door. Douglas cast Pappy a wary look when they heard the creaking of wood again. Someone was definitely nosing about on the front porch. Pappy gripped the doorknob in one hand and aimed his six-shooter in front of him with the other. He quickly opened the door and rushed out, Douglas hot on his heels. A blur of movement to the left caught his attention and he whirled around ready to shoot the lowlife.

"Pig?"

Pappy holstered his six-shooter and slapped his knee in a fit of laughter. Douglas looked just as baffled. Pappy slapped the young man on the shoulder. "You go get that girl out of the cellar. I'll take this runaway back to the barn."

Chapter 33

MELANIE HAD BEEN relieved the other day when all they found was a loose pig wondering around the property, but something hadn't felt right ever since that morning. When she worked in the kitchen, pulled weeds in the garden, rode Brooke around the property, or even picked fruit from the orchard, she had constantly felt like someone was watching her. Maybe she was just being paranoid. Or maybe someone really was out there watching. Either way, she wasn't taking chances. That's why this morning as she made the day's trek to town for supplies she took Ron, Jimmy, Mitch, Pappy, and—to her unexpected pleasure—Nick had volunteered to come as well.

As she pulled her wagon to a stop in front of the general store, she handed Pappy a list of items they needed. "I'll meet you back here in about an hour."

Pappy gave her a wary look, but bid her farewell and Melanie started making her way toward the humble looking church in the middle of town. Before she could even climb the front porch steps, Louisa Merryweather swung the door wide open.

"I've been waiting for you to come visit!"

Melanie couldn't help but laugh. "Well today you can stop waiting."

Louisa quickly ushered her in to a scarcely furnished yet comfortable sitting room. "So how have you been?" She glanced down at Melanie's bandaged arm. "Does it still hurt?"

Melanie was touched by Louisa's sincere concern. "Not at all. If it weren't for this bulky bandage I'm sure I'd forget all about it."

"And have you been thinking about what we talked about last time you were in town?"

Melanie swallowed. Every day and night she had thought of their conversation. "I have." Melanie shook her head. "Louisa, I don't want to offend you, but I don't understand how a ..."

Louisa waved her hand in the air. "I know; I couldn't believe it myself at first. My husband first saw me strolling down the street. He said the moment he saw me God spoke and told him to marry me. I told him all about my *business* but he said it didn't matter."

Melanie bit her lip. "And you believed him?"

Louisa leaned forward and looked Melanie in the eye. "Sweetheart, even after all I had done, I still knew deep in my heart I deserved something better."

Tears smarted in Melanie's eyes, but she blinked them back and tried to smile. A question burned its way up her throat and she blurted out, "But why?"

"Because one time, someone told me how God was the King and I was His daughter. Do you know what that makes me? That makes me a princess!" Louisa shook her head as she smiled. "I clung to that all the years I had to work in that dump and when I met Tom, he just had to nurture it. And he did and still does. Every day."

Melanie took a deep breath to steady her quaking emotions. If this former prostitute could find redemption, love, and happiness then maybe, just maybe, she could too.

For the next hour Melanie and Louisa talked about recent events and news. Louisa updated her on all of the town's happenings and Melanie tried to describe what it was like working a ranch full of men. As the hour came to a close, Melanie rose to leave, knowing Pappy would worry if she was late. Before she could thank Louisa for the talk, her new friend grabbed her upper arms and held her at arm's length.

"Melanie, dear, I believe it's time we find you something else to wear."

Melanie looked down at the front of her dress. "I guess it is rather worn."

Louisa huffed. "I'm not talking about the wear and tear. Come on, I think I have something."

Melanie warily followed Louisa up the stairs and down a short hall into a bedroom. Louisa opened a trunk at the foot of the bed and rummaged around until she pulled out a dark red dress. She shoved it into Melanie's arms.

"Try that on."

Before Melanie could protest, Louisa flounced out of the bedroom and shut the door behind her. Melanie sighed. She might as well just try the dress on. Melanie turned her back to the mirror and unbuttoned her gray work dress. As she stood in her shift she held up the modest red dress. It was a beautiful dress but the waist seemed so small she was sure it wouldn't fit. She sighed and pulled the dress on over her head.

Melanie dropped the hem of the dress and was shocked to feel the material reach her ankles. She took a deep breath and turned around to the mirror.

Melanie didn't try to stop the smile that was slowly spreading across her face. She turned from side to side, gazing at her reflection in the mirror astonished, that the beautiful red dress lay smoothly across her body. She had long ago covered up the mirror in her room, too disgusted with her body to look at it anymore. Melanie was so absorbed with staring at her reflection that she didn't even hear Louisa come back in.

"My goodness, don't you just look wonderful!"

Melanie spun around, surprised and embarrassed. "I had no idea my dresses were looking so bad."

Louisa bent back over the open trunk and pulled out several more dresses. "Here, take these too."

Melanie pushed the offered dresses away. "Oh, no, I couldn't."

Louisa shoved the dresses into Melanie's arms. "You can and you will. Every princess needs to feel good about herself."

Louisa linked her arm through Melanie's and led the way downstairs. While Louisa shoved the dresses into a sack Melanie wiped at the tears brimming her eyes. Melanie smoothed down the front of her new red dress. "Are you sure, Louisa?"

Louisa kissed her cheek and smiled. "Positive. You deserve to receive back some of what you give."

Melanie exhaled a shaky breath and embraced her friend. "Thank you."

As Melanie approached her wagon still sitting outside the general store she saw Pappy shading his eyes and squinting in her direction. Melanie nervously bit her lip as she tried to keep walking calmly toward the wagon. When she was a few feet away Pappy climbed down and grabbed her arm.

"Well, well, Little Missy, don't you look pretty."

Melanie tried a wobbly smile. "Thank you, Pappy."

Her other cowhands were still loading the last of their supplies in the back of the wagon. Nicholas came out of the general store carrying a large crate and stopped mid-step. A slow smile stretched across his face as his gaze swept up and down her body, making her squirm. Melanie wrung her fingers around the ties on the sack holding her new dresses.

Nick had noticed her dresses were looking bigger, but he hadn't expected her to be so small. She was still larger than other women and Nick expected, or at least he hoped, that she'd never be one of those cinched-waisted ladies a man could hold onto with just one hand. Those women seemed too fragile to him. He was always afraid if he ended up with a petite little thing he'd break her like one of Melanie's little china cups.

Nick shoved the crate he was carrying into Jimmy's passing arms and stepped toward Melanie. He gently held her good hand and lifted it to his lips. "Melanie Brooks, you're the most beautiful woman I know."

He smiled as her cheeks flushed bright red and she stammered for something to say. "That's v-very kind of you to say."

Ever since Nick had stolen a kiss with Melanie curled up in his lap on the kitchen floor, he had wracked his brain for ways to show this woman he cared. He complimented her; wrote her messages with bits of poetry he got from a book. Twice he brought her bouquets of flowers from her orchard, but never had she turned into the stuttering pool of femininity she was now.

Over her head Nick caught a glimpse of two men. One was leaning against the porch post of the barber shop with the other standing next to him. Was it his imagination or were those men staring at him? Nick held his smile pasted in place, he didn't want to ruin this shared moment with Melanie, but these men seemed out of place. As he glanced up again he got a clear look at both of them. The one leaning against the porch post was tall and lean with dark hair. The other was short and stocky with black hair and dark eyes. And neither were staring at Nick. They were staring at Melanie.

Nick frowned. Who were these men? Someone from her past? Nick stood to his full height. If these men thought they could dandy around with Melanie they had another think coming to them. He reached his arm out to protectively wrap around Melanie's shoulders, but she no longer stood right in front of him. He was so consumed with thoughts of who these men were that he hadn't noticed Melanie step away and was now staring right back at the men across the street. Nick's eyebrows slammed together and he clenched his jaw. Just who were they?

Melanie's heart pounded inside of her chest and she whirled around. The confused frustration on Nick's face was undeniable. His eyes darted from her to the men across the street. She sighed. Whatever she had felt growing between them, bringing them closer, would have to wait. The butterflies that had occupied her stomach when Nick kissed her hand had long since flown away and the space was now filled with a tight knot. She had been right. Trouble was in town and she wouldn't put it past those men across the street to have been stalking around on her property for the past several days. What she couldn't figure out was why they were together.

Melanie threw her sack of dresses into the back of the wagon. It seems the men staring at her from across the street had caught the attention of all the ranch hands that rode with her to town. She allowed the old memories to flood her mind so the solid fortress would rise up around her heart again, giving her the strength and determination to get home safely. She was surprised at how hard it had become. No longer did her heart feel like a frosted fortress of stone and ice, but it was, instead, a weak shack of twigs.

"Let's get home."

Her cowhands obediently mounted their horses, but none of them took their eyes off the men across the street. Melanie cringed. Nick grabbed her hand and tucked it securely in his arm, then led her around to the wagon. He put his hands on her waist and lifted her up to the wagon. She tried to smile down at him, but his focus was on the men across the street. Melanie took a deep breath.

Pappy quickly climbed up next to her but when he reached for the reins she snatched them out of his reach. She released the brake and clicked the geldings into motion. She glanced over at the stocky man on the porch and his smile broadened. He jumped off the boardwalk and jogged toward the wagon, waving his hand in the air.

"Mel! Hey Mel!"

Pappy elbowed her. "Someone you know?"

Melanie snorted. "Not anymore." She slapped the reins across the geldings' backs to get them to run. "Yah, get up boys, yah."

She chanced a glance over her shoulder and saw the stocky man standing in a cloud of dust, panting to catch his breath. The other man pushed off from the porch post and strolled across the street to the saloon, laughing the entire way.

Melanie's palms began to sweat. She just had to get home. She'd be safe at home.

Chapter 34

IT HAD BEEN two days since they had gone to town and Melanie hadn't said a single word to anyone. She hurried through her chores with her head down and jumped at the slightest noise. There was no doubt in Pappy's mind that whoever those men from town were, Melanie knew them—and what's more she was afraid of them. She'd reverted back to keeping her Winchester at her side at all times. Her behavior was putting all the boys on edge.

A twig snapped and Pappy whirled around with his six-shooter ready. A squirrel scampered across the yard and into a tree. Pappy sighed and tried to chuckle. Apparently he was a little jumpy as well.

Behind him the screen door opened and shut. "Pappy?"

His ward stood there wearing a pretty new green dress the preacher's wife had given her. She was wringing her hands in her apron. Pappy sighed. *Please God, give me wisdom.*

Pappy wrapped his arm around her shoulders. "Let's go talk in front of the fire." She nodded and allowed him to lead her back inside.

Nicholas was sitting in Old Brooks' seat, his eyes staring blankly at the fire. Pappy cleared his throat. "Mind giving us some pri-"

Melanie cut him short. "No, I want him here."

Nick practically jumped to his feet when she spoke. He grabbed up Melanie's hands and kissed them both. Pappy was touched by the gentle love he had seen blossoming in his nephew's heart. As Nicholas led Melanie to her rocking chair Pappy got comfortable in his chair for what he felt was going to be a long talk.

Pappy was so nervous about what was on Melanie's mind he just cut right to the chase. "Well, Little Missy, what is it you want to tell Pappy? I'm all ears."

Melanie took a deep, shuddering breath. Nick moved his chair closer and leaned over to hold her hand. She offered him a friendly smile, then looked back to Pappy.

"Those men in town the other day, I know them." Her throat suddenly felt like it was coated with thick sap. Her hands began to shake and she felt Nick squeeze her good hand. A bead of sweat rolled down her spine. "The stocky man, that was," she tried to clear her throat, "that was Jonathan."

Nick quickly stood from his chair and paced over to the window. He ran his hands through his hair. "Do you know the man who was with him?"

Her voice wobbled as she tried to say his name. A knot formed in her throat and she was barely able to whisper past it. "Tom."

Nick whirled around from the window. Anger Melanie had never seen before etched deep grooves in his face. "Tom? The Tom that …"

Melanie covered her face with her good hand. "Yes, yes, yes, *that* Tom and *that* Jonathan." The old humiliation and shame welled up inside her chest. She looked quickly between Pappy and Nicholas. "I've been so scared. I never thought I'd ever see either of them again. Let alone *together*! What if they come here?"

Melanie began to shake. How did Jonathan and Tom know each other? Why were they both here? It was all too overwhelming. Nick resumed his seat next to her and reached over to squeeze her good hand. The deep grooves of anger had softened and were replaced with concern.

"You're not alone, Melanie."

"You'll always have us, Little Missy, but most of all you'll always have Christ."

Warm tears began spilling down her cheeks. "How can you be so sure? After everything I did, I deserve whatever they have in store for me."

Nick hesitated only briefly before Pappy nodded at him, silently encouraging him. Nick lifted Melanie's hand and pressed the soft flesh of her palm against his bristled cheek. "You know, Melanie, a wise old man once told me something that changed my life."

Even with her heart and mind in a state of chaos his sweetheart didn't miss a beat. She sniffled. "What did Pappy say?"

Nick smiled. "That long ago there lived a man who could see the sins of mankind for thousands of years into the future." Nick guided Melanie's hand from his cheek to his lips. He gently kissed her palm. "This man, He saw a beautiful young woman mistreated by men and left with no other option but prostitution. He saw her heart hardened into stone because of it, and in turn His own heart broke. As this man looked into the future and saw this beautiful woman nearly devoured by the evil of this world, He declared, 'This is why I must die.'"

Melanie gasped and Nick could feel her body tremble. He glanced at Pappy but his eyes were closed and his lips moved in an inaudible prayer. Nick looked lovingly into Melanie's eyes.

"Jesus already died for you. He already paid the price for your freedom just as you paid for Esther's. Why continue refusing a gift that has already been paid in full? It's like allowing your most valued possession to collect dust in a locked trunk."

Tears streaked her face and her lips trembled as she tried to speak. "Wh-h-at do I d-do?"

Nick bowed his head as his heart burst with a prayer of thanksgiving. He looked back at Melanie and gently folded his hands around hers. "Just repeat after me." Nick bowed his head again and as he closed his eyes Pappy gripped his shoulder. Nick cleared his throat of the thick emotion clogging his voice. "Heavenly Father, I know that I'm a sinner and I need a Savior." Melanie's sweet voice whispered the words after him. "Please come into my heart and be my Lord and Savior for the rest of my days. In Jesus' name I pray, Amen."

"In Jesus' name I pray, Amen." Melanie's voice finished strong and she looked up at Nick with a smile spreading across her face. She leaned forward and softly kissed his cheek. Before she pulled away she whispered in his ear, "Thank you."

Nick's heart swelled anew with love. He made a mental note to thank Pappy for straightening him out. If he hadn't taken the blinders from his eyes he would still be mistreating Melanie.

If that were the case, then who knew if she would have ever accepted Christ as her Savior? Nick shuddered at the thought of her soul forever being lost because of his self-righteous attitude.

Pappy quickly stood and outstretched his arms. "Glory! Halleluiah! Little Missy give me a hug!"

Melanie stood up and laughed. She hugged him tightly around his waist. "Oh, Pappy, thank you. You could have given up on me, but you didn't."

He leaned down and kissed the top of her head. "I could never give up on you, Little Missy." Tears began to gather in the corners of his eyes. He reached up with one hand to wipe them away. "Land sakes, I must be turning into a water pump in my old age."

His nephew laughed as he wiped tears from his own eyes. "No I don't think it's old age, Paps. I think it's Melanie." Melanie loosened her grip and turned toward his nephew. "I think she makes us love deeper than we ever thought imaginable."

Pappy smiled. "Here's to that." He leaned down and kissed Melanie's cheek. As he did the small clock on top of the mantel chimed ten o'clock. "Woo, time sure does fly when you're praying the night away. We better all turn in for the night."

They all said their goodnights and then Nicholas walked out the front toward the bunkhouse. Pappy urged Melanie to go on upstairs. "I'll turn out the lights and lock the doors."

She smiled and kissed his cheek. "Thank you, Pappy."

Melanie rolled into bed and pulled her yellow quilt up to her chin. Her stomach had that butterfly feeling again and her heart felt light and free. If she didn't know better she'd think she floated up the stairs on a cloud. She pulled the yellow quilt up over her mouth to stifle a giggle.

Then she sighed. Such a simple prayer and yet she felt completely changed. She felt like someone had stripped a layer of grime from her very soul and in its place was a gleaming gold surface. She had to write her friends at Minnie's and tell them all of this glorious feeling and how easy it was to receive.

Chapter 35

ELANIE NEARLY DANCED across her kitchen floor the next morning as she prepared breakfast. Esther was setting the table and Melanie was whipping up scrambled eggs. Her heart felt so full of light and joy she couldn't help but hum as she worked. As her hungry cowhands marched into the kitchen, Esther and Melanie busied themselves with setting out platters of scrambled eggs, sausage, biscuits, a bowl full of gravy, fried potatoes, a crock of butter, two jars of preserves, a jug of milk, and the coffee pot.

As everyone took their seat Melanie's brow furrowed. "Where's Ron and Jimmy?"

"They were just checking on something real quick. They said to start without them."

Melanie nodded and Pappy took his cue to say grace. The men were passing platters of food around when Ron and Jimmy marched into the kitchen.

Ron nodded toward Melanie. "Mornin', boss. Sorry we're late." The two brothers took their seats and filled their plates with breakfast. Everyone had gone silent and was looking expectantly at the pair. Finally, Jimmy elbowed Ron in the ribs. Ron cleared his throat. "Boss, we saw some tracks. I thought it was just one set of footprints, but Jimmy, he's a better tracker, said it was definitely two."

Jonathan and Tom. Melanie willed herself to remain calm. She delicately dabbed her lips with her napkin, then neatly folded it next to her plate. Praying was new to her but she silently asked God to give her strength. "Boys, I think we're in for some trouble."

An immediate ruckus broke out around the table as each man tried to talk over the other.

"Who would come lurking around like that?"

"Yeah, why not just come up and state their business?"

"Maybe they're horse thieves!"

Mitch snorted. "It's probably those fellows from town we told you about."

Esther gasped and held a thin hand to her lips. "There was trouble in town?"

Melanie reached over and patted Esther's hand. "No trouble, just some curious fellows I used to know." Melanie looked around the table. Each man was now looking at her. Waiting for her to explain. Waiting for her to issue orders. What were Jonathan and Tom up to? What if they wanted to hurt her? How had they even found her? The first tremor of fear quaked through Melanie's heart.

Strong hands gripped her shoulders and she jumped. Nick's voice boomed strong and steady from behind her. "There were two men. One is short and stocky with black hair and dark eyes. The other is tall and lean with dark hair. They're dangerous con-men. From here on out, I want a man at the front door and a man at the back door. We'll rotate night watches. If the ladies need to leave the house two men will go with them. I want four men out watching the cattle. As for the rest of you, chores are now done in pairs."

Nick could feel Melanie's shoulders trembling beneath his hands. He gently squeezed her shoulders to remind her she wasn't alone. Every man around the table stared up at him in silence. Finally one of the cowhands spoke up.

"Why don't we go get the sheriff?"

Nick shook his head. "It's a day's ride to town and another day to ride back out. And that's assuming the sheriff could come right away. I'm thinking that if these boys have anything planned, they'll do it sooner than that."

Nick appointed two men to keep watch on the front and back porches of the house, then another four to ride out and camp with the cattle. He asked that the rest of the cowhands check on the livestock in the barn and make sure they were secure. Lastly, he directed each man to fire two shots if there was trouble.

After the men had dispersed to do as Nick had told them, Esther and Pappy scrambled around the kitchen gathering supplies for the four cowhands camping with the cattle. Melanie sat silently at the table.

Nick sat next to her and leaned close. "You OK, sweetheart?"

She looked up at him with tear-rimmed eyes. "I'm trying to trust in God but it's hard. I'm scared. What if one of the boys gets hurt?"

Nick sighed and reached to hold her good hand. "Don't you ever worry about yourself?"

Melanie shrugged. "I'm responsible for these men. They're my employees," Melanie's voice broke, "my friends. If something happened to them because of my past," she shook her head, "I'm not sure I could handle that."

Nick tucked a curl back behind her ear. "You're the most caring woman I've ever met." Nick leaned forward and gently kissed her lips. His heart rang with joy when she leaned forward to return his kiss. "I love you, Melanie. I always will." Nick wasn't sure where the proclamation came from. He loved Melanie with all his heart and one day he'd ask her to be his bride. But this was not the way or place he had imagined telling his sweetheart about the love he held in his heart for her.

Nick leaned forward to kiss Melanie again, but she leaned away from him. She cast her gaze to her lap and refused to look up at him. She sniffled. "I'm sorry, Nicholas, I'm just not ready."

Nick fought the doubt away with his newly reinforced faith. He knew in his heart she loved him too. He knew one day they would marry and he prayed God would bless them with a houseful of children. But in the meantime, he understood she was scared and uncertain.

Nick lifted her good hand and kissed her palm. "Love is patient, Melanie. I just wanted you to know that you're loved." He kissed her palm again and closed her fingers on the soft flesh. "Hold onto that in the meantime."

Melanie leaned back and held the hand he kissed to her heart. He recognized the love shining in her eyes and it filled his heart with joy. He pushed up from his chair and headed outside, squeezing Melanie's shoulder one last time as he walked behind her.

Melanie took a deep breath to steady her nerves. The only other man who had said he loved her had been Jonathan. And he left her penniless. She hated comparing Nick to Jonathan but her past was too real a reminder that sometimes love didn't last.

Melanie took another deep breath. Her feelings for Nicholas would just have to wait. Right now two horrible men from her past were lurking around her property. Watching her. Watching her friends. Planning to do—what? A loud crash made her jump up out of her chair. She grabbed her rifle and twirled toward the sound of the crash, her rifle leveled over her bandaged arm.

Esther shrieked and threw her hands in the air. "Sorry, Miss Melanie, I dropped some plates."

Pappy lowered Esther's hands and patted her shoulder. "It's OK, kiddo, Melanie is just on edge. Go get a bucket to throw this glass in."

Esther hurried toward the pantry and Melanie lowered her rifle. She ran a hand down her face. "I'm sorry Esther, I didn't mean to scare you."

The girl was visibly shaking. "I know. This whole business scares me."

Melanie put down her rifle and walked over to the girl. She wrapped Esther in a tight embrace. "I know, I'm scared too. But you know what?" Melanie took a deep breath. "God is with us."

Chapter 36

HE ENTIRE DAY had passed in a cloud of tension. The men walked around with their hands constantly on their pistols. Melanie and Esther stayed huddled in the sitting room, Melanie's rifle on her lap. Sam seemed to sense the tension and never left Melanie's side. Melanie had fetched Esther the derringer she brought with her from Minnie's and instructed the girl to keep it in her pocket at all times. Esther was too worked up to help with supper, so Melanie sent her upstairs to rest.

Nick and Pappy came in several times throughout the day to check on them. Every time Nicholas held her hand or squeezed her shoulder an electric jolt shot through her body. His reassuring touches comforted her in a way she had never felt before.

For dinner Esther and Melanie made a thick stew of vegetables and a rabbit Nick had brought in after supper. Esther made two batches of Melanie's never fail biscuits and Melanie used some of their canned pie filling to make an apple pie. The two men stationed at the front and back doors ate their dinner outside. Nick was adamant that the house be watched constantly. Dinner was a quiet, somber meal and Melanie missed the riotous, friendly banter of her cowhands. As everyone ate their pie and drank the last of the coffee, Nick cleared his throat to get everyone's attention.

"Tonight Mitch and I will hold first watch, then Ron and Jimmy. Douglas, I want you to sleep in the barn just in case they have plans to mess with the horses. The rest of you can sleep in the bunkhouse like normal."

Melanie put down her fork with too much force and the clang of silver on wood echoed in the large kitchen. Every face pivoted in her direction. She shook her head vehemently. "Something just doesn't feel right. Nick, Mitch, Ron, and Jimmy will take their shifts tonight. Other than that I want everyone in this house. No barn. No bunkhouse." She jabbed her finger down onto the wooden table top. "In this house."

Several jaws dropped and a few cheeks flushed pink as others rubbed the backs of their necks. "You want us to sleep in the house?"

"With you women?"

Melanie nodded. "Something doesn't feel right. Like it or not everyone is sleeping in this house tonight."

Stunned faces pivoted back to Nick. He shrugged. "You heard the boss."

After Esther and Melanie cleaned up the kitchen they instructed the men on moving the furniture up against the walls. They brought in their pillows and blankets from the bunkhouse and staked out a spot on the floor to sleep. As they all sat gathered in the crowded sitting room waiting to go to bed, Mitch opened the front door and hollered in.

"Boss, company."

Melanie stood and checked to make sure her rifle was loaded. Every cowhand in the room stood with his hands on his holsters. Douglas led Esther down the hall to the kitchen to put her safely in the pantry cellar. As she walked to the front door, Sam trotted along beside her. As she stepped through the door, there stood Jonathan and Tom, just as she expected. Nick was now in front, and Mitch had just rounded the corner on the wraparound porch to go watch the back. Melanie bit her lip briefly as she silently prayed for strength. Nick grabbed her elbow and his touch reassured her that she wasn't facing these two louts on her own.

She stepped to the edge of the porch. She was ready for answers. "How do you know each other?"

Jonathan smiled, revealing a crooked front tooth. Melanie wondered how she ever thought him handsome. "We ran into each other at a popular establishment. The girls were fountains of information."

Melanie breathed a sigh. "Minnie's."

Tom stepped forward and laughed. "Minnie and those girls sure did have nice things to say about you. They just went on and on about how their good friend Melanie Brooks was living it large down here in Sterling Canyon, Texas."

Jonathan removed his hat and looked bashfully down at his feet. "Mel, I've had three long, lonely years to think this over and I've decided life just ain't the same without you. The day I left was the biggest mistake I've ever made." He looked up at her and Melanie could see the deceit flash in his eyes.

Melanie guffawed. "You mean the day you left me *penniless*? No money for rent. For food. You left me without a second thought as to what might happen to me."

Jonathan stepped up onto the first porch step. Sam crept forward slowly and growled. Jonathan's smile wobbled and he stepped back, then flashed his smile back up at Melanie. He wiped sweat off his forehead with the back of his hand then outstretched it toward Melanie. "Mel, I'm begging you here, please marry me."

Silence filled the air and Melanie felt Nicholas go rigid next to her. Jonathan was proposing to her? Again? After leaving her penniless and not hearing from him for three years, he thought she'd just go running back into his arms?

Melanie snorted. She doubled over and nearly dropped her rifle as she was overtaken with a fit of laughter. She pointed at Jonathan. "Did you really think that would work? Did you really expect me to go running back into your arms?" She snapped her fingers. "Just like that?"

Jonathan looked taken aback. He stared back at her with wide eyes and a hanging jaw. Tom pulled him back by his shoulder and stepped forward. Tom placed his hand over his heart. "Melanie Brooks, if you won't consider Jonathan, then perhaps you could say yes to me."

Melanie immediately stopped laughing, stood up straight, leveled her rifle across her bandaged arm, and aimed it right at Tom. "Now I know you're joking, or at least you better be."

She saw Tom's throat wobble as he swallowed. "Melanie, you're the most beautiful woman I've ever come across." His gaze swept up and down her body and Melanie fought the urge to vomit in front of them all.

Nick stepped forward and blocked her with his body. She side-stepped so she could keep her rifle on Tom. Nick cocked his hip as if he were having a real comfortable conversation with

Pappy. His hand slowly slid to his holster. "You boys might want to head back to town."

Jonathan guffawed. "Oh yeah, cowboy, or what? You gonna shoot us? You'll hang for murder."

Melanie huffed. "You're trespassing; we have every right to shoot you."

Tom began stepping backward. "Come on, Jon, let's go."

Jonathan reluctantly followed Tom. A few yards away Jonathan turned back and yelled, "You'll regret this Melanie Brooks." He shook his fist in the air. "You'll regret this for the rest of your life."

When they were far enough away to not be a threat Nick turned around. He pushed her still-raised rifle down and pulled her into his arms. Melanie wrapped her arms around his waist and relished the feel of his strong arms around her. He had stood by her. He had protected her. Her heart slowed its beating and time seemed to stand completely still. It was just her and Nicholas, locked in each other's embrace.

Melanie tilted her head back. "Kiss me."

Nicholas gently cupped her face in his warm hands and lowered his head to hers. "I love you, Melanie." Her heart began beating again and a smile blossomed across her lips against her will. Nick brought his lips to hers and gently kissed her with all the love she knew he held in his heart.

Chapter 37

MELANIE HANDED NICK a warm cup of coffee. He had told her to go to sleep but she insisted she wasn't tired. She kept saying she knew something was going to happen tonight. Nick kissed her forehead as he accepted the cup of coffee.

"You sure you don't want to try and sleep?"

She smiled. "Who can sleep? The boys are all inside playing cards. Esther is cleaning out the mending basket. Pappy is whittling." She sighed and looked up at him with those warm honeyed eyes of hers. "Do you think I'm overreacting?"

Nick cupped her cheek in his palm. His hand was so large his fingers spanned out against her neck and he could feel her pulse beating rapidly. "No, I trust your instincts." He saw her shiver and his brow furrowed. "It's cold out here. You should go back inside."

She smiled up at him and mock saluted. "Yes, sir."

He winked down at her. "That's my girl."

Melanie lay curled in her uncle's old chair, Sam lay in front of her on the floor. She had dozed off, but Sam's whining woke her. She reached down to pet the dog. "What's wrong, boy?"

Pappy was hunched over in his chair asleep. Esther was sprawled out on a pallet in front of the fireplace. The cowhands were all in the parlor across the hall trying to sleep. Sam rubbed his head against her leg and whined again. She patted his head. "OK, I'm getting up." Melanie picked up her rifle and quietly crept out the back door to where Nick was on watch.

Nick was leaning against the porch post scanning the yard. She whispered across the pitch black night. "Nick."

He turned toward her. "I think I heard something."

Melanie worried her lip between her teeth. "Sam is uneasy."

Jimmy came out the back door just then for his turn at watch. He nodded at them both. "Boss. Nick."

Nick turned back toward the yard. "I thought I heard something, and Melanie says Sam is acting uneasy."

As if to prove it, Sam stepped toward the porch steps and growled at the pitch black night. Melanie leaned down and patted the dog. "Easy boy, it's OK."

Nick stepped down off the porch. "I'm going to go check it out."

Jimmy began to follow. "I'll come."

Melanie could barely make out Nick shaking his head. "No, stay at your post. I'll take Sam. It's probably nothing."

Melanie patted Sam's head. "Go on boy, go with Nick." The dog obediently jumped off the porch and ran ahead into darkness. Nick trotted off behind him. Melanie's stomach twisted into knots as they both disappeared from sight.

Melanie leaned over the porch railing for several long minutes, her ears straining to hear anything. As she waited something acidic assaulted her nose. She sniffed the air. "Jimmy, you smell that?"

He came to stand beside her and Melanie heard him inhale deeply. "Smoke."

Alarm filled her heart. Smoke meant fire. Her heart beat rapidly against her chest. Nick was out there. What if he was in trouble? What if he was injured? What if he was ...? Melanie swallowed hard. She couldn't bear to think the worst. She scanned the yard for any sign of Nick or Sam.

Jimmy pointed. "There."

Melanie looked in the direction he pointed. There, against the black night, glowed an angry fire quickly crawling up the side of the bunkhouse. As the flames grew she saw a tall figure dash across to the other side of the bunkhouse. Her heart told her it was Nick, and her mind told her he was chasing someone. Melanie flew off the porch and rang the large triangle with all her might. In an instant her cowhands came pouring out of the house. Figuring no explanation was needed she raced across the yard, her rifle tightly clutched in her good hand. When she reached the burning bunkhouse, Jonathan lay unconscious across the hard ground and Nick was wrestling with Tom.

Douglas and Mitch began tying Jonathan's hands. Ron and Jimmy rushed to help Nicholas. Between the three of them they quickly had Tom's hands tied in front of him and several cowhands began toting the two miscreants back toward the house. Melanie stared up at the burning bunkhouse. The structure was already engulfed in flames. No amount of water or effort could save it now. Nick wrapped his arm around her and she craned her head back to look up at him. She cringed at his swollen eye and bleeding lip. "I was so worried about you."

He tried to smile but winced with the effort. "I was worried about you, too." He chuckled. "I knew once you saw the fire you'd come running right toward it." Nick turned her away from the burning building. "It's too late to save it. The barn should be safe but we can move the animals just in case." He tugged on her good arm. "Come on, let's check on the others."

By the time they got to the house the boys had Jonathan and Tom's feet tied up and they were sitting in a corner of the kitchen. Ron, Jimmy, and Mitch sat at the table receiving gentle ministrations from Esther for minor cuts and bruises. Douglas was watching as if he were sorry he didn't have something for the girl to gently tend as well.

Melanie marched up to their captives. Anger shone in her eyes, and she asked the one question repeating itself in her mind. "Why?"

Jonathan snorted. "I said you'd be sorry."

Melanie slammed her fists onto her hips. "So because I wouldn't marry you, you burn down my bunkhouse?"

Jonathan looked up at her with a smug expression. "Yup."

Nick stepped next to her and wrapped his arm tightly around her waist. "You know, you could have killed a lot of good men tonight. If it weren't for Melanie insisting they sleep in the house tonight, they would have been in that bunkhouse. They probably wouldn't have awakened until it was too late."

Tom smiled up at her. It was the same smile he flashed at her as he walked down the hall the morning after he invaded her body. "That was the point."

Nick felt Melanie tremble. He squeezed her tighter and leaned down to whisper in her ear. "Go upstairs, they aren't worth talking to." She began pulling away, but the taller man spoke up.

"Although, I wouldn't mind settling for just killing you."

Melanie turned back toward him, her head cocked to one side. "Well, I'm so sorry I can't accommodate you."

Tom smiled. "Sure you can, beautiful."

Nick didn't see Tom pull a small pistol from his boot until it was too late. Nick was a fast draw, but Tom already had his gun drawn and aimed so Nick did the only other thing he could to protect the woman he loved.

Nick spun to face Melanie and wrapped his arms around her. As they both fell to the ground Nick felt a searing-hot pain explode across his back. Somewhere in the kitchen Esther screamed as gunfire erupted and filled the silence. Nick used his remaining strength to shift his weight to completely cover Melanie with his body. His efforts caused a breathtaking pain to slowly spread across his entire back. A life he would never get to share with Melanie flashed through his mind. He saw their wedding day; Melanie dressed in a simple calico, her hair down and curling around her face. Six strapping young boys all built just like him slowly faded into non-existence. Melanie, old and gray, sitting in her rocking chair by the fireplace tending to her basket of mending. A grief more painful than the mind-numbing pain shooting up and down his back gripped his heart in a vice. If he could give her nothing else before he died, he could give her the one thing no other man had; his love. As a tear rolled down his cheek he whispered to Melanie and prayed she heard him over the gunfire. "I love you Melanie, and I always will." A weariness Nick had never known before began sucking away the pain and he succumbed to darkness.

Chapter 38

THE DEAFENING SOUND of gunfire ceased and the air filled with an eerie silence. It felt like hours ago that Nick tackled her to the ground, told her he loved her, and then went limp. When he was conscious, his large muscular frame was heavy, but now that he was passed out he was crushing her. She gasped for a breath. "Pappy?"

"I'm here, Little Missy. Boys get him off her."

Mitch, Ron, Jimmy, and a few other cowhands worked together to gently heave Nick off of her. Melanie sat up and gasped for a breath. Nick still wasn't moving. He lay on the floor, his face a deadly gray.

Melanie choked back tears. "Nick?" She leaned over his still body and rested a hand to his cheek. "Nick? Nick please talk to me." Melanie looked up at Pappy. The old man had tears in his eyes. He slowly knelt down on the other side of Nick's body. He pressed two fingers to Nick's neck. Melanie squeezed her eyes shut. She would never forgive herself if he was dead.

Melanie heard Pappy exhale deeply. "He's alive."

Melanie's eyes flew open. "He is?"

Pappy nodded. "But he needs the doctor."

Ron and Jimmy rushed out the back door and Melanie knew they were going to saddle horses to head to town. Melanie leaned down and softly kissed Nick's forehead. "Please don't die, Nick, please."

She heard someone whimper and looked up. There sat Jonathan, huddled in a corner staring at Tom's dead body. Tom was slumped forward and still gushed blood from a couple dozen bullet holes. Melanie glared at Jonathan. "You see what your wickedness has caused?" Jonathan turned his head and vomited in response.

Ron and Jimmy had several horses ready in a few minutes. The cowhands threw Jonathan and Tom over the back of two saddles and handed the leads to Ron and Jimmy. Melanie grabbed Mitch's hand as he strode to the back door to join Ron and Jimmy. "Bring back the doctor and don't spare the horses."

Mitch nodded. "Yes, boss."

Melanie looked around for Esther. The girl was trembling in Douglas's arms. Melanie swallowed her sympathy for the girl. "Esther, run upstairs and bring down as many clean sheets and blankets as you can carry. Douglas you go too, bring down a mattress."

When Esther and Douglas returned Esther quickly made a bed up in the front sitting room. It took several cowhands to lift Nick's large body off the floor and carefully carry him down the hall and into the sitting room to the bed Esther had made. Pappy knelt at his side while Melanie gently washed his face with a cool cloth.

As the sun began to rise Nick began to stir. He tried to move and groaned in pain. Melanie gently ran her hand down his cheek. "Shh, my love, be still."

Nick huffed in what Melanie thought was supposed to be laughter. "I hope I'm the love you speak of."

Melanie smiled. "You will be if you promise to live."

Nick opened his eyes and squinted up at her. "I saw the life we could have had and I ..." Nick snapped his eyes shut again and groaned in pain.

Melanie's brow furrowed as fear gripped her soul. Nick could be dying. Why had she wasted so much time with uncertainty? Her heart sang with love for this man, yet she had withheld that love in the foolish belief that all men were evil. Well, no more. Despite the ache that filled her heart, she was determined to love Nick all she could before he died. "Nicholas, I'm so sorry. I should have told you. I was just so scared." Tears clouded her eyes. "I love you. I love you with all my heart." She rushed on. "Please say you'll marry me."

Nick tried to chuckle but began coughing with the effort. "I was kind of hoping to be the one to ask that question."

Melanie lovingly cradled his face in her hands. "Oh my love, I don't care who does the asking so long as the answer is yes."

Nick reached a shaking hand up and grabbed her good hand. He pressed his lips to her palm. "How could I say no?"

Melanie smiled down at him. "Then rest now. Rest and get better because you have a wedding to attend."

Pappy paced the front porch waiting for the doctor to finish working on Nicholas. Melanie sat on the porch steps with shoulders slumped. They had both been praying all afternoon. Pappy heard Melanie sniff and saw her swipe at her nose. He sat down next to her and wrapped his arm around her shoulders. "He'll be OK, Little Missy."

She looked up with red-rimmed eyes. "I hope so, Pappy."

Pappy squeezed her tight. "He will be. You gave him something to fight for."

Her forehead wrinkled. "I did?"

He smiled down into her sodden face. "You asked him to marry you." Pappy actually managed to laugh. "I think you made that boy just about the happiest man in Texas."

The door behind them creaked open and the doctor's nurse stepped out. Pappy helped Melanie to her feet. The nurse was wiping her hands on a clean, white towel. "Well?"

The nurse looked grim. "The doctor is still trying to extract one of the bullets. It may still be several hours before you can see him. The doctor asked me to come out and suggest you go around back to the kitchen and make the noon meal. It might help keep your mind busy."

This wasn't what he wanted to hear. He wanted to see his nephew, awake and alive and thriving. Pappy sighed defeat and nodded. "Come on, Little Missy, let's go around back."

His ward didn't argue. She turned on her heel and allowed Pappy to lead her around the porch toward the back door. Some of the other cowhands were already waiting around the table and Pappy promised to tell the boys what the doctor said as soon as he had a cup of coffee between his hands.

A couple of the longest hours later, Dr. Williams smiled up at Pappy. "Your nephew will be just fine. I was able to remove all three bullets. He's lost quite a bit of blood, so he might be weak for a while."

Pappy shook the doctor's hand vigorously. "Thanks, Doc, thanks so much."

Melanie stepped forward, her lower lip tucked between her teeth. "He'll live?"

Doctor Williams turned to face her. "Yes ma'am, right as rain in a few weeks. Fact of the matter is, that little pistol he was shot with didn't carry much punch. The bullets didn't penetrate very deep and the bleeding could have been much worse." The doctor looped his suspenders over his shoulders as he laughed. "Sure will be sore for a while, though."

Doctor Williams' nurse stormed out the door shaking her head. "That man is impossible."

From inside the house Nick's voice rang out. "Where's my bride? I want a kiss from my bride!"

Pappy chuckled and pushed Melanie toward the door. "You better go see your future husband, Little Missy, before he tries to come out here and find you."

Melanie's face blushed a beautiful pink as the cowhands chuckled. She embraced Pappy with a crushing hug and kissed his cheek. "Thank God he's OK, Pappy."

Pappy leaned down and kissed her forehead. "Thank God, indeed." He gripped her shoulders and spun her toward the door. "Now go on, go see your man."

Epilogue

ELANIE TIPPED HER head back to look at the groom. His smile beamed down on her face like warm sunshine. Never in her life had she thought she'd feel this complete. She had spent countless hours dreaming of it, but never had hope grown strong enough for Melanie to truly believe a day like this would come. If she were to have a single regret on this blissful day it could only be that her dear friend Charlotte wasn't standing amongst their family and friends. For a split second her heart ached and she wondered how her tender friend was doing. Melanie straightened her shoulders and the corner of her lips turned up as she quickly decided she'd take the first opportunity to go visit Charlotte and insist on bringing her to Texas.

Nicholas gently squeezed her fingers and Melanie looked up into his handsome face as he began repeating his vows—vows to always love her, cherish her, protect her and respect her. Melanie sighed blissfully and smiled at Nicholas.

Her heart fluttered about in her chest as she repeated the same vows back to him—vows she not only said with words but committed to with her very soul. Nicholas leaned down and Melanie's stomach burst into a thousand butterflies. His lips softly pressed against hers and somewhere in the distance she heard Reverend Merryweather announce them as Mr. and Mrs. Nicholas Henderson. Melanie's heart soared and she wrapped her arms around her new husband's neck.

As they pulled away from each other, Nicholas gently tucked her hand in the crook of his arm and led her down the aisle. Pappy stood front and center, ready to embrace them both while wiping tears from his eyes.

"I never understood how a wedding could make people cry." He embraced Melanie tightly. "But now I do. My heart is so full of happiness for the two of you."

Melanie kissed Pappy's weathered cheek. "Thanks, Pappy."

Nick extended his hand to Pappy. The old man shook his head and drew Melanie's husband into a fierce hug. "Not today, son. Today I need a hug."

Nicholas chuckled and the sound was music to Melanie's ears. He clapped Pappy on the back, "Anytime, Paps, anytime."

As the newlyweds continued down the aisle toward the waiting wagon, their cowhands shouted their excitement and happiness with "yee-haws" and "yahoos." Nick assisted Melanie into the wagon and quickly climbed in after her. He wrapped his arm tightly around her shoulders and she leaned into the comfort and renewed strength of his body. Nick drove the wagon around the back of the house and down the path that led to her secret orchard. He pulled the wagon to a stop and jumped down, then turned to lift Melanie down. She smiled as the warmth of his hands on her waist seeped through her dress and into her very bones.

"Thank you, husband."

He leaned down and kissed the tip of her nose. "My pleasure, wife." His smile grew mischievous. "I have a surprise for you."

Melanie raised an eyebrow. "Oh?"

He winked down at her. "But you have to close your eyes."

Melanie couldn't help but giggle as she closed her eyes. Nick grabbed her hands and began leading her in a slow walk. When they finally stopped walking, he spun her around and held her close to his chest. He whispered in her ear. "Open your eyes."

As she opened her eyes she saw a blanket laid out across the ground with a small picnic basket resting in one corner. Melanie gasped. "Oh Nick, you shouldn't have. They're expecting us back for supper."

Nick squeezed her shoulders. "Don't worry, we'll be back in plenty of time for supper." He grabbed her hand and led her toward the blanket. "Why don't you see what's inside the basket?"

Melanie lowered herself to the ground. "I wonder what Esther packed us."

Nick laughed. "What makes you think Esther packed this basket?"

"Well if we're going to eat, I certainly hope it wasn't Pappy."

Nick clutched his stomach as he laughed. "I'll remember to tell him that. But who said we were eating?"

Melanie looked at her husband, baffled. "Well what else could be in a picnic basket?"

Nick didn't say. He just pushed the basket toward her. Melanie smiled up at him, her handsome, courageous husband. As she lifted the lid to the basket she spotted something yellow.

As she lifted the lid completely, Melanie was surprised to see a yellow rose bush wrapped securely in burlap.

She gently touched the petals. "Oh, Nick, it's beautiful." She looked up at him. "But I thought roses couldn't thrive in Texas."

He reached over and gently cupped her cheek in his hand. "It's a yellow Texas rose and I hear it does just fine in Texas soil." He gently rubbed her cheek with the pad of his thumb. "The man that sold them to me said yellow was the color of happiness and hope. I figured that was a mighty fine way to start off a marriage. By the time we get home for supper the boys should have the rest planted all around the porch."

Melanie cupped her hand over Nick's. "Nicholas you have made me the happiest woman in Texas."

He leaned close and his breath tickled her cheek. "Just Texas?"

Melanie's face burst into a smile and she lunged to wrap her arms around her husband's neck. "No, the world!"

JOYIN
PUBLISHING INC
Where joy finds a voice

To order additional copies of this book call:
1-888-273-4JOY
or please visit our website at
www.ajoyin.com

If you enjoyed this quality custom-published book,
drop by our website for more books and information.

www.ajoyin.com
"Where joy finds a voice"

www.ingramcontent.com/pod-product-compliance
Lightning Source LLC
Chambersburg PA
CBHW031940010726
47493CB00007B/2004